sto

Dave Groenemann
2018

WOMAN ALONE

One Woman's Journey
Through the Murky and Magical

Jan Groenemann

BALBOA.
PRESS
A DIVISION OF HAY HOUSE

Balboa Press books may be ordered through booksellers or by contacting:

Balboa Press
A Division of Hay House
1663 Liberty Drive
Bloomington, IN 47403
www.balboapress.com
1 (877) 407-4847

Print information available on the last page.

ISBN: 978-1-9822-0157-9 (sc)
ISBN: 978-1-9822-0159-3 (hc)
ISBN: 978-1-9822-0158-6 (e)

Library of Congress Control Number: 2018903936

Balboa Press rev. date: 04/20/2018

CONTENTS

Dedicated to Mom

PREFACE

WOMAN ALONE, MY first novel, is a response to my greatest life lesson: be true to your own revelation; only you have the answers to your questions concerning your life purpose.

Jude Bennett's story could be the story of every woman growing up in a culture that teaches the fundamental, Christian concept of female inferiority. Having grown up within this tradition I often found it a struggle to find my unique path. I have always felt the presence of a loving Higher Power, and, as I evolved spiritually, I found my concept of God changing as well. As a result, I not only found myself, but my power as a woman, and my joyful place in creation.

There is a sense in which Jude's struggle speaks to everyone experiencing the polarization of belief systems within our contemporary American culture. It seems all too often when we believe we have the truth, we assume our way must be right for everyone. Time and a great deal of honest reflection have taught me otherwise. I respect the path that works for others, but I must find my own way.

I believe that sense of "inconsolable longing," as C.S. Lewis termed it in the prologue to *The Pilgrim's Regress*, is what triggers both our creativity and our spiritual seeking. Traveling that road can be intensely passionate. But we must be humbly cautious in our enthusiasm, for the very journey that is ours may in some way be a hindrance for another.

So, *Woman Alone* is my way of encouraging readers to ask these age old questions for themselves: who am I and what is my purpose in being here?

Jan Groenemann

ACKNOWLEDGEMENTS

WOMAN *ALONE*, ONE of the greatest challenges of my professional life, could not have happened without the help and loving support of many generous people:

Bob Scarfo, my editor, gave me invaluable help in editing, proofing and arranging content from the beginning.

My Writer's Group, Teddy Norris, Esther Fenning, Frank Prager, Bob Hornbuckle, Scottie Priesmeyer, and Hannah Zane, provided important feedback that helped me rethink and rewrite.

My readers and friends, Holly Carson, Amy Kartmann, Nancy Rickert, Sandy Alford, Pat Elliot Tait, Tom Hawkins, Joyce Yarborough, and Sharon Hawkins, gave me feedback and encouragement.

My son, Garic Groenemann, and my niece, Cortney Tatlow, assisted me with the final proofing and editing.

I am grateful to every person who helped to shape who I have become at this point in life, especially my closest friends and my three sons: Jason, Garic and Jeremy.

And finally, thank you to those at Balboa Press who made the dream of seeing *Woman Alone* in print a reality.

I said, please reveal this to me
I am dying in anticipation.
Love said to me,
That is where I want you:
Always on the edge
Be silent….
Love said to me
There is nothing that
Is not me.
Be silent.
—Rumi

CHAPTER 1

We are destined to be opened by the living of our days. —Mark Nepo

THE COLD DAMP **of her pillow pulled Jude Bennett out of a restless sleep.** At least she had dozed. She sat straight up, alone in the center of the king-sized bed. She had been having a terrible dream. So terrible her cheeks were damp with tears; she didn't want to think about it. But she knew. How strange, after all these months of struggle, just like that, she knew she had to end it. She had to end her marriage. She wiped her cheeks with the edge of the sheet and tried to get her bearings. Edward? Across the room she could see bare wood where his fingers had worn away the finish on the top drawer of the Broyhill chest. They had bought the chest as an heirloom before they married. Slowly everything came back to her. She had allowed Edward to come home again, and they had fought. He was sleeping in the guest room. Jude pulled herself out of the warm bed and reached into the closet for a robe. It was March. Yesterday had been warm and sunny, but a cold front had moved through overnight. She rubbed her eyes, combed through her hair with her fingers, and walked into the guest bedroom. For a moment she stood looking down on Edward. She had no idea of the time. It was still dark, so it was early. She knelt beside her sleeping husband, amazed that with all he had put her through, was

1

still putting both of them through, his sleep seemed undisturbed. His skin was smooth beneath a trimmed, graying beard, his salt and pepper hair barely tousled. He had the broad shoulders of a former football player and a thick head of hair, a gift from his mother's side of the family. Their son had inherited his father's hair.

This was how a cheating husband looked? Tranquil, even innocent. Her resolve was stirred.

"Edward." Her voice came out in a hoarse whisper. "Edward, wake up." This time she spoke more forcefully. Still, he didn't stir. "Edward," she spoke again, shaking his shoulder.

He groaned and turned toward her, squinting as he attempted to focus. "What?" he mumbled. His eyes closed again.

"Edward, I have to talk to you. Wake up." This time her voice was elevated, urgent.

Edward widened his eyes as if trying to force them to stay open. "What's wrong?"

The irony hit Jude. "What's wrong?" she repeated. "What's wrong is that I can't keep doing this with you."

With her words he came fully awake. "What do you mean?"

"What I mean is, I love you Edward. I really hope you can get your head on straight and figure out what it is you want. But we're stuck, and I can't stay stuck with you any longer. It's killing me. I want a divorce. I have to get on with my life."

"How can you divorce me?" he growled, grabbing his pillow and giving it a sling. As Jude caught it against her chest, she was forced backward against the wall.

Righting herself, Jude responded, "It's been months, Edward, and you won't let go of your mistress. You're back and forth. You tell me one thing and her another. You even lie to our therapist. I can't...no, I won't do this anymore. I'm filing for a divorce."

Without looking at her, Edward pushed her aside, got out of bed and grabbed his clothes.

"You'll regret this!" he shouted, storming out of the room.

He was irate, as if she was the one who had wronged him. Sitting on the floor beside the bed, she heard him start the shower. She felt numb as a realization came over her. He felt no remorse. This was who he really was.

Jude replaced the pillow on the bed, rested her elbows on the still warm sheets and looked out the window of the small suburban home she shared with her husband of more than twenty years. Everything looked different, clearer, as if the window had just been washed. There were buds on the Bradford pear. The gnarly redbud on the hill was in full bloom. Relief washed over her.

II

It had taken her months to finally say *enough*. It would have been good had it ended there. But marriages seldom die easily. And in this marriage the wounds had been long hidden, like a cancer that shows no symptoms as it slowly metastasizes. For Jude it would require some time to absorb the knowledge that her life had been a lie. She could feel the anger building within her! She had put everything into her marriage, built her life around her husband! She deserved honesty! If Edward wanted other women, then he should have been honest with her, should have freed her. He had been her first and only lover. She had saved herself for the one love of her life. And now she felt foolish. Once they became sexually intimate, her religious teachings had kicked in: joining sexually made you one, sex was the real consummation of commitment, this joining was until death do us part. She knew now just how naive she'd been.

Looking back, she had at times felt something wasn't right. There had been subtle hints. With two kids it was difficult to have privacy. There was the time she had bought that new bustier the week that her young children, Jennifer and Grant, were visiting their grandparents. She remembered the feel of the transparent lace, the flattering cut, the anticipation she felt at knowing Edward would get a real kick out of it.

"Wow, look at you!" Edward raised his eyebrows as Jude walked into the room. He had just come in from work, and she surprised him with a candlelight dinner wearing her new purchase. Jude's face lit up with a smile. She knew she looked good. Edward took her face in his hands and kissed her.

"You look amazing," he sighed. "I'd love to spend the evening enjoying you, but I—I have a dinner meeting I can't miss."

"A meeting?" Edward never had meetings in the evenings. "You mean you can't have dinner first?"

"My boss asked if I would take his place on the city zoning commission while he's out of town. Didn't I mention it to you?"

Jude's smile faded, her shoulders slumped. "No, you didn't mention it to me."

She felt a knot form in the pit of her stomach.

"I'm sorry honey. I'll make it up to you, I promise."

He walked away. She felt the blood drain from her face. "Shit, what is this?" she whispered under her breath. "Something isn't right."

They had always had a great sex life, but recently something was different. Wasn't it supposed to be the woman who wanted less sex as she aged? Edward had once pushed for sex on an almost daily basis. Was he having an affair? That seemed so unlikely. Hadn't they kept romance in their lives more than most couples?

Edward hadn't seemed to notice she was holding back tears as he left for his meeting. She intended to stay up to greet him when he got home but eventually fell asleep and didn't hear him come in. The next evening he had taken her to dinner; they made love afterward.

There had been other things that triggered uncomfortable feelings. Jude taught life learning classes two nights a week for a local university. Jennifer, their youngest, often called Jude, worried that Edward was hours late getting home. He always had an excuse. There had been subtle clues. Jude was just too naive, too deep in denial to catch them. Edward insisted when they entered therapy together that his affair with Helen, his secretary, had been going on for a little over a year. Jude now knew better; the affair with Helen had not been the only one. Worse yet, Edward's involvement with Helen had not stopped for the entire eight months he and Jude had been in therapy. Once their therapist learned this, he refused to continue working with Edward and suggested they each needed some space.

Shortly after Edward moved out into a furnished apartment, he asked Jude to meet him at the hospital to visit his sister who was fighting pneumonia. Edward insisted they tell his sister that they were separated. He was so calm about it. Jude watched the horror come over Donna's face.

"You're telling me this while I'm lying here in a hospital bed? Eddie, what are you doing? Do you have a girlfriend?" Edward hung his head. "I can't believe this," Donna continued, "You two are the perfect couple!"

Jude had often thought this. That they were the perfect couple. What was wrong with her that she had been so blind?

III

There are always two sides to every situation: two sides to an argument, two sides to a divorce…. How many times had she heard this? She learned to just keep silent as she sat through hours of therapy listening to Edward telling a very different story of their marriage than she knew. How could two people see things so differently? At times she had even questioned her own memory, her own sanity.

"When there are two such different perspectives on what has happened, the truth is usually somewhere in between," Jim, their therapist, had asserted. Eventually Jim would apologize to Jude for this.

"You shouldn't even want a long term relationship with your husband," Jim had said after learning that Edward had not been honest even in the therapy sessions. Jude could still feel the knot that had formed in the middle of her upper belly. These were very strong words from a therapist who was supposed to help her save her marriage.

"He's so good at it, Jude, that I'm sure he began lying long before he knew you. I pride myself on seeing through the men I work with, but he completely fooled me, too." Compulsive lying was, according to Jim, a part of Narcissistic Personality Disorder.

Jude had continued seeing the therapist, trying to understand how she found herself in this situation. She was a religious young woman. She had expected her family to be involved in church together, and it seemed Edward wanted the same thing. He gave her no reason to believe otherwise, and had accepted a position as Deacon in their church. But Edward had never been the man she believed him to be. She just couldn't wrap her mind around it. Regardless of how happy, how content he appeared to be with their life together, something else had obviously been going on in his mind. The truth was she'd never really known her husband of twenty years. What was wrong with her? How could she have fallen in love with someone so dishonest? And how could she not have realized something was so wrong?

CHAPTER 2

We think that accomplishing things will complete
us, when it is experiencing life that will.

—*Mark Nepo,*

THE COLD OF **the window glass against which Jude was leaning drew her back to the present.** She looked out onto a totally different world from the one she had shared with Edward. That was twelve years ago. Spread out before her was the expanse of Lake Michigan. Sail boats dotted the deep blue of the water, and white cumulus clouds were scattered across the horizon. Jude stood at another crossroads. The recent death of her mother had brought her face to face with her own immortality and she was struggling to adjust to being the matriarch of her family. As the oldest of her siblings, and both her parents now gone, she was next in line to experience ageing and death. She felt suddenly old, and life seemed very short. Was there time to do all she planned? Six months after her mother's death, and at age fifty-four, she felt caught in a surreal slow motion as if trying to move forward after having the breath knocked out of her. She kept getting pulled back into the memories of her mother's last few days.

"Oh, look at that," Jude's mom said, pointing at the basket of flowers Jude had set on the night stand.

"What is it, Mom?"

"Oh, never mind. There's nothing there is there? You don't see it." Her mom shook her head in frustration. "I thought I saw Jennifer's face in that basket."

Jude felt a discomfort in her chest; her heart ached. The doctors claimed it was a urinary tract infection that created her mom's hallucinations. She saw strange little children staring from impossible places and reached out trying to catch the side table and the chair as it lifted and floated out the door of her rehab room. Jude felt it had to be something more. Her mom had called Jude the week before, telling her that she was in the lower level of the old barn on the farm she and Jude's dad had owned.

"Jude, you have to help me," her mom had said.

"What is it Mom? Where are you?"

"Jude, I'm standing on this old dinette chair. I can't get down."

"Mom, why are you on a chair; where are you?"

"I'm in the barn. Your Dad is here with me, and Aunt Zella. Jude, I'm scared. I can't get down."

Both Jude's dad and her mother's Aunt Zella had been dead for years. Realizing that her mom had awakened from a bad dream or was hallucinating, Jude knew she had to speak to her from that perspective. "Mom, put your hand on the back of the chair and try to sit down. Can you do that?"

"I...I can't reach it, Jude. ... I'm...I'm going to fall."

"Mom, just stay calm. You can't reach the back of the chair?"

"No. I'm standing up on the seat and it's too far down. Jude, please help me."

"Mom, can Dad help you?"

"No. He doesn't seem to hear me."

Jude knew her mom had to be in her rehab room; she was on the phone.

"Okay, Mom. I can help you," she said calmly. "I'm going to stay on the phone with you. I'm right here. And I want you to call for help. You're in rehab and someone will hear you. Can you do that?"

"Yes," her mom answered in a weak whisper.

"Call for help as loudly as you can, Mom. When the nurse comes, give her the phone. I'll talk to her."

Jude's heart broke listening to her mom's shaky voice calling, "Help. Help. Help."

Within a few seconds a nurse came into the room. Jude's mom thrust the phone toward her, "My daughter wants to talk to you."

"Hello?" It was the nurse.

"Hello, this is Mrs. Hayward's daughter, Jude. She's having hallucinations and thinks she's standing in a chair and can't get down. Can you talk her down?"

"Well, she's lying in her bed all covered up," the nurse responded.

"But she doesn't think that's where she is. Will you just talk with her and help her understand she's in bed and okay?"

"Sure will, honey. She's just fine. Don't you worry."

Jude hung up the phone as tears began to stream down her face. Don't worry, the nurse had said. She would never forget the sound of her mom calling for help.

Jude had spent every day with her mom for three weeks, and in the early morning on Sunday, before she could get there, at 5:37 AM, her mom slipped away, gone forever, as if she had floated right out that over-sized, left-ajar door with the furniture. Jude knew it was what her mom wanted. She realized that the dying often chose to go when their loved ones stepped out of the room. But it felt unfair. Jude felt abandoned. It hadn't been easy to arrange her schedule so that she could be with her mom. She hadn't wanted her to die alone.

"Judith Renee Hayward," her mom would call to her when a young Jude forgot to finish her chores or was caught up in her drawing and didn't hear her mom asking for help. But Jude was the nickname from her father that had stuck. She left the farm in southern Illinois because of her dreams, and also, she was restless, even bored. She was seeking a more expansive world as she entered college at Northwestern University for a degree in fine arts.

Her dad insisted if she wanted his financial help, she must study something practical, like business. "Besides," he asserted, "You'll just get up there and meet some boy and that will be the end of college."

It was her mom Jude told when she switched her major from business to studio art. Later, the business minor would benefit her career as an artist. "Things happen as they need to," she would think to herself even back then. She was eighteen when she entered the university, but she and her mother had remained closely connected. The two of them were able to discuss almost anything, though her mom often teased her with, "I don't know where you came from Judith Renee. You're a mystery to me!"

"You don't need a man in your life. A man can hold you back," Jude's mom had said after Jude's painful divorce. Yet, her mom built her entire life around Jude's father until his early death at age sixty-seven. It wasn't until then that Jude saw her mother's independent nature emerge.

There's no choice but to accept death, but Jude had hoped for some sign, some indication of her mom's lingering presence. Friends told of how their recently deceased loved ones appeared to them in a dream or stood at the foot of their bed with a special goodbye. But Jude's mom had not appeared. Now, months later, with her face pressed to the cold, glass-paned window looking out across Lake Michigan, Jude felt a presence behind her and chills ran up and down both arms; she was sure she felt her mom.

"Mom, is that you?" Jude whispered under her breath. Her eyes filled as memories of her mom flooded her thoughts. An early morning call from Jude's youngest brother, almost half a year ago now, had announced that their mother had been hospitalized. The entire day passed before Jude could reach her by phone.

"Jude, something is very wrong, I can feel it," her mom said in a weak teary voice. "Can you come? I think I need a mommy."

Jude felt panic sweeping over her. Her mom was always the strong one. This didn't sound like her at all. Jude quickly taped a note to the gallery door, packed her bags and drove the six hours to the small Mt. Vernon hospital. When she walked into the private room her mom's eyes brightened. Jude rushed to her and wrapped her in a warm hug. "I'm here to mommy you," she whispered in her mother's ear.

But by the time Jude's mom was released from the hospital and settled into rehab, she had made up her mind. It was time, she told Jude. In hindsight, Jude realized that over the previous six months or more her mom had been letting go. She had lost interest in *Days of Our Lives*, the TV soap opera she had watched for as long as Jude could remember. She no longer enjoyed conversations on *The View* or *Meet the Press*. She was not even much interested in talking with her friends on the phone. Even when Jude made her morning call to her mom, she found her less newsy, more tired, and sometimes even irritable. Jude felt a pang of guilt remembering how there had been times she dreaded making that daily call.

On their last day together, Jude's mother sat in a wheelchair, wrapped tightly in a new robe, handmade booties on her feet, like the hundreds she had crocheted for friends and family. She had often distributed these "made with love foot warmers" at local nursing homes. Get well cards lined the windowsill and hung by scotch tape across the wall. A basket of assorted plants and a Peace Lily sat on either side of the window. It was Jude's way of trying to make the sterile room feel homier. Her throat constricted with emotion. Her mom had taught her to see the good in everyone and every situation. She was Jude's example of unconditional love. It was so difficult to see her giving up.

"Mom, I know how you must be feeling." A wave of emotion washed over Jude. "But that's not the way it works." She felt irritation building within her. "You can't just decide you want to die. There's no button to push. You have to try and make the best of things. The doctor says you're getting stronger every day."

Jude's mother rolled her eyes and sighed in frustration. "We both know I'll not be able to go home and live on my own. And I don't want to live in some nursing home."

"Mom…"

"Honey, I don't want this to upset you, but I just need to get this over with."

"You have other options," Jude insisted. "You can stay with me for as long as you want, Mom. At least until you feel able to live at home on your own again." Her mother shook her head, unwilling to consider an alternative.

The room was heavy with silence as the two women seemed stalemated. But Jude realized this wasn't a time for argument. "Mom," Jude said softly. Her mother raised her eyebrows in a questioning look. "Will you promise me one thing? When you do go, promise to contact me if you possibly can?"

Jude's mother shook her head and rolled her eyes again. "Well, don't sit around waiting for that."

Jude smiled. Her mother smiled back and chuckled; a wave of love washed over Jude. "Oh, Mom, I wish there was something I could do." But she knew there was only one resolution to her mother's struggle. Her mother was right.

They had talked many times about what it might feel like to die and what might happen after death. Jude had grown up with the same Christian concepts of heaven and hell as her mother, but as she grew older she had been drawn toward a more mystical path. She felt that death was less traumatic than most imagined it to be, a transition, not an ending. And she no longer believed in a hell, except for the kind of hell people create here on earth. Why didn't that make this easier?

"I don't know where you get some of your ideas," her mother had said teasingly, after one of their discussions on spirituality which included reincarnation. "I guess I've just never thought about as many things as you. Life has always been pretty simple and straightforward for me. It's been enough to just deal with all the changes. I remember your Grandma talking about watching the first car come down the highway, backfiring and scaring the horses. Just think of it, cars, then planes, then rocket ships flying men to the moon. So many changes, and now gays want to marry each other, and we have a black man and even a woman wanting to be President. I have to tell you that I felt pretty uncomfortable a few years back when Obama was first elected, watching that crowd of black people yelling and cheering at his inauguration. It was a little scary, like maybe they were taking over."

"Mom, that's a racist statement," Jude had said.

"Well, I'm not very comfortable with a black man as President; but I'm not racist, Jude, and I'd rather he be President than a woman."

"Why is that, Mom?"

"I just don't think a woman has any business running for President."

Jude gasped. "Mom, how can you feel that? You know there are women more intelligent and presidential than many men!" But Jude had watched as her mom acquiesced to her father's every whim. It was according to the Word of God that women were inferior to men, were to be submissive to men. It had to do with Eve taking a bite of that apple.

II

Jude had fought long and hard to get here, to this Michigan Avenue loft apartment over her own gallery. Maybe she'd figured it out: a woman had to love herself, find herself, and depend on herself. As much as she had once wanted to believe it, no one was coming to her rescue. Why did women of her generation tend to believe they needed rescue? She'd not only found success as an artist, but also a sort of peace. Peace. She reached for the Old Country Rose pattern tea cup that had belonged to her mom. With her thumb she traced the delicate lines hand-painted in deep rich colors…deep pink and yellow roses. In spite of its delicacy, the cup had a good feeling, smooth and solid, and a flawless glaze. A deep longing swept through her. She couldn't quite pin it down.

Jude turned the cup in her hands and ran her forefinger over a small chip. This had been one of the few material things her mother had ever wanted: a set of Old Country Rose china. Jude had bought her the first place settings. The other thing Jude remembered her mom wanting was a red 64 ½ Mustang. Jude smiled to herself. She wished she'd had the money to surprise her mom with that Mustang. "Wouldn't that have blown your mind Mom?" Jude mused.

Jude had wanted so much more. Still wanted more. Something more. Standing on the forty-sixth floor in an apartment open to the sky and water, she was surprised to find herself feeling, what? Restless? Unfulfilled? Forty-six floors below on the door of her gallery was written:

Woman Space

Jude Bennett, Gallery Owner and Resident Artist

"I'm a damn good artist and a successful business woman," she asserted to herself. She loved the gallery. It was through Woman Space she offered opportunities in the form of financial support and exposure for emerging female artists who were struggling to support themselves and often, one or more children. These were single mothers with little or no help from the fathers of their children or from other family members. She'd never forget the first struggling artist she discovered and promoted in the gallery. Diana Buffett did such unique sculptures from recycled materials, but no one had taken her work seriously. Diana had shyly approached Jude, sharing that she was going through a divorce and had to sell her work in order to have a chance to keep her two kids. Their father had abandoned them. Jude saw Diana's potential, gave her a space in a back room where she could do her work, gave her part time work in the gallery, and did a marketing blitz and opening focused on Diana's work. Jude would never forget the shock on Diana's face at the end of that opening. Every sculpture sold. The press pushed to interview the artist. Diana was on her way. It was then Jude realized, for the first time, the real purpose of Woman Space.

Jude knew firsthand the roller coaster of supporting herself with her art. During her divorce from Edward, he had done his best to control and manipulate her with money. It was as if he thought he could force her to drop the divorce if she were desperate enough financially. She knew how important solid, physical and financial help could be when a woman was trying to escape a bad situation.

Jennifer had once said, "Mom, why are you so worried about money? You always sell a painting if you really need to." Jude smiled, thinking how things seemed so simple to a child. It had taken a long time to learn to trust that there would be enough.

Just over two years following her divorce from Edward, her friend and mentor, Emily Rosen, had called her into her office at the Rosen Galleries where Jude had done her internship after college and worked part time as her children got older.

"I have some good news and some bad news, Jude," Emily had begun. "They've found a lump in my breast, and I have to begin treatment. It's cancer."

"Oh, Emily...when did you find out?"

"I met with my doctor yesterday. Jude, I'm going to need help."

Jude walked to Emily and put her arms around her. Emily was like a second mother. She had helped Jude survive financially since the divorce. "Anything you need," she said.

"I'm going to need a lot of help with the gallery. I need you as my director. I'm not sure how much I'll be able to be here. I'll feel good if I know you're in charge."

"Oh, wow, Emily, it would be an honor to be your director. I...I just hope I'm ready."

"Yes, you're ready!" Emily said without hesitation. "I have no doubt, and I know you need a consistent salary. It will be good for both of us."

Jude hesitated. As if Emily was reading her mind, she added, "We'll work around Jennifer's needs, Jude."

Jude felt tears begin to trickle down her cheeks. "Oh, Emily, I'm so sorry. I'm excited about being your director, but so sorry for why you need me."

"You're like a daughter to me, my dear. I can't tell you how much stress it will take from me to know you're overseeing the gallery."

Already Emily had taught Jude the details of the business and promoted her work above most of the other artists. She had allowed Jude flexibility with her part-time hours in order to see to Jennifer's needs and complete her Masters of Fine Arts degree. Jude excelled as gallery director.

Emily died from a return of the cancer seven years later. Jude was shocked to learn that Emily had willed to her the Emily Rosen Galleries. With the gallery came a paid two-year lease to the prime Chicago space and to the loft apartment.

"Make your dreams happen, Jude," Emily had written in a letter that accompanied the gallery papers. Thus, Woman Space was born. It had not been an easy transition, and two years was a short time in which to totally transform a business. She had initially exhausted herself, both physically and financially. Now, the inheritance from her mother would allow Jude to pay off the loans she had needed in order to set up the women artists' scholarship programs. It had been a daunting undertaking, but in Woman Space Jude had found a sense of purpose, and perhaps, finally, financial stability.

Jude sat her mom's tea cup back in its saucer on the end table. Emotion again swept through her.

"Mom, I still miss you so much. Is there something missing from my life or am I just grieving? I have so much to be grateful for. What's wrong with me?"

Jude's children were also doing well. Her son Grant had graduated from medical school and accepted an internship at Duke University. Jennifer, who'd been diagnosed with Juvenile Diabetes as a toddler, had been the one most thrown off course from the divorce, but she now had her degree in physical therapy and was married to Doug, a great young man.

So, why, Jude wondered, was she feeling so unsettled? Surely the hard part was behind her. Earlier in the evening she'd had a long phone conversation with Andrew, a cowboy of a man, who had her laughing one minute then swept with a mix of emotions the next. Maybe the confusion came from her attraction to Andrew, who was everything she had worked to escape: conservatism, fundamental religion, country boy.

"So you no longer attend church?" Andrew asked.

"No, not for some time. You might say my worship is my morning meditation and yoga," Jude responded.

"Well, don't you miss the fellowship of the people, Jude?"

"Andrew, I feel such fellowship with my friends and family—even those who work with me at the gallery. We're there for one another, sort of like a church. And I like to spend my Sunday mornings in meditation and walking in nature."

They had such differing philosophies, still she felt drawn to him. She was amazed at his openness, even his faith. Something about him touched her deeply. And she had to admit she felt youthful and full of vitality when she was with him.

"A—maz—ing grace, how sweet the sound…" Andrew was singing on the phone. "I know you have to miss all those old gospel songs: 'In the Garden', 'I'll Fly Away', 'How Great Thou Art'."

A wave of emotion swept over Jude, and tears began to roll down her face. Suddenly she felt such confusion and a terrible missing of her mom. Her mom had to be at work here. The cowboy was her doing. It would be just like her to throw this wrench in Jude's plans. She sensed her mother was looking down on her smiling. Her mom had loved the Gaithers, the Oak Ridge Boys, and all old gospel music, and, more than anything, she would have liked to see Jude back in church. She had to be the reason this man had come into Jude's life.

"It's not that I really loved that old music," she said, trying not to sound choked up. It didn't work.

"What's wrong Jude? Are you okay? I'm so sorry; I've made you sad."

"I'm fine, Andrew. You just make me think of my Mom. What I did love was singing in harmony with Mom and Dad. I've spent hours singing acapella, three-part-harmony on the rides Mom and I took with Dad to deliver milk to the Carnation plant. I'd sing soprano along with Mom's alto and Dad's tenor."

"That's so cool, Jude. That had to create a real bond for you with your parents."

"Yeah... it did. We even performed at 'singings' held in several small local churches in surrounding communities."

"My parents only sang at church," Andrew responded. "I think it was more a duty for them. You were lucky, Jude."

"I know. There was a lot of singing in our home. Even when I was a kid I knew the words to most songs on the radio, and Mom used to play the piano while she and Dad sang together after we kids were in bed. I'd lay there listening. Sometimes it made me cry. Some of those songs just made me think about when Mom and Dad might die—to me they were funeral songs."

"Now I'm tearing up, girl. There is a sadness to some of those old songs; makes me think about my childhood too...."

Who would have imagined she'd meet a man who would get emotional about old songs—and on the phone. They had talked for an hour and a half. Andrew stirred so many feelings in her.

"Well, you asked for my help," a voice softly whispered. It sounded just like her mom. Jude felt chills run up her arms. "Here it is, the best way I know to ground you."

She felt the chills again as she pushed herself away from the windows with both hands. It had been a long time since she'd opened herself to a romantic relationship. Could she even do so again? She certainly didn't feel a need to be grounded. She was flying high, both from the view of the city and the lake and in her work. Forty-six stories high. She laughed to herself. Glancing at her phone she saw that it was 1:36 AM. Her long-time friend Sharon was in town, and Jude was to meet her for breakfast.

Jude picked up her glasses. It had been a long day, and she was ready for bed. Embroidered Japanese screens separated her bedroom from the living and entertainment space where she kept her easel set up for painting. Right now the spacious open rooms were filled with ambiance from the lights of the city; come morning they would be flooded with sunlight, giving her space an openness that fed her need to feel free and unencumbered by city living.

Jude walked into the bathroom off the bedroom and turned on the faucet. What she needed was a hot soaking bath. Lying back in the body-conforming tub always allowed her to let go of whatever was weighing on her mind. She adjusted the water temperature and turned to stare at herself in the mirror. It was difficult to realize she was only a few years away from sixty; she was often told she didn't look her age. She wondered how truthful that was as she studied the lines around her tired eyes and reached for her hairbrush. Her hair made her think of her maternal grandmother whose deep red curls Jude had been told she had inherited. But she could only remember her grandma as fully gray. She removed her makeup as she studied her skin; it was still firm and sometimes even glowing. Certainly she loved life, and that showed in the sparkle of her green eyes. She was blessed with high energy and, fortunately, good health. Jude had everything she wanted. Well, almost everything. There were times when she longed for a man's strong arms around her, an embrace that made her feel a sense of belonging as she shared with him events of the day. She missed more than anything the comfort, the affirmation, of touch. But she could not allow her infatuation with another man to get her off track.

A man had too often been a distraction for Jude. She thought of the plans she had for travel upon graduation from college, but meeting Edward Bennett had changed all of that. She sometimes wondered just how committed she'd been to her artistic passions. Like many of the women she knew, she had ultimately allowed a man to chart her course, forgetting what felt so important to her and following Edward as if he played some magical flute. Their whirlwind romance literally swept her off her feet, into a single-engine Cessna, and off on their honeymoon, airport hopping from Kentucky Lake to the Florida Keys. She was so in love at twenty-two.

Thoughts of Edward could still trigger feelings of betrayal and abandonment, though it seemed another lifetime when they were together. They had grown in different directions. And Jude realized that she had allowed the chemistry between them to cloud her mind. Maybe there was something to that theory that because a woman was the gender that committed the "original sin" women would always feel a need for a man to guide their lives. The thought irritated her. Edward was very intelligent, an engineer with two master's degrees, but he was not a "seeker of spiritual truths." He had no interest in psychology or philosophy. For him religion was as simple as going to church; and in the years since they divorced they had become opposites, she growing more liberal both in politics and religion and he moving toward a radical right and a rigid fundamentalism. Most likely their relationship had been doomed from the start. She'd been shocked to learn that Edward had a series of affairs scattered throughout their marriage, yet, he considered himself the "religious" one now.

Still, she liked to imagine that Edward had loved her to the best of his ability, and they had created two beautiful children. And it was because of Edward she learned to fly. She could still feel the magic of gaining speed until she lifted off the ground and punched through the clouds.

"Your marriage has lasted twenty years due to your tolerance," the therapist had told her. It was not a compliment.

Following the divorce, Jude had put her full focus on creating and marketing art in order to support herself and Jennifer, who was halfway through her junior year of high school. Jennifer, since the age of eighteen months, had to have daily insulin shots and careful monitoring of what she ate. With the stress of her chronic illness, family was an especially important foundation for her. Jude needed to keep things as normal for Jennifer as was possible; she had to create a solid career.

Jude was single two years before she found the courage or the time to date, and had it not been for meeting Josh Weldon she might never have found the courage. She had met Josh, a psychologist and writer, at a conference on creativity in Santa Fe where they had been asked to co-lead a discussion group. They became immediate friends and colleagues. Josh edited the book Jude was writing on creativity and personal growth and helped her find a publisher. In turn, Jude illustrated a book that Josh was writing, and for a brief time they co-facilitated workshops. Josh was happily married, which made him safe in spite of the strong connection between them. Jude came to love both Josh and his wife, Clare; they restored her faith in the possibility of a good marriage. She felt she was open to meeting a man, even to marriage. In fact, eventually she was engaged, but the relationship didn't last. When she fell in love again and that relationship also ended she decided she was probably happiest on her own. Her work became her passion.

Divorce was the impetus that moved Jude to commit to becoming fully herself as an artist, entrepreneur, and independent woman. Her marriage had revolved around Edward's needs and her children's needs.

The financial stress of ending her marriage had actually catapulted her into becoming a successful artist. Would the loss of her mother, which brought with it an acute aloneness, now open her to finding the love of her life? Did she still believe in that possibility?

III

Morning came quickly. Over the muffled noise of honking horns and squealing tires, Jude could hardly hear the *Breakfast with Mozart* CD set to awaken her. The city was impatient. As she sipped her morning coffee, she found herself longing for the quiet of her modest home and studio with the Japanese garden that had been hers before her life exploded into success. Still, she knew she was where she was supposed to be; she loved her work in the gallery downstairs. It gave her a sense of doing good in the world, and she still found time to create. She cut her reverie and her coffee short. She had to meet Sharon.

Jude finished her second cup of coffee across the table from Sharon Ellis. They were catching up over their monthly breakfast. Sharon lived in Kansas City, but her daughter lived in the Chicago area and Sharon flew in to visit on a regular basis.

"Chicago's energy can really drain me. I'd love a getaway place on the outskirts of the city," Jude said. "I'm finding it really difficult to get enough sleep or solitude in the loft."

Sharon smiled over the top of her expresso. "Girl, you always manage to manifest what you need. Do you have specifics on what you want?"

Still feeling some of the heaviness of the night before, Jude sighed as the waitress refilled her cup. "I'd really like to live closer to the kids. I think if I found the right property I might talk Jennifer and Doug into moving here. Doug would be a good caretaker of the property and, as you know, Jennifer has this dream of doing equine therapy."

"What about Grant?" Sharon asked, squinting her eyes in thought. "What are his plans? Won't he complete his internship soon? Will he look for a residency in Chicago?"

"I know he'd like to find something here. And if he does, a country escape would benefit him, too. I'm thinking I might convince all of them to go in on property with me. I love that area just west of where Melody lives, but I doubt I could afford anything there on my own. What's the name of that small town?"

"Western Springs," Sharon interjected.

"It has everything I want—-gently rolling hills sprinkled with small lakes and woods. I really want a house on a lake. I keep dreaming of doing yoga on the deck and skimming on glassy early morning water in a kayak. Sometimes I drive out there just to get away from the city."

Sharon shook her head in agreement. "Melody and I often hike out there when I'm in town. There are some great trails—there's a lot of state owned forest in that area, too."

"I know," Jude said. "I've been looking into the cost of buying a few acres."

Jude thought about telling Sharon about meeting Andrew, but no, she wasn't ready. How many times had she gotten excited about meeting a new man only to be disappointed? There would be plenty of time to tell Sharon if a romantic relationship developed. Instead, she sneaked the bill and stood. "I'm buying this time!" Due to Sharon's stubbornness, Jude was sure she was over due to pay. It was a game between them. Sharon had been there for her through so much and for so many years.

"Jude," Sharon called as she caught up to her at the register. "Are you going to the Jungian workshop on Shamanism? It's this Saturday."

"Oh, I completely forgot about it!" Jude had intended to go.

"I'll call and see if they still have space if you want to join me. I think it would be good for you to get away from the gallery."

"Actually, I probably can get free on Saturday."

Sharon interrupted her, "Don't add a tip. I left it at the table."

"Okay. If there's still room I'll come."

"Good, I'll check into it." Sharon dug in her purse and pulled out a brochure. "Here, this will give you details. I think there's a list of supplies you'll need, too."

"Okay. Let me know as soon as you know about space. I'm pretty sure Maggie can manage the gallery on her own."

Sharon often pushed Jude's boundaries, though in a very positive way. She was always handing Jude a thought-provoking book, and she was the one who had encouraged Jude to have a psychic reading. Later she had talked Jude into a past life regression which had been a life-changing experience! Now Sharon was "sure" that Jude would relate to Shamanism. Jude was, after all, part Cherokee and certainly related to totem animals and psychic dreaming. They had both come a long way from their childhood religion, good or bad.

Jude wrapped her arms around Sharon. "Girlfriend, what would I do without you? You're always expanding my mind. I love you."

Sharon let out one of her full musical laughs and said, "You do the same for me, Jude. I love you girl."

"See you Saturday if it works out. Oh, tell Melody hi for me. How's the remodel going?"

"The renovation is amazing. I'm just hoping their marriage survives it," Sharon laughed.

Jude waved to Sharon as she got in her car, then opened the brochure she still held in her hand. Shamanism. She had read a lot about it, even had a session with a Sedona Shaman once on a Spirit Quest. She found it both intriguing and confusing. Did shapeshifting mean literally turning into a wolf or deer? Guess she would find out on Saturday.

IV

It was on a property-hunting drive west of Chicago on the outskirts of Western Springs where Jude met the cowboy. He owned the ranch next to the forty acres she was viewing; the two properties shared an eighty-five acre lake. Jude was waiting for Andrea, her real estate agent, to arrive so she could take a third look inside the house when Andrew came riding down the long drive on a beautiful roan appaloosa mare. She could see his smile, even at a distance. He was handsome, with reddish blonde hair blowing across his forehead. He gently pulled his mare to a halt, slid down from the saddle and reached his right hand toward her.

"I'm your neighbor, Andrew Jamison. I heard this place sold, and I felt I should say hello since we'll share a lake."

"Jude Bennet," she said, taking his out-stretched hand. "I haven't exactly bought it yet; I'm waiting to get a contractor out to look at the possibility of moving some walls."

His hand was large and his handshake firm. Jude thought of the hand of Michelangelo's Adam reaching toward God. She noticed callouses on his fingers and wondered what kind of work he did, but his nails were clean and well-manicured. He smiled broadly. She smiled back. Then, realizing she was still holding his hand, she let go and lowered her eyes. She felt drawn to the sensual energy emanating from him.

"Well, I hope it all goes through as you want. This place needs some TLC, but it's basically sound. It's a great horse property. I hear you're an artist. Are you a horse lover, too?" Even his voice distracted her. He had a soft, subtle southern accent. Was he aware of the effect he was having on her? Was he married?

"It seems you've heard a lot," Jude said with a laugh. "And yes, I love horses! You own the place across the lake? You raise horses?"

"Yes, I've been here almost ten years breeding and training fox trotters. I also take on any difficult horse—-sort of like a horse whisperer," he added with a glint in his eye. Andrew had a youthful energy and was tanned and toned from spending hours training horses.

Yes, she thought, he knows exactly the effect he has on a woman.

Still, Jude liked him. He came across as genuine. "Where are you from?" she asked.

"Ava, Missouri. My great grandfather bred the first registered Missouri Fox Trotters and started the association there. I moved here after my wife and I divorced."

"So, you've always been a horseman? That's how you make your living?"

"There's a lot more money in training horses here—well, at least there are a lot more horse people with money in this area."

So, he was single. Jude found herself wondering if he felt the chemistry she was feeling. It had been so long since she'd felt herself responding to a man. She hoped it wasn't obvious.

"My first horse was a fox trotter," she managed to say. "But it's been a while since I've ridden. I'd like to own horses again."

"So will you have horses if you move here?"

"That's one of the reasons I'm hoping to get this property. Maybe you'll help me find the right horse once I get settled in?" Had she really just invited him to help her look for a horse?

"I'd be more than happy to," he smiled a knowing smile.

Jude felt a blush wash over her cheeks. With more reserve she thanked him for his welcome. She was glad to meet a neighbor. And a sexy neighbor at that.

"Once you get settled in, I'll have a group of friends and neighbors together to introduce you," Andrew assured her. "You'll like this community, sort of a small town atmosphere."

They shared more small talk, and Andrew agreed to keep his eyes open for a horse for her.

"Good luck to you. I hope you make a good deal," he said as he put his hat back on his head.

"Thanks, Andrew. It's good to meet you."

"You too, Jude. You'll have good neighbors here."

The cowboy swung onto his horse and trotted back down the drive. Jude followed him with her eyes, smiling at how proudly he held himself in the saddle. She felt like a school girl. Definitely, it had been too long since she'd met a man who stirred her.

Apparently, Andrew felt the same. Within a few days he called to ask her to dinner. "I hope you don't mind that I got your number from Dan Grayson," he said with a chuckle. "I couldn't let you get away, in case you ended up not buying the property. Will you have dinner with me?"

CHAPTER 3

"Now I'm starting to think he wasn't supposed to be my whole life, he was just this doorway to me." — *Barbara Kingsolver*

SEVENTEEN-YEAR-OLD JUDE RODE **bareback, her hand wrapped in Fanny's mane as the sorrel mare galloped across the open meadow**. There wasn't a cloud in the late summer sky as tall Indian grass and blue stem whipped across their legs. The memory was so vivid Jude could almost feel the sting of the meadow grasses. There was only a bareback pad between her and the mare's sweaty back as they "hightailed it," as her dad would say, red ponytails flying, to the woods on the far side of the six acre opening.

Jude pulled the mare to an abrupt stop at the edge of the clearing. Both were exhilarated and breathing heavily. They had moved as one energy across the field and now exchanged the same air as they attempted to catch their breath. A bee tangled in Fanny's tail; the mare switched hard and the bee flew by Jude's face. As she watched its escape across the meadow, she noticed how the subtle yellows and grays of the grasses melted into the soft neutrals of the woods. A red Cardinal, brilliant in its contrast, flitted from a tree branch and flew across Jude's view.

"Red bird, red bird, fly to the right, I'll see my honey before daylight,"

Jude chanted to herself and laughed. But she had no honey in her life right then. The next day she would leave for college, and a gallop across the meadow would become a rarity. She felt a wave of sadness flow over her.

Jude felt safe and loved with her attentive mother and strong father, and she and her two brothers were close. There was the added benefit of extended family that lived along a four-mile stretch of county road Z, known to the locals as Hayward Ridge. Jude's maternal grandparents lived on the east end of the gravel road, Jude and her family were next, then came a smattering of Hayward aunts, uncles and cousins, followed by her paternal grandparents. She would always have their love and support, but she would be more than six hours away from the quiet farm life in southern Illinois. She would miss them all terribly. And she would miss Fanny.

As a child she had been so sure that it was her destiny to own a horse that she prayed daily for one. She fantasized walking to the pasture to bring the cows in for milking and finding a horse, her horse, waiting for her. She was twelve when her dad allowed her to use her own hard-earned money to buy Fanny, a sorrel with a white star on her forehead and white stockings on both back legs. A mix of quarter horse and Missouri Fox Trotter. Jude had trained her. She could coax Fanny to lie down, roll onto her back, and allow Jude to sit on her belly.

Jude, with her open smile and long red hair, had been swept off her feet more than once by a boy. The first crush lasted all her freshman year, but he was a senior and went on to adulthood without her. The second serious love, a drag-car-racing, big-hearted bad boy, asked her to wear his class ring her senior year, to be "engaged to be engaged." He was four years older and was set to inherit his family's cattle ranch. But Jude was going away to college to be an artist. It had been her dream since she was four. She couldn't say yes, and he understood this to mean she was moving on. It still sent a sting of pain through her to think of him. She would pine for him all through college. He married one of her best friends, and then was killed in action in Vietnam.

Jude had been religious and, even as a child, carried on a continuous conversation with God. Still, hers were the same childhood dreams as most girls growing up in the late 60's: fall in love with Mr. Right, have two or three children and live happily ever after. But there were other things she had to do first.

It was the summer after her first year of teaching that she met Edward Bennett. Edward's best friend, who was dating Jude's post-college roommate, introduced them. When their eyes met, each felt a connection neither had felt before. For Jude this was the first time she had experienced the feeling that she might not be happy without this person in her life. They were married six months later.

II

Jude had prepared to realize her long-time dream of becoming an artist with a Bachelor of Fine Arts in Studio Art. Because of her dad, she ended up with enough hours in business that she could almost declare a double major. In addition, she was fascinated with philosophy and psychology and was constantly questioning the meaning of life. Now, seven years out of college, Jude was a mommy, a nurse, and knee deep in diapers.

"I am grateful I can stay home with Grant and Jennifer," Jude said to her friend Sharon. "It's just that I sometimes feel my brain is shriveling from trying to relate on a toddler level all day."

"Me too," Sharon interjected. "I get desperate for intellectual stimulation!"

"Edward comes home and zones out. I think he resents he has to drive downtown to work every day while I get to stay home. He really doesn't appreciate that I had to give up a part of myself for motherhood, or how hard I work keeping up with two kids and the household. He just sees me as living an easy life."

Sharon, who was ten years older than Jude and had set aside her own career as a teacher to be home with her children, wiped her four-year-old's nose with an already used Kleenex and stuffed it in the diaper bag. "I know what you mean, Jude. I joined a book club to try to keep my mind fresh, but half the time Dave doesn't get home in time for me to make the meetings. He doesn't see anything I do as all that important."

Jude was a voracious reader herself; she and Sharon often discussed books that seemed to literally jump off the library shelves in an effort to speak to them. Both shared Christianity as their basic philosophy of life, but it seemed their growth as individuals kept expanding into much broader realms. They had met at the church Jude and Edward joined upon moving to the Chicago suburbs. For the first time, Jude could openly discuss her questions and philosophy with another person who really "got her." They read and discussed such authors as Martin Buber and Thomas Merton with whom they shared a natural curiosity. They found God speaking through a gradual spiritual progression, which they nurtured in one another. Thomas Moore's *Care of the Soul*, M. Scott Peck's *The Road Less Traveled*, the list went on. One philosopher spoke so intensely to Jude that he appeared in a very vivid dream:

> In the dream she awoke in the middle of the night to a raging storm. She walked into the kitchen and turned on the faucet, noticing intense lightning out the large kitchen window. Instead of water, blood came from the faucet. But rather than fear, Jude felt excitement and walked to the sliding patio doors to look out at the storm. She wasn't even shocked to find that instead of the deck she and Edward had built onto the back of their house, there was a pier going out into a wild sea. From the flashing lightning she could see that on the pier stood a small man with a long white beard. He was holding a rope attached to a tiny dingy with one hand and with the other he was waving wildly for Jude to come.
>
> "I can't come. What about Edward?" she had called back.
>
> "Don't worry about Edward," the old man yelled above the crashing waves.
>
> "He'll come when he's ready."

Jude had not recognized this man in her dream until, in the middle of *The Essential Kierkegaard*, she discovered several pages of photos. There she saw a photo of the old man she had seen at the end of the pier. It was Soren Kierkegaard.

"Jude," Sharon exclaimed as Jude was relating the dream, "you know the old man's message is true. Edward can't come with you on this journey. You think so much differently than him. I'm sure the dream is telling you not to let him hold you back."

"I did think about that possibility; but the idea scares me, Sharon."

"Well, I don't think you really have a choice. We all grow at our own pace."

The alarm sounded on the five-alarm wristwatch that Jude wore. It was time for Jennifer's afternoon snack. Jude pulled a box of cookies out of the pantry without interrupting her conversation with Sharon.

"You know you aren't going to stop asking questions," Sharon continued. "Or reading everything you can get your hands on."

"Oh, that reminds me," Jude interrupted. "Listen to this." Jude handed Jennifer six vanilla wafers and reached for her open notebook.

"This present moment, since it knows neither past nor future, is itself timeless, and that which is timeless is Eternal. Thus, the eternal life belongs to those who live in the present," she read from the notes she had scribbled from Ken Wilber's *The Spectrum of Consciousness.*

"Milk, Mommy, milk." Jennifer, her twenty-month-old, interrupted. Jude pulled a carton from the fridge and poured milk into a plastic juice cup and sat it on the table near Jennifer.

"I feel we are most likely living heaven or hell right now—which, depends on the state of our own minds."

"There's no doubt," Sharon chimed in. "You know heaven isn't somewhere out in space."

"And God isn't some old man in the sky," Jude added. They laughed at the absurdity of the idea.

"I'm guessing He is a She!" Sharon said, with a sparkle in her eyes.

"Well, even the Bible says we create what we think about. As a man thinks, so is he, right?" Sharon added. "I think it's likely we do create our own heaven or hell. Where did you hear about this Wilber?"

"I signed up for a newsletter on the latest concepts in philosophy, and he was featured in one of the issues. To some degree at least, I believe what he's saying is true, but we're talking about each of us creating our own reality and being responsible for what we experience. How does this fit with Jennifer, just a baby, having to deal with diabetes? She can't have made that choice."

"It doesn't seem to fit with every situation, for sure," Sharon added. "Even the innocent deal with hell on earth; I don't know how you rationalize illness in children. Or what about those who are subjected to violence or abuse? Or why would God allow an innocent child to starve? I don't see a logic to this…that is…unless we made the decision about what we are to experience before we came here."

"You mean as in reincarnation?"

"Yes," Sharon continued. "What if we choose to experience painful things?"

"Well, I can't understand why this happened to Jennifer." Jude's voice trembled.

Sharon wiped Brad's nose again and placed him, with his two matchbox cars and a stack of books, into Jennifer's play pen, then re-joined Jude at the table.

"I just can't believe this has happened to us," Jude said in barely a whisper.

"Are you doing okay with the diabetes, Jude?"

Jude reached to fluff Jennifer's curly hair. "I'm not sure it's really soaked in yet, Sharon…just what this means, that she'll have to have insulin shots and blood checks several times a day just to stay alive, and for the rest of her life. And the insulin reactions really scare me. I have to have this shot kit, Glucagon, on hand to give her if she loses consciousness or goes into convulsions."

"I'd like to learn to give her shots, Jude. Then you could get away once in a while. I can't even imagine how it feels to be constantly on guard like that. I'm sure you need a break at times."

Jude's eyes filled. "I love you dear friend. What would I do without you? I'd really appreciate you knowing how to care for Jennifer."

"More coo-kee?" Jennifer looked up at Jude. She liked dipping her cookies, and vanilla wafer was smeared across her face. Jude wiped the sweet rounded face as Jennifer's big blue eyes stared up at her. Tears pooled at the edges of Jude's eyes.

Sharon walked around the table and hugged Jude. "I'm here, girlfriend, whenever you need me," she whispered. "Right now I do have to go. Got to get home and start dinner."

"Thank God I have Sharon in my life," Jude thought as she closed the door behind Sharon and Brad. "I think I might go mad if I didn't have her to talk to." She smiled thinking about how fortunate she was to be at home with her children. With Jennifer's diagnosis, daycare was not an option. Grant would be arriving home any minute from kindergarten; he loved to have his milk and cookies as soon as he got in the door.

"Eternity in the present," she whispered under her breath. "Be present in this moment, 'chop wood carry water.'" She laughed aloud. For Jude chopping wood and carrying water meant cook, clean, do laundry, bathe babies, and, literally, keeping her baby girl alive. Edward didn't get it, what it took to be a stay-at-home mom, especially one with a chronically ill child. All he seemed to think about was how he deserved flying whenever he wanted, or drinking with the guys. It seemed to Jude that he took every opportunity to get away from the house.

Jude heard the school bus stop in front of their small suburban home. She opened the door to the smiling face of her five-year-old son. "Mommy, I'm hungry! Can I have some milk and cookies?"

"Yes, you may, big guy. Come here." Jude swept Grant up into her arms, Superman book bag and all. She was learning that being present with her children was as much a part of her personal growth as reading Wilber or Kierkegaard.

While Grant had his cookies and milk, Jude moved the ink and watercolor wash drawings from the dining table. These days she had to squeeze in her artistic pursuits between meals. She would have to start dinner soon. She hoped Edward would be home on time, or at least that he would call if he was going for after-work drinks.

After dinner, with clean up done and dishes in the dishwasher, Edward sat in his recliner reading while Jude bathed both children, got them into their pajamas, brushed their teeth and read *Pokey Little Puppy* aloud to them.

"Daddy, Daddy," Grant called out. "Come and tuck me in." Edward stood in the bedroom door. Jude smiled up at him as he came in and reached first for Grant, then Jennifer.

"Sweet dreams my bambinos," he said in a Cookie Monster voice. Both children screamed with delight. Edward could be so good with them. He obviously loved them and certainly gave them more attention than Jude

JAN GROENEMANN

had received from her slightly detached father. Edward is a good daddy, she assured herself. Together they tucked the children in their beds.

As Jude turned out the lights and pulled each door within a crack of closed, Edward reached for her, pulled her to him and kissed her demandingly.

"Feel like a little romance tonight?" he teased, as he began to fondle her breasts and kiss her neck.

"Wait, wait." she playfully pulled Edward toward the living room. "Come and sit with me and tell me about your day. Help me switch into adult mode."

Suddenly, as if losing interest, he walked past her and back to his recliner. "I want to finish this last chapter," he said.

Feeling rejected, Jude sat on the sofa across from Edward, watching his face as he read. Did she really know this man? Sometimes, something she couldn't put her finger on, felt, what? A little off. He was a good man, a deacon in the church where they went every Sunday morning, Sunday evening and Wednesday night. He loved his children. He loved her. They had great sex. They enjoyed a lot of things together: biking, boating, even horseback riding until moving to the Chicago area where it was too expensive to board horses. And she was glad that he loved to read. There was a togetherness that came with sitting quietly in the same room, each into their own book. She just had to let it go. She picked up the small aged book Sharon had found in the library and brought for Jude, insisting it was a "must read." It was old and out of print. "*The Cloud of Unknowing,*" Jude whispered the title to herself.

III

The shamanic workshop facilitator was leading a guided visualization, or as those studying Shamanism labeled it, a Shamanic Journey. They had begun with deep breathing and relaxation. In her imagination Jude was waiting on the edge of a clear expanse of lake surrounded by trees in full foliage. The vision was so clear, the shimmering of the trees as they moved with a soft breeze, scattered clouds, and sky reflected on the water. Except for the sound of birdsong, all was silent. Jude was waiting, as instructed, for her totem animal to appear. She wondered if she would actually find this sort of visualization beneficial. There was always a worry that she made these experiences up in her mind. As she was questioning, a dog that looked somewhat like a wolf materialized in the scene. She wasn't surprised, as it had been a wolf dog that she saw previously in a meditation while in Sedona. It had seemed very real then as well, and feeling a strange sensation, she had opened her eyes and looked down on the trail below to see a man walking a dog that looked exactly like the wolf in her meditation. The wolf that came to her now was the same, grays and white with touches of brown. He walked to her and nuzzled her hand.

"Is it a good day to journey?" she asked, still following her instructions.

The wolf spoke: "For you every day is a good day to journey." And Jude laughed aloud.

The wolf turned and ran ahead up a winding and narrow path that led from the lake up the hillside. Jude hurried to follow. She had been told by the facilitator to watch for the doorway to the first chamber, and sure enough, one appeared. It was an arched wooden door, rough and weathered. The wolf sniffed at its base, and it opened into a small stone-walled chamber. Jude entered. The chamber was empty except for an elegant antique desk that sat in the center. This, the facilitator was saying, is your Chamber of Contracts. Jude was instructed to look around the room for any unfinished contracts. The top of the desk was clear, and she found the single drawer empty. She was feeling the room to be empty of any contracts at all when she noticed a paper that had been plastered to the wall. She walked closer to find an old contract between her and Edward. Across it was stamped "Fulfilled." She pulled the paper from the wall in pieces. The wolf sniffed at the scraps of paper, grabbed them from her hand and ate them. Obviously that contract was no longer valid. She thought it interesting that there were no others in the room. It was time to leave.

As they left the chamber, the wolf bounded further up the hillside and stopped to wait for Jude at a second door much like the first. As she pushed, the door slowly swung open to reveal a second chamber. "This is your Chamber of Wounds," she heard as a whisper. At that moment the room began to spin slowly as if moved by a soft wind. The whisper again filled the room with the words, "Your wounds are only as deep as you imagine; in truth they are moments of teaching that carry you through life as a Great Wind." Jude thought of those wounds that had most affected her and how she could always look back and see her lessons. She was filled with a knowing of the truth of this message as the room began to spiral upward. She and her totem guide were carried with the spiraling wind. When the spinning stopped, they stepped out of the chamber directly into a brilliant light. The voice whispered, "Welcome to the Chamber of Grace."

As Jude attempted to adjust to the bright light, she saw that it was morphing into the form of an eagle. The great wings encompassed her. The wolf stood beside her unafraid. The Light Being had obviously been the source of the whispering voice. Again it spoke: "Your true self is a being of light, of higher consciousness, Christlikeness, your ultimate guide." Jude recalled the words of Jesus: "I am the light of the world….." Jesus instructed his followers to "let your Light shine," not to hide it. What did it mean that the Light Being was in the form of an eagle? Jude was a student of Native American totems. Eagle eye meant seeing keenly, clearly. Eagle totem was a reminder of one's own ability to soar to great heights. Eagles were considered messengers from heaven, an embodiment of the Spirit of the Sun. Those with an Eagle totem needed to have a willingness to use their ability, even if it meant getting "scorched" a little as one flew high, and a willingness to see one's true emotions. Eagle was a demanding totem. Its four-toed feet reminded one to stay grounded even when soaring to the heights. Eagle people could live in the realm of the Spirit, yet remain connected and balanced within the realm of the Earth.

Again the Light Being whispered: "You must trust in ALL THAT IS. Trust that whatever comes is from ALL THAT IS. You are to know that you can ride the winds, have no fear, risk, soar, but remain grounded."

"Now, allow yourself to come back to the present," the facilitator was saying.

Jude breathed in deeply. She thought of her mom whispering to her that sending Andrew was the best way she knew to ground her. Soar but remain grounded, the Light Being had told her. The journey had been revealing. She had read about Shamanism, but this was her first Shamanic experience. She was anxious to discuss the experience with Sharon. She found it amazing that the Shamanic Journey was so like the visualizations she taught in her creativity workshops. Perhaps she had been calling on her Native American heritage in her own work without realizing it.

CHAPTER 4

Throw your dreams into space like a kite, and you do not know what it will bring back, a new life, a new friend, a new love, a new country. —Anais Nin

THERE WERE SO **many memories swirling in Jude's head.** Did all this introspection have to do with losing her mom? Or was it meeting Andrew? Why was she feeling so drawn to the past? She certainly had no wish to go backward, neither to her childhood nor her marriage. And she didn't regret saying no to marriage since her divorce from Edward. She recalled the message from the workshop experience. She was to trust that everything came from ALL THAT IS. This meant from a Higher Power, from God. Certainly she could see how everything she had experienced to this point had brought her to Woman Space and a work that felt very purpose-filled. Everything had fallen into place. She felt positive anticipation about what might unfold next in her life.

The ringing of the phone pulled her out of her reverie. She reached to answer: "Woman Space, Jude speaking."

"Jude, it's Andrea. We'd better get an offer in on the Grayson property near Western Springs if you're serious about it. Three other parties have looked at it over the weekend."

"Oh, I'm very serious! I've been meaning to get my contractor out there to see if I can open up the living area. Let me see if I can reach him and get him to meet me there today."

"Better make it this morning!" Andrea exclaimed. "I'll go ahead and write up the offer so that all I'll need is your signature if everything checks out?" There was urgency in her voice.

"Yes, let's do that." Jude cleared her desk and zipped her keys into her purse. "I'll call Carl on the way out. Maybe we should let the listing agent know I want that place even if I have to outbid someone for it." If she didn't go for her dream now, it might never happen. It wasn't often that you found a property on the water that included a house with great possibilities. Forty acres would allow for room to eventually build a retreat center. Jude was designing a plan that would offer a holistic range of programs helpful to the Woman Space artists in creating stable lives and careers. Several of them needed training in business management, and life coaching would also be beneficial. Several of these artists came from abusive situations, so therapy could prove helpful as well. Acquiring the property was the first step.

"I'll make the call, Jude; you get Carl out there and have an answer for me when I arrive."

It was early, and her gallery assistant, Maggie Dennis, would not be in for another hour. Jude sent a text to let Maggie know where to reach her, pulled on her jacket, grabbed her purse and scarf and rushed out the door. Her mind raced ahead as she tried to be patient with the slow movement of the elevator. She rang the building attendant asking him to bring her car around to the front hoping that would save a few minutes.

Her phone was ringing Carl's number as the attendant opened the door for her. "Jude, what can I do for you?" Carl spoke in his usual gruff manner.

"Hi, Carl. Could you possibly meet me at the Grayson property right away? Andrea says I need to move on it immediately, and I need you to tell me if it's feasible to move some walls to open up the space."

"You can move any wall…for a price." He teased. "But yeah, I can meet you right now if you want. I just had a meeting cancelled, so my morning's pretty slow."

"I'm on my way as we speak, so meet me there."

"You got it." Carl hung up.

Her stomach filled with butterflies and chills ran across her shoulders as she neared the long tree-lined lane leading to the main house. This was definitely the place. Carl's silver Jeep was already in the drive when she arrived. Could she really be about to buy her dream property? The thought excited her all the more. She had grown up on fifteen hundred acres, but it had taken almost forty years for her to afford this forty.

II

Jude dreamed of living on acreage and had tried to convince Edward that it would be a good investment. But she watched in frustration as land prices inched higher while Edward spent money on flying lessons, then on airplanes. Looking back she realized how very different their priorities had been.

Edward's value as an employee had prompted his company to send him to school for an advanced degree, which had required a good deal of travel. He loved flying himself to the sessions that were scheduled in various parts of the country. Jennifer, their second child, had just been born when Edward began to build hours toward instrument certification. Flying had become an obsession, and so buying a four-seater airplane had been top priority. Over the years of their marriage they had owned three different planes, each a step up from the last, and thus, anything extra they had between them went into Edward's passion.

In fact, their first major disagreement came because Jude had not been in favor of buying that first plane. "Edward, a plane will take every extra penny we have," she had argued. "How will we ever have a family vacation?"

"We'll fly places. A plane is a time machine. And we can see your family more often."

Jude knew how loud the engine was when flying. It was impossible to carry on a conversation. Family vacations tended to go by the wayside. But when a husband and wife can't agree, someone has to make the final decision. According to both of their upbringings, it would be Edward. After all, the man was the head of the household. And with Jennifer's health issues, Jude had no choice but to be a stay at home mom which meant Edward was the sole breadwinner.

That conflict was just the beginning. Jude had felt confident in Edward's love for her, but she eventually learned that he was a womanizer. There had been times that Jude sensed something wasn't right, had even attempted talking to Edward about her uneasiness. But Edward managed to convince her all was well. "We have a better relationship than anyone I know. What are you worrying about? You're becoming a worry-wort like your grandma," he had said. And there was nothing she could put her finger on.

It had been Edward's strange behavior on the phone while traveling to a school that had brought things to a head. Jude felt that knot in her stomach that she always got when something wasn't right. Edward seemed awkward when they talked and had neglected to say his usual "I love you." When Jude confronted him, he got disproportionately defensive. She knew something was wrong. She later learned that Edward's secretary was traveling with him, and they were involved in an affair. Eventually Edward became so enmeshed with his secretary—who left her husband believing Edward was leaving Jude— the marriage fell apart. They had been nearing their twentieth anniversary.

Jude was devastated. But she felt she had no choice but to divorce Edward. She couldn't stay with him while he insisted on continuing his involvement with another woman. There were no savings, and Jude refinanced in order to buy Edward's share of their small suburban home. This decision had ultimately forced her into the world's concept of a real artist, one who could sell enough art to pay the bills.

III

Andrea and Carl had gone. The offer on the property was made. That she could actually manage to make this purchase on her own gave Jude a great deal of satisfaction. She stood looking out onto the lake. She could envision a studio sitting at the edge of the water where she could paint in total solitude. Her best work had always come out of the silence. Light danced across the water as if there was a shimmering below the surface.

She could live here. She belonged here. She dropped her jacket on the polished hardwood floor in the large empty family room, slipped out of her shoes and stepped forward into a yoga sun salutation. Sunlight poured in through the open French doors, casting dancing shadows across her face. She could feel the warmth on her closed eyes. She whispered, "Our Father who art in heaven," as she leaned backward extending her arms toward the ceiling. "Hallowed be thy name," she slowly came forward into a standing forward bend. She continued the Lord's Prayer as she focused on each position, a combination she had learned at a yoga retreat years ago and had started her day with since. Jude felt her energy growing with each asana, validating that she could accomplish whatever she set her mind to. Buying this property would move her toward the pinnacle of her dreams.

"For thine is the kingdom, the power and the glory forever and ever. Amen," she whispered under her breath as she finished the last movement and ended with her hands in a prayer pose. Someone clapped softly. She turned to see Andrew standing in the doorway.

"Hey there, neighbor," she greeted him. "Come on in and have a look. I'm waiting to hear if my offer is accepted; I'm so hoping this goes through."

The cowboy moved toward her with long, relaxed strides and a wide smile. He was holding something behind his back. Jude cocked her head to see as he swung his hand toward her with a fist full of wild flowers. "I thought you might like a celebration. I happen to know your deal is going through. Jack Grayson and I have known each other a long time, and I twisted his arm because I really want you for a neighbor." He reached for her with his free hand and twirled her around.

Jude laughed aloud. "I wasn't expecting such a fringe benefit!" She hugged Andrew and then reached to take the flowers. "I'll have to wait 'til I get back to the gallery to get these in water."

"I have a vase in the truck; let me run and get it." Jude watched as Andrew jogged out to his black late model Ford pickup. What a character, she thought as he pulled a large wicker picnic basket from the rear seat. And a romantic at that.

"You've thought of everything!" Jude teased, pleasantly surprised. The basket contained a fried chicken lunch with all the trimmings, a bottle of Pinot Noir, and a pewter vase that Andrew filled with water from the sink.

"I have water already?" Jude exclaimed.

"Yes, I asked Grayson to leave it on. I told him I'd vouch for you. Come on, let's have a celebration." He spread a red and white checkered table cloth on the floor in front of the French doors that overlooked the lake and motioned for Jude to seat herself next to it. He set the vase of flowers in the center.

"This is so sweet," Jude said as she took utensils rolled in a cloth napkin that matched the table cloth from the basket, while Andrew opened the bottle of wine. "I'm impressed!"

"Actually, it all came as a set," he laughed. "I picked it up at Target on the way over— basket, napkins, utensils…guess I'd better rinse the utensils."

"But I would have expected you would cook the chicken yourself," she added in a teasing tone. "Kentucky fried?" Andrew looked up with a sheepish smile.

How could she resist someone so charming? Jude had expected she was finished with men. She was determined to put most of her energy into her work: Woman Space and her own creative endeavors, with enough left over for friends and family. She had not had the best of experiences in the romance department, and she didn't know if she'd fully trust a man again.

"Just enjoy this." Was that her mom whispering in her ear again?

"Already dreaming about how you'll remodel this place?" Andrew interrupted her thoughts.

"Yes, I am. Carl assures me it won't be a problem to move these two walls and make this one big open space looking out over the lake."

"That'll take a good sized beam." Andrew ran his fingers through his hair as a thoughtful look crossed his face. "You do have great views from here. Will you have a deck across the back?"

"Yeah. And I think I'd like it partially covered so I can enjoy it in the rain."

Andrew got up, chicken leg in hand, and stood at the windows. "You might like skylights in the porch roof to magnify the sound of the rain."

"I love that idea," Jude said as she joined him.

They stood looking out onto the lake, an expanse as smooth as glass even though it was mid-day. "I imagine a flower garden with a path to the water and a pier going out several feet for morning yoga. Oh, and a tie off for a kayak. Over here." Jude motioned with her hand to the left of the main view as she spoke, "Right on the water I want a studio large enough for painting and holding small workshops, its deck connected to the pier."

"I have an extra kayak you can have if you want it," Andrew interjected. Jude turned, meeting his eyes; they laughed aloud. This just kept happening between them. They were so alike in many ways in spite of their differing philosophies. She had once held similar fundamental Christian views but that seemed years ago.

Andrew leaned down, kissed her forehead, and then said, "I'll help you get settled in, whatever way you need." As Jude looked up at him, he pulled her close and kissed her lips. His broad shoulders enveloped her. The feel of him stirred a buried desire. Sensing this, Andrew's kiss became more passionate. She felt her body awaken. These sensations had been dormant for so long she'd thought she might not feel them again.

Feeling a bit overwhelmed, Jude pulled away, laughing nervously. "Okay, we'd better slow down."

Andrew let her go, and touched her cheek. There was gentleness in his eyes. He's a good man, she thought, but I don't want things to move so fast.

CHAPTER 5

We waste so much energy trying to cover up who we are when beneath every attitude is the want to be loved, and beneath every anger is a wound to be healed and beneath every sadness is the fear that there will not be enough time. —Mark Nepo

A STRONG WIND WHIPPED up white caps on the lake as Jude and Andrew sat beneath the giant old sycamore at its edge. After measuring and staking the location where the new studio would sit, Jude was visualizing how the sycamore would mark the western boundary of the dock that would be attached. A gusty wind grabbed at her hair as she attempted to tame it into a pony tail. The wind, combined with planning for her lake side studio, seemed a metaphor of her life. So many years of chaos that now seemed to be settling into a flow that felt much like the still after the storm. She was planning for a future she could actually see materializing. She wondered if anyone ever had real control. She'd learned that wind just might change things up at any moment. Andrew's voice pulled her from her thoughts.

"You're even more beautiful windblown," Andrew said as he caught a stray strand of hair and pushed it behind Jude's ear.

"You're not so bad yourself." Jude laughed, appreciating Andrew's own windblown good looks. God, she was so attracted to his looks. And she was so comfortable with him. He seemed as excited as she about the country house remodel, and obviously enjoyed helping her measure and plan. It was fun having a creative partner as she brought to life her dream of a studio and retreat. A sweet sexual tension played between them.

"I think you have me charmed," Jude said, smiling into Andrew's eyes.

"I'm the one who's charmed." Andrew leaned forward and kissed her lightly. Jude found his kiss as enticing as his rugged good looks. She felt herself tempted to melt into him, to stay there in his arms. But she reminded herself that she hardly knew him. It was chemistry that was pulling at her at this point. There was something electric between them, but she had followed that path before, had fallen in love with a man who turned her on physically and emotionally only to learn later it was not enough. What she wanted, longed for, was a relationship in which she felt a compatibility on a soul level, a spiritual connection. She reminded herself that kind of connection took time.

"I do like the fringe benefits that come with this property." Jude laughed playfully as she pushed Andrew backward into the grass and then laid back next to him to stare up into the sycamore branches which spread out in a wide circle above them. The gnarley old tree's white-washed limbs were just beginning to fill out with spring leaves, as if it too were readying itself for the next stage of life.

"Look at those clouds. They're really moving today!" Andrew folded his arms behind his head to put his full focus on the sky.

Jude watched the billowing and changing forms. A shape resembling an elephant formed with its long trunk trailing off to the east; just as quickly the elephant morphed and disappeared as a white stallion appeared to the north. "Look at that horse form!" Andrew exclaimed. "Remember that old movie, *Thunderhead*, wasn't it?"

Jude laughed, "I remember that movie. Oh, and *My Friend Flicka*. As a kid I watched them both over and over."

"Yeah," Andrew chimed in, "I loved those movies. Guess I've always been crazy about horses. You, too?"

"Me, too." Jude turned to appreciate Andrew as he concentrated on the clouds.

"Wonder what will appear next? Oh, over there," he pointed to the south. "There's a white buffalo."

"Good magic!" Jude whispered as she turned to look. A chill ran down her arms. She was feeling it now, the good magic. She sighed deeply. "My life feels like these clouds right now, moving faster than I know how to adjust. As soon as I begin to get comfortable with one change another materializes."

"Hmmm," Andrew responded thoughtfully.

"But it's all good." Jude sighed and turned to look again at Andrew's profile as he studied the sky. "This sky, these clouds, this old tree, reminds me there must be something at work far beyond my comprehension….a Higher Power. I see God most like this—moments in nature."

"Yeah, I see God in nature," Andrew responded. "But I guess I feel Him most when I'm praising Him with my church family." He paused, studying Jude for a moment. "I've been visiting some new churches; I've found one I'd like you to visit with me." Again he paused to look Jude in the eyes. "Would you do that? I'd like us to find a place we could go together, even if only on Sunday mornings."

"I understand you really want that Andrew, and I've felt a lifting of the Spirit when I was in church. But I'm not sure I belong in a church anymore. So many churches I've been part of split over unimportant issues. And my concept of God has changed over the years to be… more inclusive. I think maybe I…I sort of have my own religion." There was a long pause. "Maybe I'm becoming a pagan," Jude teased in an attempt to lighten the mood. She turned toward a silent and serious Andrew, studied his perfectly shaped nose and added, "Hey, I feel my spirit lifting just looking at your profile, talk about a perfect creation." She traced Andrew's nose with her finger and smiled into his face as he turned toward her.

"Now you're just giving me trouble, aren't you?" He pulled her to him as if to kiss her, but instead, began to tickle her ribs.

"No, no, no!" Jude wrestled away from him giggling hysterically.

Andrew followed, this time pulling her to him as he kissed her. A tremor of desire ran through her body. She did love having a man in her life again. She just wasn't sure how to deal with his need for her to go with him to his church. She felt that on any given day she was in her church: the studio where she was surrounded by art, and now surrounded by nature under this incredible Sycamore at the edge of her lake. She felt God all around her and talked to him constantly, like an old friend.

Suddenly serious again, Andrew sighed and said, "Jude, I'd like you to consider using Jeff Becker for your remodel and the building of your studio. He comes with excellent references; he's done a lot of projects for me. I trust him."

"Andrew, Carl has done all the work on Woman Space, and I'm very happy with everything he's done."

"He doesn't have the experience my guy has."

"Please, we've already had this conversation Andrew, and I don't really want to discuss it further. I promised this job to Carl before I even knew you. He dropped everything several times to check out a property for me, and he's already helped me lay out the changes I want made."

Jude watched something change on Andrew's face; he fell into a long silence. He does have a few control issues, she thought to herself, but what handsome, self-made man didn't like to be in control? Like Jude, Andrew had grown up poor. His father was a farmer, horse breeder, and preacher. Andrew was a PK, as they called preacher's kids when she was growing up in Southern Illinois. PKs were known for being a bit arrogant and intent on having their way. She didn't know Andrew well enough to know if this was true of him. But she knew he had worked hard to pay what had not been covered by a scholarship toward his MBA, and he was very sure of himself. She liked that.

Jude had had enough of men who were uncomfortable in their own skins. In her experience such men were drawn to strong, independent women, but ultimately were intimidated by what had attracted them in the first place. She expected there was little that intimidated Andrew.

Jude's phone broke the silence. "Hi, Maggie, what is it?"

"I need you here at the gallery Jude. Can you come right away?"

Jude heard the urgency in Maggie's voice. "I'm at the country house. I can be there in maybe twenty minutes, depending on traffic. What is it?"

"It's Gavin Crane, Madi Crane's ex-husband. He's here and demanding to talk to the person in charge. I've tried to calm him down, but it isn't working. I don't think he likes a black woman telling him what to do. Can I tell him the boss is on the way?"

"Yes. Should I contact 911?"

"That might not be a bad idea, Jude."

"Okay, I'll be right there." Jude sat up, made a quick call to 911 and gathered her things.

"Is everything okay?" Andrew asked, concern on his face.

"Maggie's having some trouble with an irate ex-husband of one of our new artists. He's some sort of radical guy who believes Woman Space is the reason his wife left him. Madi has a restraining order against him, but it seems that isn't working. He's at the gallery demanding to see the person in charge. I'd better go handle this."

Maggie, Jude's gallery assistant, was a very attractive black woman, who at fifty-seven and five feet nine inches tall was very capable of handling most situations. But she had been a battered wife herself before she got up the courage to leave her husband of twenty-five years. She had come to interview for the position as Jude's gallery director with a black eye, one of the many reasons Jude had hired her.

"I'm going with you," Andrew asserted, grabbing his jacket and throwing the tools into a small canvas bag. "You never know what someone like that might do. It could help to have a man along."

"That's true. I'd really appreciate it. I've talked to this guy on the phone, but I've yet to meet him. He sounds a bit unstable, and I'm guessing he's been physically abusive with Madi and the kids, though she hasn't come right out and said so."

Jude was finding that an unexpected aspect of Woman Space was dealing with angry exes who didn't want their women to become independent. This was the third incident in as many years, and most likely would not be the last.

"Come on, I'll drive," Andrew said as he directed Jude to his truck. Thankfully the traffic was light, and they made it to the gallery in fifteen minutes. Andrew dropped Jude at the front door. "I'll park in the garage and be right in," he said.

Jude paused a moment, straightened her hair and gained her composure. As she walked into the gallery, she saw through the glass partition that Gavin Crane was pacing back and forth in the office. Maggie stood in the doorway, as if keeping a safe distance.

"Mr. Crane," Jude greeted him as she walked through the office door. "I'm Jude Bennett, the owner of Woman Space. How can I help you?"

"You need to tell my wife that she's not going to be involved in this business!" he shouted. "Not only is she doin' the devil's work with all this painting, she's being influenced to be disobedient to her husband by you people. This is your fault. You're responsible for me losin' control of my wife!"

Jude caught the wild look in the man's eyes. His left eyebrow twitched slightly. Her own adrenalin began to flow.

"Mr. Crane, I understood that you and Madi were divorced." Jude said calmly. "We're trying to help her build an income so she can support herself."

This only infuriated him more. "What God has joined together let no man put asunder!" he yelled, as he slapped a large worn Bible down on Jude's desk. "No piece of paper tells me whether she's my wife or not. She's the mother of my children, and I've taken care of her for eleven years!"

Jude could see the veins protruding on his forehead, and her heart pounded. Out of her peripheral vision she saw Andrew come in from the parking garage and pretend to be looking at the artwork near the office. Crane was too absorbed in his anger to notice Andrew, or that Maggie walked toward the front door. Hopefully the police would arrive any minute. Jude had to figure a way to stall him without making him more irate. She walked to the coffee pot and poured a cup of coffee. Her hand shook slightly; she was glad her back was to the angry man.

"Do you take cream or sugar, Mr. Crane?" she asked without emotion.

"No. Just black."

Jude thought she heard a slightly softer edge to his voice.

As she turned to hand him the coffee, she could smell alcohol on his breath. "Please, sit down with me and tell me what has you so upset."

Thank God, Jude thought, as he sat down in the chair to the front of her desk and took a sip of coffee. She took a seat putting the desk between them.

"Look here," Crane began, "Madi and I are going through a rough spot, that's all. She thinks she wants to get away from me, but it's all this craziness about being an artist. There's no way she can make it on her own selling these god-awful wooden totems. Nobody makes a livin' doing art! She's losin' her mind, and I'm responsible for her. She's my wife, and she's one of my flock."

"Your flock?" Jude asked.

"I'm a preacher of God's word. I know what's best for my family, and you're gonna tell her she can't display her work here. She's goin' home with me!"

"I'm sure we can work this out. Is the coffee okay? Strong enough?"

Crane nodded.

"Okay. Let's think this through, Mr. Crane. How long have you and Madi been married?"

"Eleven years. And I've been very good to her…took good care of her and the kids. I provide everything she needs. Her place is in the home takin' care of the kids and makin' sure we have good meals and clean clothes. I thought lettin' her buy some carvin' tools and bang around on some wood would keep her happy, not turn into an excuse to desert us all."

"And how many children do you have?"

"Four; a girl and three boys. My wife is needed at home."

"How long have you been having marital trouble, Mr. Crane?" Jude spoke in a soft calming voice.

"Well…." he seemed to stop to consider just how long it had been.

"Take your time," Jude encouraged him. "We just need to think this through from the beginning." Out of the corner of her eye, she saw a Chicago policeman enter the front door. Maggie was speaking to him as she escorted him through the gallery toward the office.

Noticing Jude was distracted, Mr. Crane followed her eyes to the officer. He mumbled something under his breath about "all these blacks surrounding him."

"Excuse me just a moment, Mr. Crane." Jude stood and walked to the office door.

"Is there a problem here?" the officer asked.

Crane stood, looking confused.

"I think Mr. Crane is just a bit upset," Jude responded.

"You'd better come with me sir. We'll get to the bottom of this at the station." The policeman reached for Crane's arm, keeping his other hand on his revolver. Seeing the revolver, Crane threw the hot coffee in the policeman's face. "Ain't no nigger taking hold of me!" he yelled and bolted out the office door. Fortunately, Andrew was ready for him. He tackled Crane to the floor and held him down as the wincing police officer pulled his arms behind him and cuffed them. Crane was breathing heavily but remained silent. The coffee cup had shattered on the floor; Maggie began to clean it up.

Jude grabbed a hand towel and motioned to the officer.

"No. I'm fine," he said, shaking his head.

Andrew and Jude followed the officer as he pushed a silent Mr. Crane ahead of him toward the door. At least Crane was sober enough not to fight the officer further.

"Oh, wow," Maggie sighed as they closed the door behind them. "I just knew he was going to blow up and start breaking things! Thank God it was only a coffee cup! Jude, you handled that beautifully."

"We handled it beautifully," Jude said, giving Maggie a hug. She wiped a bead of sweat from her forehead and realized her hands were still trembling. This was not something she wanted to deal with every day. And what if Andrew hadn't been there?

"We couldn't have managed this without you." She turned to Andrew and gave him a hug. "You're my hero."

"Mine, too," Maggie added.

Andrew put his arm around Jude. "Have you thought about hiring a security person as part of your staff? I think it might be a good idea."

Jude felt her energy begin to calm with Andrew's comforting arm around her. Yes, she had thought about hiring security, and today was a sign not to put it off any longer.

"I'll make some calls Monday morning. Thanks, Andrew. I'm really so grateful you came along."

"Come on, it's almost closing time. Why don't you lock up, and I'll take you girls for a drink."

"Sounds good to me," Maggie added.

They sat in a small, quiet café a block from the gallery. The soft music and single fresh flower in a vase on the table were calming. Jude attempted to make small talk as she could see Maggie was pretty shaken.

"I'm so sorry you had to deal with this, Maggie, including his insults."

"No problem, Jude. You get used to it."

"I'll never get used to people like him, such a jerk, yet, feeling so superior."

They all needed time to allow the flow of adrenalin to slow, but the subject kept coming back to Gavin Crane.

"Was he disrespectful to you before we arrived?" Jude asked.

"Oh, just the usual innuendos and superior attitude. Probably didn't like that I was a woman first of all, and that I was black just added to his irritation."

"He didn't like that the officer was black either," Andrew added. "A real bigot, that one."

Jude sighed. "It's lucky the officer got there when he did. I was only managing to stall him."

Eventually, with a little time and a little wine, they relaxed enough to order a light dinner.

"I'll check tomorrow to see what part of the budget we can adjust in order to cover the cost of a security man." Maggie spoke, her voice still shaky.

"And I'll make some calls to a couple of friends who might have suggestions," Jude said, reaching to stroke Maggie's shoulder. "I won't allow you to be put in this situation again. Woman Space is growing; today's incident was one of its growing pains."

Jude turned to glance at Andrew. He was intensely focused on his phone. "Here," he said sliding the phone toward her. "This is the best security company I know of. Ask for Gail Wilson; tell him Andrew Jamison referred you."

Jude looked at the information and handed the phone to Maggie who wrote the name and number in her day planner. She slid the phone back to Andrew. Jude caught Andrew's eye. "Thanks again," she whispered, touching his hand. Andrew smiled softly, and taking Jude's hand, squeezed it.

"Well, that was a bit more excitement than I needed. Thank you both for getting there so quickly!" Maggie sighed.

As they finished with their dinner, Jude pushed her plate to the side. "I think I'll get a few things from the loft and go back to the country house tonight." She turned to Maggie. "Do you want us to drop you home? You could get your car tomorrow."

"No, no," Maggie responded. "I'm fine now; but thanks for dinner."

Jude and Andrew walked Maggie to her car in the parking garage then took the elevator to Jude's loft where she packed a small overnight bag.

"Are you okay, Jude?" Andrew asked.

"I am. But I do know having you here made a big difference."

Andrew smiled and hugged her. "Come on my lady." He took her bag so she could lock up. "Let's get you back to the country and tucked in for the night."

Jude had a lot on her mind as they made the drive back to the country house. She had to get security in place for the gallery, and she needed to get Carl started on the renovations. The house was in decent condition, and certainly it wasn't a problem for her to be there overnight, but she needed to get the renovations completed as soon as possible. She wanted to schedule workshops in the new space by fall, and she hoped this would be the first year her family would spend the holidays at the country house.

"I know you're very independent, but it's always good to have a little extra muscle around," Andrew reminded her as they pulled up to the house.

Jude reached across the car and squeezed his upper arm. "Come on my muscle man; let's have another glass of wine before you go."

Laughing, Andrew put Jude's arm through his and walked her up the path to the front door. She took a deep breath of the cool evening air. A sliver of a new moon was hanging over the lake, and she enjoyed the soft scent of Andrew's cologne. "What is that cologne?" she asked.

"Cool Water. Do you like it?"

"Very nice," And very appropriate, she thought.

She still felt a bit shaken, but it did feel very good to have a cool, calm man beside her.

II

Andrew opened a bottle of Shiraz while Jude changed into leggings and a loose jersey top. She ran a brush through her hair and touched up her lipstick. She felt exhausted.

"You look revived," Andrew said, smiling as she entered the kitchen.

"I don't feel so revived." Jude took the glass of wine Andrew pushed toward her. "That experience really drained me." She moved across the room and sat with her legs folded under her on the comfortable worn sofa that was one of the few furniture pieces in the house. Andrew snuggled in beside her. As they sipped their wine, Jude felt the tension slowly draining away. She realized that dealing with situations like the one with Crane was a part of being involved in the lives of women like Madi. It occurred to her that it was time to look into an on-staff therapist as well as security.

"Feelin' better?" Andrew asked, putting a warm hand on her shoulder.

"I think so. I just need to wind down. That really got my adrenalin flowing!"

"Here," Andrew said taking her glass and setting it on the floor. "Let me give you a shoulder rub. You look as if you could use one."

Jude turned her back to him, and Andrew began to massage her shoulders in a deep circular motion. "Oh, god, that feels so good," she moaned. He worked his way across the width of her shoulders then up her neck relieving tight muscles with each stroke. "Where did you learn to do that?"

"I often use massage to calm a nervous horse." He laughed.

Between the wine, which was beginning to take effect, and the incredible pleasure of his touch, Jude couldn't help but giggle. Thinking of Andrew massaging a horse provided a sense of comic relief. "You're a horse whisperer and a horse masseuse?" They both laughed aloud.

The circular motion of Andrew's kneading fingers moved down her arms. There was something about the way he held her as he massaged, protective and possessive. She felt a tingle down her spine. Suddenly his lips were on her shoulder then working his way up her neck and behind her right ear. She felt her nipples harden, and then an ache that centered between her legs created a triangle of sexual energy. Andrew turned her gently to face him. Kissing her neck, he pulled her shirt over her head and kissed her eyes, her cheeks, and leaned to kiss her breasts as naturally as if he had done so a thousand times. *A Thousand Splendid Suns* ran through her mind. No, that was a book she had read at some point; but the "splendid" fit. How splendid she was feeling at this moment. She turned to him, her eyes searching for his. She caught his gaze as he found her willing lips. She could feel her body open to him full with pleasure and the ache of desire. It had been so long. And there was something more.

She trusted him. She even felt she might love him. The thought sent a tiny panic shivering through her.

Whether she slid herself beneath him or he pulled her into place she couldn't remember, but he was tugging at her leggings, and then she was helping him, pulling them down around her ankles, kicking them free. Then he was touching her, kissing her. The fingers of his wonderful Michelangelo hands were all over her, in her. She could stand it no longer. She pulled him to her.

Her pleasure had been intense. Andrew was smothering her with kisses as she strained to meet each kiss with one of her own. Their joining felt right. She had so missed the intimacy, the belonging that she felt at this moment, wrapped in Andrew, her body soothed, satisfied as it intertwined with his long arms and legs.

"Oh, my sweet Jude," Andrew moaned. "That was incredible."

Jude was breathless, speechless. She had known this was inevitable, but she had not expected it tonight. Andrew lay behind her, holding her tightly against him. They lay quietly, skin to skin. Jude breathed in the smell of him. "I think we were both ready for that," she whispered.

Andrew gently stroked her shoulder and sighed.

"I do have a question," Jude said as she turned to face Andrew. "How do you reconcile your religion with drinking wine and having spontaneous sex?" She smiled a teasing smile.

Andrew chuckled. "I am human," he answered. "And besides that," his face became serious, "I'm falling in love with you, Jude. Are you ready for that?"

"I don't know." she answered.

III

She didn't allow Andrew to stay the night. There was only a full-sized bed in the house, and she insisted they would both sleep better if he went home. The truth was, she needed some alone time, some processing time. She had met Andrew almost three months earlier, and they had spent a lot of time together since. But she was not sure she was ready for this step, this intimacy. For her it was a commitment. The eagerness with which she had made love with him surprised her. Suddenly she felt very vulnerable. The thought that she might love him, and he loved her—she was not at all prepared for what that might mean. "Okay," she whispered aloud, then reminded herself that this didn't have to change anything. There was no hurry; he lived across the lake. They could take this really slow. And there were many kinds of love. She had loved a few men, and each relationship had been unique to the person whom she loved. This love between her and Andrew would take time to develop, to take specific form. She had no desire for a traditional romance. At this point in life Jude needed a depth of friendship, a spiritual connection. Though the chemistry was certainly there and friendship was developing, she couldn't imagine that she and Andrew would connect on a spiritual level. She yearned for an overlapping and merging of mind, body, and spirit. But perhaps being neighbors and lovers afforded the perfect opportunity to develop a deep intimacy. She tossed and turned, finally falling into a restless sleep.

IV

It had not been an easy journey from housewife to big city gallery owner. Getting married, having children, this had been part of her perfect world, but after Jennifer was diagnosed with Type I Diabetes she had not been sure how being an artist would fit. Being the perfect wife and mother meant building her life around her husband. She would just begin to get known in an area, winning awards with her paintings, selling work, and Edward would be transferred with his job. Jude would start all over again. She was, by necessity, a stay-at-home mom; Jennifer needed special care. And she had been happy until Edward changed. He had become restless and defensive. She had thought he was going through a mid-life crisis. Whatever it had started as, it ended up a marital crisis.

At first, Jude determined to stick it out, to do whatever it took to save her marriage. But Edward's confusion became emotional abuse. He didn't want a divorce; Jude should hang in there until he figured out how to end things with Helen. But he didn't end things. The craziness continued.

It had been a very intense dream that had shaken her into a decision. She and Edward had separated. Their therapist felt they needed some time apart to sort things out. But Jude had allowed Edward to come home. They argued. Angry and exhausted Jude fell into a restless sleep, made even more so by a nightmarish dream:

> She was buckled into the passenger seat beside Edward who was doing loops and spins in their Cessna 172. Feeling more nauseated with each maneuver, Jude yelled, "Stop, stop!" Edward stalled the plane and allowed it to dive into another spin. "That is all I can take!" She leaned forward unlocking the door and pushing hard against the wind pressure in an attempt to open it. She couldn't get it opened while buckled in. She let the door slam shut in order to undo her seat belt. Edward didn't seem to notice. I wonder how you are going to feel when I'm gone, she was thinking to herself as she again pushed at the door with all her power. She finally forced it open enough that she could squeeze through. Grabbing the strut with her right hand, she managed to pull herself out of the plane, and then allowed herself to drop. She was free falling, her screams fading into the night.

Jude jerked awake. Her first feeling was one of great relief at the realization she had been dreaming. It had been so real; she had felt herself falling, knowing she would die. She was thinking that with her death Edward might finally realize how much he was hurting her. Her second thought was that she had to end the marriage.

Jude's income had barely covered Grant's dorm fees in college at the time she told Edward she wanted a divorce. At the same time, Emily Rosen was fighting for her life as the cancer had returned. She needed Jude full time at the gallery, and she would allow Jude to schedule her hours around Jennifer's needs. Working full time, painting enough to keep her inventory at the gallery, and keeping the household intact while being there for Jennifer and Grant was difficult. She could laugh now at how upset she had been to find she couldn't remove the cork from a wine bottle with the corkscrew Edward always used. And how many times had she been frustrated to tears over trying to wind the cheap garden hose into the storage container? Starting the ancient lawn mower was another story. But those were minor challenges. Making a budget, only to find there was inadequate income to cover the absolute necessities, had been the big challenge. Often, she wished she would be rescued: win the lottery, fall for a generous man—but her life hadn't unfolded in that way. Jude's "happily ever after" had been cut short, and she found herself having to handle all the details: keeping the house and car running and the bills paid, getting the support and therapy Jennifer needed, helping Grant stay on track with his school work, keeping the small suburban house a home for all of them. Edward used his assistance, his money, to manipulate Jude. He convinced himself that if only Jude would cooperate they would get back together. "Why had she divorced him?" he whined more than once. He just needed her to stick with him until he figured the right way to let Helen, his mistress, down gently. He couldn't just dump her, he told Jude. "She needs me more than you do."

Jude now knew that each chance she gave Edward had been a waste of time and energy. It simply delayed the inevitable. She was enabling him to stay stuck between the two relationships. This was co-dependency, but she had been afraid, too. Afraid of being alone, and afraid of all she would lose once Edward was gone. And she was so confused. Why did he keep begging her to let him come home if he didn't still love her? And if he loved her, why did he hang on to Helen? It was a crazy-making situation, and it took time for Jude to accept that something was irrevocably wrong. She had learned, too, that a marriage was like a separate entity. It didn't simply end when you decided it needed to. It died slowly, painfully as if gasping for another breath. Giving up on her marriage had seemed an unbearable choice, but in the end, it had been a choice for sanity.

With the ending of her marriage, Jude convinced herself, if that door closed, it must be that there was something better in store for her. But her wounds were deep. It took more than two years after the divorce was final before she felt ready to date again. When dating seemed to bring a line of equally self-absorbed men, Jude had lost trust in her own ability to choose someone caring and compassionate. What was wrong with her that the "so charming" narcissist was drawn to her? And she to him? Did she find good men boring? Was she an excitement addict? She had to take at least partial responsibility for this string of failed relationships. She was not interested in an exciting fling, she wanted depth of connection. Yet, she kept falling into these less than authentic relationships. What did she need to learn?

On some level, through each relationship, Jude was led to see herself, to know herself more fully. She knew that life was ultimately a spiritual journey: Spirit spoke to her through the books she read, through her art, so there was no doubt that the Divine was also speaking through each relationship. What was she missing?

Jude had been single for four years when Brandon Wilson walked into her studio to sign up for drawing lessons. She had dated a few men by this point, and she was tired of trying to figure out why this man or that man behaved as he did. But Brandon moved slowly, taking months after they met to ask Jude if she would like to drive to one of the local wineries for music and lunch. She felt safe to say yes. It was a beautiful fall afternoon. The leaves were reaching their peak of color, and the air was crisp and cool. Brandon was a gentleman, and they found they had art, music, and a love of nature in common.

"I do need to tell you," Brandon said with a smile, as they sat across the table from one another at a lovely outdoor winery, "I'm sure I never want to marry again."

By the questioning look on his face, Jude knew he was wondering if that might be a deal breaker for her. Instead, she gave a sigh of relief and said, "I feel the same. And the truth is I'm relieved to hear you say that."

He laughed nervously, then reached across the table and took her hand. "I do know that I'd really like to get to know you; I'm just afraid you may be out of my league."

Jude laughed "What does that mean?"

"What that means is that I feel a bit intimidated by all that you've already accomplished." Brandon responded. "You have more education than I, and my job in advertising in no way compares with your accomplishments as an artist or your position as a director in a very upscale gallery."

While Brandon's admission raised a small red flag in Jude's mind, her wish for the kind of relationship he and she both seemed to want allowed her to ignore it. "Well, what it means to be an accomplished artist is questionable," Jude said laughing again. "Emily Rosen saved my life by bringing me in as her gallery director shortly after I divorced. Otherwise, I might be a bag lady by now."

Brandon brought her hand to his lips and kissed it gently. "Okay. Do you want to do this, then? Want to see where this chemistry that I hope you're also feeling might take us?"

Jude smiled and nodded. "Could be fun, don't you think?"

The relationship unfolded slowly. Jude was learning to trust again. Brandon was not the kind of guy who would cheat on her, and he wasn't a narcissist. She wasn't sure how she knew this, but she did. And they did have a lot in common. Even their children liked one another.

On a drive to visit Brandon's parents in Wisconsin, they listened to a CD by Gary Zukav titled, *The Seat of the Soul*:

The new female and the new male

are partners on a journey of spiritual growth....

Their intuition guides them....

They are friends. They laugh a lot. They are equals.

Caught up in Zukov's words, Jude wondered if perhaps she had finally met an equal, a friend, a partner on her spiritual journey. "This is what I wish for, Brandon."

He turned and smiled at her. "Me, too; someone who's a good friend first and a partner in all these ways."

A sense of excitement permeated the car.

"Are you up to driving awhile?" Brandon interrupted the CD.

"Sure," Jude responded.

Brandon pulled his five-year-old Suburban to the side of the Interstate. He got out and walked around the back of the vehicle as Jude did the same. They met at the edge of the highway. Brandon took Jude in his arms and kissed her. Jude was filled with anticipation.

I'm falling in love with this man, she thought. This feels so right. She saw in his eyes, as he released her, that he felt the same though neither of them spoke.

They got back into the Suburban, and as they buckled their seat belts, Brandon broke the silence: "I think I've found my soulmate," he said.

Jude smiled.

It was on one of many drives in the country, about two years after their first date, that Brandon announced his son and fiancé had set a wedding date. "And Reese wants to know if they might buy my house," he said to Jude. "Which leads me to ask if maybe it's time for us to try living together?"

Jude hadn't expected this, but the idea was intriguing. They did get along well. A love had developed between them that felt comfortable, and yes, maybe even long term.

"You took me by surprise. But maybe it's time."

As if the question about living together had only been to build his courage for what he really wanted to ask, Brandon added, "I wonder how you might feel if we got married instead of just living together?"

Now, Jude was shocked. Brandon moved so slowly: it was months before he even asked her out, then another couple of months before he attempted to kiss her.

"Is this a proposal? You've really taken me by surprise, Brandon. Marriage? I thought neither of us were interested in marriage."

Brandon chuckled. "Well, I've changed my mind. I can no longer imagine my life without you, Jude. Will you marry me?"

Jude was silent for a moment. She loved Brandon. Enough to marry him? Maybe. Maybe that wasn't such a bad idea. "Okay," she finally answered. "Yes, I'll marry you. But can we have a long engagement?"

They both laughed aloud. It was as if each had made it over some invisible hurdle and with it came great relief. They giggled together like children. Brandon reached for Jude's hand, turning to look at her eye to eye. "I love you, Jude Bennett. I love you, and I want you to be my wife."

A proposal tooling down the Interstate. It wasn't the most romantic, Jude thought. But she smiled as she responded: "I love you too, Brandon, and I want to be your wife. Yes. Yes, I will marry you."

It was an exciting time, trying to blend their furniture and find personal space for each of them. There were tensions, of course, and Jude realized that by allowing Brandon to hang his stuffed Bass over the fireplace she had passed some sort of test.

As they should have been settling in together, Brandon became strangely quiet and withdrawn. But he couldn't tell her what was upsetting him. Even a simple conversation would somehow go wrong between them. And the things he so loved about her? Her artwork took up too much space. She was too close to her children. And everywhere they went someone knew her and wanted a piece of her. He complained that nothing was left for him.

"Something is going wrong between us," Jude said softly, as she stood in the bathroom door watching Brandon trim his beard. "I don't think it has to do with what is and what isn't art." They had just argued over the breakfast table about that subject. "I think we need to see a therapist. Can we do that?"

"Yes, but I want to see my therapist, not yours," Brandon said angrily.

Brandon arranged for them to see a female therapist that he had been seeing for some time. But following the first session, Brandon insisted she and Jude ganged up on him. In a private session with Brandon the following week, this therapist suggested that he might do better with a male therapist. The second was another therapist of Brandon's choosing, this time a male. When the new therapist confronted Brandon about his issues with women, Brandon was finished with therapy. "What if I have some fatal flaw that is the reason for my divorce and for every other failed relationship in my life?" He said.

"But wouldn't you want to know what that was and try to change it?" Jude asked. "I'm sure I have my own issues here. I get scared! Are you saying you will give up on us rather than consider there might be something you need to do differently?"

"No!" he shouted. "I will not pursue this further."

Without further therapy Jude was fearful of staying in the relationship. It wasn't working. But she needed to know if there was something she was doing wrong. She had her own list of failed relationships. She made an appointment with the therapist she and Edward had gone to. He knew her background, her flaws. She made a list of questions she needed answers to and made an appointment. She arrived thirty minutes early and sat in the car going over her notes.

After reading through her detailed notes, Jude said aloud, "What am I doing here? This relationship isn't working." Two different therapists had pointed out that Brandon had issues with women that he was bringing into the relationship, but he refused to do further work alone or together. She folded the list and put it in her purse and went inside.

There she sat, across from Jim Daves. It had been more than five years since she had sat here with Edward listening to his lies and wondering how it was that the two of them saw things so differently.

"Jude, it's been a while. How can I help you?" Jim greeted her.

"I came here to find out what I'm doing to mess up the relationship I'm in, to figure out how to fix it. But as I sat in my car, going over my notes, I realized that I don't want to do this anymore. The relationship isn't working. I just need to get out of it."

"Good for you, Jude," Jim said smiling.

She then began to share the details of the relationship with Brandon, including their sessions with the two therapists.

"I think you learned something important, Jude," Jim said softly. "You were in a twenty-year marriage with a very narcissistic man because of your tolerance. I know you, Jude. You are more than willing to look at your own issues. But it takes self-examination on the part of both partners. Don't stay in relationship with a partner who refuses to do the work his own therapists are telling him he needs to do. You've made the right decision."

The relationship was over. Jude hoped it was the right decision. It had been six months since she and Brandon had moved in together. She wasn't sure what went wrong, but she did accept that it wasn't right. She felt like a bird with rubber bands around her wings. She could do nothing to please Brandon, yet he could not tell her what he needed, nor would he work to determine what was wrong. She was not walking on eggshells with another man.

She supposed she didn't regret it, but she did wonder if she would ever make another commitment to a man. She felt convinced she would never trust herself enough to do so.

"You have to trust your inner self, my girl." Was it her mom again? Or was it her intuition? "You teach others to listen to what you call their inner knowing. Don't doubt your own."

This was true. Jude was often having a discussion with one of her artists on connecting with that still small voice of guidance. So why did she find it so difficult to trust her own intuitive nudges? In retrospect she could see how her intuition, her inner voice had been speaking to her throughout her marriage, and especially through the trauma of divorce. She knew something was not right with Edward, but she was compelled to keep giving him another chance, and another. Eventually her intuition began to literally scream at her, as in the dream in which she jumped from the plane. And she could see that her intuition had been waving the red flags as she got involved with Brandon. In the future she had to do more than hear it. She had to act on it. She knew this was what it meant to truly trust herself.

Jude had entered into a relationship once more after Brandon and before she met Andrew. That relationship had been with Xander Voss, with whom she had fallen in love. But Xander had lied to her about many things. She ended the relationship immediately upon learning how dishonest he was. Maybe she was supposed to be alone.

As Jude draped the dish towel over the oven door handle, she looked across the room at Andrew napping in the over-stuffed chair near the fireplace. They had been together almost four months. She walked to the fireplace, quietly stirred the fire then seated herself in a chair near him. He was a handsome man with sharp features, his tanned skin and arms glowed in the late evening light, and his red-tinted blond hair mingled with gray fell over his eyes. He slept peacefully, a pleasant curve to his lips, as if he was content. She had no doubt that he loved her, and how could she not love him? He was a very attractive man, financially secure, and gentle. He was one of the good guys, and God knew she deserved a good guy. Her eyes followed the outline from his forehead to the angle of his nose, then down to his Adam's apple. Desire began to stir in her. Jude sighed and turned, staring out the window of Andrew's lake house at the peaceful lake view. Could Andrew be that missing link, that one thing she felt was lacking? Perhaps every failed relationship, every disappointment had been leading to him. Maybe the key was to love and accept one another in spite of their differences, to love unconditionally. She felt sure her mom would approve. Andrew was like those men who surrounded her as she was growing up, strong, thoughtful, a godly man….and a bit controlling. But then, didn't she sometimes feel the need for someone to take over, take care of things. She sighed deeply. She was tired. It would be so nice to just let someone take control for a while. With Andrew she could finally relax and put her focus on enjoying the work she loved and her family. He would worry about the details.

It was interesting that just when she had determined she was supposed to be alone, to put all her focus on her family and Woman Space, Andrew literally rode into her life on his horse. It was as if her knight came with her dream property. She felt a knot begin to grow in the pit of her stomach. Certainly Jude knew by now that being swept away by a knight on a horse was fantasy. She laughed aloud. She just needed time. If she was to let Andrew fully into her heart, then he would have to prove himself a very patient man.

VI

Maggie was busy checking inventory on a new shipment of artwork when Jude arrived at the gallery.

"How are you feeling?" Jude asked as she switched on her computer then joined Maggie to uncrate more art.

"I'm fine, really. And I'm relieved to have a security guy on site. Daniel is working out great."

"I'm thinking about adding a therapist to our staff as well," Jude responded. "I'd like the peace of mind of knowing we won't have to handle another situation like the one with Gavin Crane without help. But I'm worried about Madi."

The door chime rang announcing someone had entered the gallery; Jude looked up to see Madi Crane walk in.

"Speaking of Madi," she whispered to Maggie. "Madi, we're back here!" Jude called. Even at a distance she could see that Madi looked somewhat disheveled. Jude laid down the inventory checklist and walked toward her. As their eyes met, Madi seemed to crumble and began to sob.

"Madi, what is it? Are you okay?" Jude rushed to comfort her, leading the tall, rather thin, young woman to a nearby bench, and sitting down beside her. "What happened?"

"It's Gavin." Madi began to tremble uncontrollably. "Gavin killed himself last night." She put her head in her hands and again the sobs came.

"Madi. Oh my God, Madi! That's terrible! Do you know what happened?"

Madi took a moment to gather her composure. "Apparently, after the police questioned him and said he would be in trouble if he didn't let things be, if he didn't leave me alone, he became despondent. He's been missing a lot of work. Last night his brother found him. It appears that he took his deer rifle and shot himself in the head."

"Oh, Madi! I'm so sorry!" Jude had worried that Gavin Crane would stalk Madi, or that he might try to kidnap the kids. But she hadn't imagined he would hurt himself.

Maggie walked over to join them, handing Madi a cup of hot tea. "I'm so, so sorry, Madi." She sat on the opposite side of the girl from Jude.

"Thank God the kids and I have been living at my parent's home. We've been there since the night he hit me; I took the kids and got a restraining order."

Jude put her arm around Madi's shoulders. Jude was the one responsible for sending Gavin Crane away with the police. Had she done the right thing? Of course, she had! Otherwise, it might be Madi and the kids who were dead!

"You aren't alone, Madi," Jude assured her. "We're here for you. We'll help you in whatever way you need, and your parents are there to help you with the kids. You'll get beyond this, Madi."

"I know. I know. I just feel so bad about Gavin. Now the kids have no daddy, Jude."

"Madi, you have to remember that their daddy hurt them… and you," Maggie said emphatically. "You couldn't stay and allow that to keep happening. You did what you had to do. He was a sick man."

Madi covered her face with her hands. "I've wished him gone. I—I feel so guilty. What am I going to tell the kids?" She sobbed.

"You'll figure that out," Jude consoled. "Just thank God he didn't try to kill all of you before he killed himself. This is not your fault."

"I know, it's just all so unreal. How did I end up in this situation? I loved him so much, and he was so good to me until Leah was born. How can someone change so drastically?"

"People don't usually change that drastically, Madi. I'm sure all along he was struggling to hold in all that anger."

"I think having kids stressed him so much he couldn't hide the turmoil going on inside." Madi dabbed at her eyes.

"He tried to control all of you because he couldn't control himself." Jude hugged Madi tightly. "I'm going to call a friend of mine who's a therapist. I want you to have a few sessions with her. She can help you sort this out. Okay?"

Madi shook her head. "Jude, I can't afford therapy."

"You don't worry about that. You'll be okay, better than okay. You and the kids can make a good life. I know it doesn't feel possible right now. You've suffered a terrible trauma, but girl, your artwork is selling like crazy. I have a big check for you on my desk."

Madi looked up at Jude, a faint glimmer of hope on her face. "Come on," Jude said taking her hand and leading her toward the office. "I want to show you how you're going to make a living for yourself and your kids."

The decision was as easy as it was obvious. Jude hired Madi part time at the gallery, and she had already talked with Gracie, a friend and Woman Space board member, about hiring Madi to clean for her. Between the two positions, they could keep her busy pretty much full time until her art sales became more consistent. Madi needed time to do her sculpting, and thankfully, her parents had room for her and the children and could help with babysitting. Jude was already working with the board to build a network of potential employers for the women who became affiliated with Woman Space; now they would see how well it worked. And Woman Space would cover the cost of therapy. Madi would be okay. It would just take some time and lots of love and support. She was a gifted artist, and Jude was sure she would eventually be able to support herself with that gift.

VII

The sun was setting as Jude walked the path to the lake. She sat, yoga style, under the Sycamore and imagined her studio with its deck attached to a pier going out into the water. She thought about Madi and hoped she could recover from the trauma, though she knew, from her own experience with Edward, that the wounds would always be there. Her thoughts turned to the twenty-two other women whose artwork was now on exhibit in the gallery. Twenty-three lives that Woman Space would change for the good. She was feeling good, very good.

"Thank you, thank you, thank you," she whispered under her breath as the red ball of fire and light set behind the woods on Andrew's side of the lake. A red hue spread across the water toward her as the stillness of night descended. She finished her bottled water and stood, reluctant to leave, but knowing she needed to get back to the loft. She looked up through the now silhouetted branches of the tree. The old Sycamore was becoming her friend. One day soon she would spend more time here. But right now the house was a mess with the teardown for the remodel, and she needed to be in the gallery early in the morning.

CHAPTER 6

Sing and dance together and be joyous, but let each one of you be alone,
Even as the strings of a lute are alone though they quiver with the same music.
—Kahlil Gibran

A HEAVY FOG HUNG **over downtown Chicago**. Sitting on her small private balcony sipping her morning coffee, Jude was literally in the clouds. Living in a high rise was proving to be an ethereal experience. She could stand, detached, with her face to the glass watching the city below slowly come to life in the mornings. At times, she felt like an observer rather than a participant in the world. Of course, she realized that the line between living and watching was very thin. She struggled with her introverted self so as not to let her pause for introspection and solitude grow into a wall between her and life. She was, at these times, literally, a "silent witness," a term she often used when she attempted to step back and see her own life and her decisions objectively. It helped her to allow fear to evaporate and to see an experience as clearly as possible for what it was.

With Edward she had finally seen that staying in her marriage was destructive. It had been from the space of the silent witness that she could separate her emotional need to save her marriage from the reality of the situation. She could see that her marriage was no longer healthy or nurturing for her. Detaching as the witness allowed her to hear the voice of intuition and guidance, but she was often reluctant to trust enough to act on it. She felt she had made progress when she acted quickly to end the engagement to Brandon once it was not working for either of them.

Jude was trying to see Andrew in this more detached, objective way. She was acutely drawn to him, his looks, his manner, his masculinity. But he was a religious conservative who referred to President Obama as "Jude's President" because she had voted for him twice. Voting for Obama was something Andrew would have never considered. In politics and religion they agreed to disagree. And there were other such topics, abortion, for example. Andrew believed abortion should never happen other than when the life of the mother was at stake, and even that was questionable. Jude felt she would never choose an abortion herself, but she felt it was not another's right to tell a woman she could not make that decision if it was what she felt compelled to do. On gun control, Andrew was absolutely adverse to government regulations concerning guns in any form; he was very much a cowboy in that respect. In contrast, Jude couldn't understand how anyone could be against background checks as an attempt to keep guns out of the hands of unstable people. And Jude could not understand why many who insisted they were Christians were so against programs that assured adequate health insurance, food, and housing to those who could not otherwise afford them.

The list could go on, and Jude knew these differences represented two different ways of viewing the world. They could, in the long run, become bones of contention between the two of them. That Andrew was quite far to the political right put him in a category with Edward. Was that a red flag? Should she be concerned? At times these questions haunted Jude. Black and white thinking was an indication of a mindset that made Jude uncomfortable. She found this perspective inhibiting and stifling, a hindrance to personal growth, and even to the creativity that was her world. But as "the witness" she knew it was not a matter of making a right or wrong choice, but rather that your choices could take you more deeply into who you truly were or could distract you from your authentic self.

In hindsight, Jude could see that she had often chosen to ignore potential incompatibilities if she found herself attracted to a man. Well, love could do that, she rationalized. And on an unconscious level, the fact that she had become sexually involved with Andrew also played a role in her commitment. So, in spite of the differences between them, she allowed their relationship to grow quite intimate in the months following her purchase of Applewood, the name she had given her forty-acre ranch. Andrew was as excited as Jude with the renovations that were taking place, and he was proving to be tremendously helpful.

The name Applewood was inspired by the small apple orchard near the house. Applewood also seemed appropriate since it had been a full moon rising behind the old apple tree at the far end of the meadow that had inspired Jude's first childhood mystical experience. Jude found the gnarly wood of the old trees fascinating. She hired Madi Crane, who did beautiful figures in wood, to create a sculpture from a tree that was so damaged with disease that it needed to be removed. If anyone could give that old tree new life, a second life, it was Madi. The sculpture was an abstracted form that emphasized the curves of the feminine body. The feminine figure's arms lifted to the sky in a dance-like movement. The dancer now stood near the front entrance of Woman Space. In her carved, up-lifted hands, she held a clear glass globe, a blown glass sphere, created by a second gallery artist, Adrian Benz. The "Life Dancer," as she was titled, was a perfect logo for Woman Space.

The phone rang, "Woman Space. Oh, Maggie, hi. Yes, I'll be down in a few minutes. Is everything okay?"

Maggie was a calm, well-organized lady and a wonderful watercolorist herself, but tonight was an important event, and Jude was needed to make final decisions. "Everything's fine. I know it's early, but the caterer will be here soon, and I need you to sign off on the menu for tonight."

"Give me twenty minutes." Jude hung up and took another sip of her coffee, thinking about all she had been organizing to move Woman Space onto the international stage. Taking one last sip she sighed, hating to leave the view. Tonight Woman Space was hosting a third anniversary black tie gala. Important and wealthy people would be there. Jude, along with her board of directors, had put a huge amount of work into contacting arts centers and guilds in Great Britain, France, Italy, and Germany over the past year. They were exploring potential interest in offering Woman Space programs to qualifying artists in their locations. If Woman Space could inspire adequate funding, they would partner with these centers and guilds to locate, fund, and bring artists to Chicago to promote their art. The program would give Woman Space artists and Jude international visibility while introducing emerging female artists to Woman Space as an international venue. The event was getting great press. Jude and the gallery had been featured in both *Chicago Magazine* and *Entertainment Weekly*.

Maggie, obviously a bit stressed, was speaking with John, the head caterer, as Jude walked in. "Oh, here she is." Maggie turned to include Jude in the conversation.

"Good morning, John," Jude said reaching for the caterer's handshake. "I'm so grateful that you worked us into your busy schedule. This is a big night for Woman Space, and I wanted the very best."

John smiled. "Woman Space is one of my top priorities, Jude. You're doing wonderful work here."

She had known John since going back to work for Emily Rosen. It had taken a long time to get Woman Space on his "regulars" list. Now he catered all of their events, and tonight would be the biggest yet. The menu was light but gourmet. The decor in the gallery was minimalist with white candles and greenery on the tables and elegant centerpieces on the servers....beautiful without distracting from the art work.

"This is perfect, John," Jude said as she signed off on the details.

"Jude, I do have a favor to ask of you," John said with a smile. "I'd like to purchase one of your paintings for the new restaurant my cousin Alfie is opening. I want it to be my grand opening gift to him."

"John, I appreciate that! What's the name of his restaurant?"

"Gabrielle, in the River North area."

"Oh, that should be a great location. Just find me in my office when you finish with Maggie, and I'll show you the new work." Jude had relegated her own work to the back gallery for this event; she wanted to showcase the women Woman Space was promoting. She loved to barter, as doing so often made her work available to buyers who might not otherwise afford it. Bartering was also a wonderful way to build strong work relationships, and at times it also saved her money. This was not the first time John had bartered for one of her pieces.

Jude left John and Maggie to finish up the details on the menu and went into her office to check for messages. There were several waiting for her attention. The *Chicago Tribune* editor wanted to be sure his journalist would have first chance at the story. An agent for Oprah Winfrey wanted to pin down an interview for the OWN network. Jude found herself amazed, almost daily, at the opportunities that were coming her way. Could this really be her life? She was finishing up her call with the OWN network agent when John knocked on her door.

"Come on in John. Have a seat. I'll be with you in a second."

John sighed as he seated himself in the comfortable chair facing Jude's desk. Jude smiled at him as she hung up the phone. "Do you have a size or particular price range in mind?" she asked.

"Actually, I have a specific painting in mind. I'm so hoping you still have it. It had the feel of landscape with spheres and a red-tailed hawk."

"Earth Song!" Jude exclaimed.

"Yes, that's it! Tell me you haven't sold it."

Jude flipped the pages of her inventory book and found a photo with details of the painting. "Is this the one?"

John leaned forward, "Yes. That's it!"

"It's a part of the show in the back gallery. Do you want to see it? I can have it delivered the first part of next week."

"I don't need to see it; the photo is enough," John said. "I remember it very well. Just send it to this address." He handed her a business card with the contact information for the Gabrielle Restaurant. "Once you apply the cost of the party, we'll settle the remainder."

"I really appreciate this, John, and I wish your cousin great success." She scribbled a note to send a card and fruit bouquet for the restaurant's opening.

"Thanks, Jude. This works equally well for me," he responded. "I know the painting will be an amazing addition to the restaurant, and Alfie will love it."

Jude walked John to the entrance of the gallery. "I'm so happy with how you've handled the details of this event," she said as she hugged him.

"Thank you Jude. I'm really impressed with all you've accomplished here. Kayla Levine is the daughter of a very good friend of mine. She was in such a terrible state until you and your staff helped her build the confidence to take her art seriously. My friend, Maud, that's her mom, can't say enough good things about you. You should be very proud of yourself."

"I'm so happy with how things have turned out for Kayla; but you must know that all I did was to encourage and support the talent that was already hers."

"Maybe so, Jude. But your help made all the difference in her life."

"Thanks, John. That's what I hope to make happen for these talented women who simply need a break."

John hugged Jude again. "I'll do what I can to contribute. It's a good cause. And I'm very impressed with your art as well! Alfie will be so excited!"

"Thanks, again, John." Jude closed the office door behind him thinking how much she appreciated his validation of the work she was striving to accomplish through Woman Space.

II

By evening the gallery had taken on an aura of the exotic. Amy, a close friend and colleague, sat near the entry playing the harp; waiters offered delicious fruits and appetizers and tables glowed with candlelight. Beautifully dressed people wandered from painting to painting, and conversations were stirred as guests met the artists. Jude noticed that Maggie and Madi were already busy finalizing sales.

Jude stood to the back of the room, again the silent witness; she was thinking about how far she had come with this gallery. She had been a young girl just out of college when she interned for Emily Rosen. In spite of taking several gallery management courses, she'd actually learned the practical aspects of running a gallery from Emily, who was near the age of Jude's own mother. She had been both mentor and friend to Jude. How she wished Emily could be here tonight. Without her generosity there would be no Woman Space.

"Well, this appears to be a very successful event," Andrew announced as he walked confidently to Jude's side and leaned over to kiss her cheek. He was striking in his tux. As he came closer, Jude noticed his satin cummerbund had a pattern of small crosses. His cuff links were tiny silver crosses as well. She felt a pang of something, embarrassment maybe? She experienced the same feeling that came over her when Andrew insisted on praying loudly in public over his food. To Jude a public display seemed inauthentic, as if he needed to advertise that he was religious. But she had come to know Andrew well enough to know he was serious about his faith. Perhaps her discomfort came from being reminded of when she was part of a very fundamental church which pushed its members to literally go door to door as if trying to sell religion to others. It had never felt right to her.

Thinking of Andrew again, she scolded herself. Who was she to judge? She did believe that each person had the right to deal with the Divine on their own terms and in their own way. Pushing her discomfort aside, she smiled at Andrew and took his arm. It felt good to have a handsome, confident man by her side. There was, after all, no perfect relationship.

"Come with me, handsome," she said smiling. "There are some people I'd like you to meet." They made a striking couple as they crossed the room, stopping to speak with small groups of guests. Jude's teal gown highlighted both her striking figure and red hair that hung loosely around her face. She led Andrew toward the Mayor and introduced him. Andrew had an easy way with people, and Jude left the two of them chatting.

An hour and a half into the gala, Jude walked to the podium that was set up near the food tables and spoke into the microphone. "Ladies and gentlemen, may I have your attention?" There was no hint in her voice of the nervousness she was feeling. "I want to thank you for supporting Woman Space International by your attendance tonight." She went over in detail her plans for taking what Woman Space had to offer Chicago area women artists to other parts of the world. Then she read a list of distinguished guests who had already made significant donations.

"Finally," Jude continued, "I want to announce the establishment of the Emily Rosen scholarship in honor of my dear late friend and mentor, without whom there would be no Woman Space. This scholarship will be awarded annually to a promising young talent to help her manage financially while getting established as an artist. I so hope Emily is looking down on us and knows all that has grown from her contribution toward what we celebrate tonight."

There was hardy applause as guests converged on Jude with compliments and congratulations as well as pledges for contributions. As quickly as she could manage, Jude worked her way back into the crowd. As she headed toward a group of Woman Space board members, someone grabbed her arm from behind. She turned to find herself face to face with Xander Voss. He laughed as he saw the surprise on her face.

"The last person on earth you would expect to see, eh?" He spoke in his soft Dutch accent, smiling his familiar smile with the lifted right brow.

Jude felt momentarily weak in her knees. "Xander, this is a surprise!" She struggled to quickly regain her composure as she put her right hand over the hand still holding on to her left elbow. She saw a flicker of emotion move across his face as he quickly loosened his hold on her arm.

"It is good to see you, Jude, and good to see you so successful. I'm quite impressed."

Determined not to be thrown off balance by Xander's unexpected appearance, Jude took his arm and led him toward the back gallery.

"Come. I want you to see my latest work! You'll see for yourself just how well I'm doing."

The back gallery was large and open with carefully designed lighting. Jude's recent work was displayed in a minimalist fashion to most effectively give attention to each piece. She knew Xander would be pleased.

The exhibit was titled *Exploring the Goddess*; Jude's approach to painting was powerful and brilliant with light and color. Her own spiritual journey had led her to the conviction that the Divine Spirit expressed itself through each individual as expressions of the Divine in the world. And so, each painting in the series, *Exploring the Goddess*, was an exploration of the female expression of God.

She felt Xander catch his breath and was almost sure she felt him tremble slightly. Gently, he removed her hand from his arm and walked toward the first painting, stopping to read the artist's statement under the title. Jude watched in silence, observing how he studied each piece, seeing the stirring of emotion on his face. Xander had always connected with her paintings. It made her feel pleasantly validated. And though she hadn't thought about it before, she knew Andrew could never appreciate her work on this level. A wave of sadness washed over her.

There was history between Jude and Xander Voss, though she had neither seen nor heard from him in four years. Anyone observing their interaction, as Jude walked him through the exhibit, would have known they were more than acquaintances and might have wondered if they were more than friends. Jude still felt it, the tension and the chemistry. It had always been there between them, even on their first meeting. But she was no longer susceptible. She had learned that great chemistry does not mean a great relationship.

Jude watched as Xander took his time viewing each painting. She knew when he squinted his eyes and wrinkled his brow he was trying to determine why she had used certain colors, or he was questioning just what she was trying to say with the mood she had created. When he stood motionless, ten feet back from a painting for an extended time, she knew he was seeing a piece that particularly spoke to him. If he took much time at a distance then moved ever so slowly closer, he was looking for the surprises he knew she built into her work that were only to be discovered as one drew near. She loved the way he took in her art, as she had loved the way he once took her in, enveloped her, loved her. She had loved Xander, the man she knew he could be. But she didn't like the Xander who had lied easily and couldn't commit in relationships. That Xander had hurt her, had driven her away.

Jude smiled; she still enjoyed him, the way he carried himself with a hint of royalty. She enjoyed watching him, his emotions never hidden, and delighted in the way he delighted in her art.

"Come and have some food and wine," she invited him, once he had taken ample time to enjoy her work.

"I can't stay," he said smiling, his dark eyes dancing. "But I had to come and let you know how proud I am of you. Congratulations, Jude. You've made it big. I've seen the articles about you even as I've traveled. Your name is getting known internationally for this work you're doing with Woman Space. Enjoy this time—you've earned it!"

Xander took her hand and pressed it to his lips. Instantly, Jude flashed back to how it felt to be kissed by those lips; a flush moved across her cheeks. With his free hand Xander pressed a small, neatly wrapped package in her palm and wrapped her fingers around it. She was grateful to have her focus drawn to the gift.

"Open this later, after the celebration," he whispered. His smile was perpetually flirtatious. He turned as if to leave quickly.

"Wait," she caught his arm. "Are you staying in town a while?"

"No, I'm catching a plane out tonight, heading for a conference in Canada. I'm speaking."

"It's good to see you, Xander. I wish you all the best."

"And I you…..always, no matter what." He smiled that charming smile, his words not lost on her. In the past he always left her with, "I love you, always, no matter what."

She stood, watching him until he disappeared into the crowd.

III

Andrew's truck was parked in the drive as Jude drove up the lane to Applewood. The property was being transformed. Trees and shrubs had been trimmed, a new stone walk had been laid leading to the solid oak entry door surrounded by a leaded glass transom and side lights. A fresh coat of warm gray paint accented with white trim gave the exterior an impressive facelift. Jude pulled her Subaru beside Andrew's pickup and shut off the engine. As she picked up her purse, the small package Xander had placed in her hand the night before tumbled out onto the seat. She had been so caught up in the gala celebration after Xander left she had forgotten about it. She picked up the neatly wrapped package, turning it in her fingers. The wrapping was light gray with black writing in French. *Vous tous les meilleurs, vous tous les meilleurs* was repeated over and over on the surface of the paper. I wish you all the best. Wasn't that what she had said to him as he was leaving last night? She pulled the black ribbon from the package and peeled back the paper to reveal a small dark gray box. Lifting the lid she found a heart-shaped stone nested in soft gray paper shreds. The tag beneath it said it was made of rhodonite crystal. Jude knew rhodonite to be the stone most associated with healing and forgiveness. Xander would know. She turned the stone heart slowly in her hands, feeling the smooth quality of the polish. The pinks were deep and rich, punctuated with grays that swirled through the surface. It was beautiful. Was this Xander's way of saying he was sorry— and perhaps even asking her to forgive him? She smiled. She had forgiven him long ago, but the thought was nice. And it was good of him to show up at something as special to her as last night's opening. She placed the stone back in the box and put it in the glove compartment.

As Jude walked up the path to her house, her mind quickly filled with the remodel and the anticipation of seeing the changes to the interior. Her instructions to Carl had been to open the floor plan to the fullest possible view of the lake. She was to approve the new layout today, before the plumbing was rerouted for the kitchen and powder room. She pushed open the unlatched door and was greeted with one large open room flooded with sunlight. Andrew stood near the new back windows deep in conversation with Carl. The discussion stopped when Jude entered. The room seemed filled with tension.

"Is all going as planned?" Jude asked as she allowed her eyes to take in how much larger the space now looked.

"What do you think?" Andrew rushed to greet her with a kiss. "Carl and I were just discussing where the kitchen should go."

"Well, I've made that decision." Jude walked to the windows then turned to survey the room.

Carl handed her a blueprint, "This is what Becker has drawn up, but I don't feel this is what you had in mind."

"Becker knows what he's doing," Andrew interjected.

"Why is Becker involved in this?" Jude said. She and Carl had already discussed the layout as she envisioned it. And she had made it clear to Andrew that Carl would do the work. She took the blueprint and spread it out on the dining table, the only piece of furniture in the room except for the worn sofa. "I want to see the lake when I'm in the kitchen. I agree with Carl. The kitchen goes here." she said, pointing on the drawing to the back right end of the room. "There are plenty of windows to allow each area, living room, dining room and kitchen to share them." She heard Andrew sigh deeply.

"I just think you should let Becker make big decisions like this, honey. I convinced Carl to let Becker do an architectural drawing. He's a professional architect."

Jude smiled sweetly. "I've been dreaming of this house for a very long time, Andrew. Just trust that I know what I want."

"Okay, it's your house." Andrew was visibly disgruntled.

She couldn't feel too irritated at Andrew's need to control. He'd been tremendously helpful in this renovation. It was only normal that he felt invested. But she had envisioned the design for this remodel from the moment she first saw this property. This room would have visual and physical access to the lake from the living room, dining room, and kitchen.

A huge stone fireplace would stand against the left wall with an "L" shaped sectional that allowed one to sit by the fire and view the lake at the same time. The large wooden slab dining table, on which the blueprints were now spread, had been purchased with the money she received from her first $5000 painting sale, many years ago now. The table would be the center piece of the dining area. The kitchen, separated only by a large island, would fit into the back right corner. The cabinets would be a light gray topped by gray granite countertops with swirls of black, dark gray, ochre, and a greenish brown. She could see it as if it was already finished. She had a gift, an ability to see the finished project before it was even begun.

Jude walked to an area adjacent to the stairway that led to the master suite on the second floor. Here the hall would open to six bedrooms, each with a small private bath. She could host her entire family here, and during retreats guests would stay in the main house. "The powder room will go here." Carl made notations on the blueprints.

"Take a look at what's up here," Andrew said, pulling Jude toward the stairs. At the top was a long balcony that looked down over the entry; behind that double doors opened into a large master suite with a window wall looking out over the lake. The bathroom, off to the right, had a matching wall of windows and a huge modern freestanding tub centered against them.

Jude laughed with delight. "It's as wonderful as I've imagined! Andrew, don't you just love it?"

Andrew took her by her shoulders and smiled, "I love seeing you love it, and I love you." He bent to kiss her.

She did love this man. Seeing Xander had been something of a closure. Andrew was so good to her, so protective. Maybe at times he was a bit possessive. But over the last several years, she had become so independent that perhaps she mistook protective for possessive? She had not fully trusted her judgment of men for a very long time, probably not since Edward, and certainly not since Xander. At least, she and Andrew shared core values. That he was a religious conservative was not a bad thing.

CHAPTER 7

If I dare to hear you I will feel you like the sun and grow in your direction
—Mark Nepo

A VERY YOUNG JUDE **was conscious of the warm dirt between the toes of her bare feet as she walked the corn row, stooping to push her forefinger an inch into the soil.** She dropped in a seed and then used her hand to carefully cover it with dirt. She loved the feel of the warm, moist earth, the softness, the aliveness. The act of planting a seed and watching for it to peak its head above the ground fascinated her; she would rush out each morning to measure its progress. She finished with a pat of her palm to the sun-heated soil then moved half a foot's length down the row to bury the next seed. Planting the garden was a family event. Her mom, dad, and brothers each worked silently down a row of their own.

Always there was a bounty of food on their table, which was one reason Jude never realized how poor her family was as she was growing up. They raised chickens for eggs and fried chicken dinners, or her oldest brother's favorite, chicken and dumplings. Pork and beef were also raised on the farm. Jude and her brothers each had pigs as 4H projects. They even built a house for each sow, complete with a name on a wooden pig cut from plywood in Grandad's woodworking shop. Jude then painted each plaque to match the resident. Grandpa Hayward's orchard grew apples and peaches, and there was fresh milk daily for making butter.

Jude's favorite chore, however, was feeding the baby calves born each spring. The newborn calves would run to greet her when she arrived with the food bucket equipped with a large nipple. On the farm, there were chores morning and night, rain or shine. Jude scrubbed her hands twice then sniffed her fingers, fearful they might smell of the barn, before running to catch the bus for school. She and her brothers returned from school to repeat their work ritual each evening.

Jude had loved so much about growing up on a farm. There was nothing as fresh as the brisk morning air and nothing as majestic as watching storm clouds gather. So often she lay flat on her back staring up through the clouds trying to imagine where the universe ended and what might be beyond; and wondering too, how it was that she was here in this place, in this body, with these parents when she might have been born anywhere in the world.

Jude loved the animals, especially her horse, Fanny. She also loved the feeling of having worked hard as a team with her family then coming home at the end of the day to wrestle and play and share a big meal together. Now a city dweller, she often missed the country. Of course, she missed it least in winter. So often, looking out over the Windy City, she recalled freezing hands and feet as she helped milk seventy dairy cows in an unheated barn or helped her brothers carry an ax to break the ice on the pond so the cattle could drink.

Jude missed her horseback rides in the fields and woods, and she fondly recalled those times when she could just sit quietly staring out her bedroom window. The old house had been built by her great uncle. She remembered the heat of the wood stove and snuggling into toasty-warm blankets in the evening. Later, as the wood fire faded to embers in the early hours of the morning, she was captivated with the frost-formed, crystalline designs on the insides of her bedroom windows.

It was in that very bedroom, on a mild fall evening, her head at the foot of the bed so she could watch the moon rise out her east window, that she had what she knew now as her first mystical experience. As the moon made its slow climb, silhouetting the apple tree at the far end of the orchard, Jude heard the hoot, hooting of a barn owl. She thought, in her childish innocence, how beautiful this moment was and how God's creation filled her with awe. Slowly she felt a most unusual sensation, not exactly uncomfortable, but as if she was expanding from the inside out. The expanding feeling grew into a bursting sensation in her chest, as if she was filled with a presence that might explode right out of her. Her feet and fingers tingled as chills ran up and down her arms. She felt suspended, and at that moment, she knew: God was not just "out there." God was inside her, inside everything, in everything! Everything was One. Everything was God! For nine-year-old Jude it was a life changing moment.

Jude learned trust from those who were trustworthy: her parents and grandparents, her aunts, uncles and caring neighbors. And because they were who they told her they were, she believed in their faith. But the reality of God had come to her in that moment. From that point on she communed with the Spirit through such solitary experiences with nature. She talked to God while swinging in her tire swing, sitting in her treehouse, riding her horse through the woods and meadows, or lying on her back staring at the sky. These talks seemed more than prayer.

There had been one complication. Jude found it confusing that her mom and dad argued over which church they would attend on Sunday mornings. She found it easy to accept Christianity as the One Way, as it was the only religion she knew. But she found it difficult to understand why God allowed so many conflicting doctrines within Christianity. Jude's dad delivered milk to the Carnation Company on many Sundays, but when he was free to attend church the family went to the small Baptist church in sight of their home. Here she saw her Grandma Hayward and her aunts and uncles on the Hayward side of the family. Revival meetings and Vacation Bible School also required her attendance at this church. However, on the Sundays when her dad had to run the milk route, she went with her mom to the Church of Christ a few miles away. This upset Jude's dad, and on these Sundays he was often out of sorts and sullen. He didn't speak to her mom, sometimes for a couple of days. Jude found this upsetting, and being the only daughter, and a very sensitive child at that, she took on the role of peacemaker, playfully teasing her parents into games or pleasing them with a drawing or painting. She didn't yet know her need to "fix things" created in her a tendency toward co-dependence. Later, she was reminded of this during her marriage when she caught herself trying to please Edward in order to keep the peace.

When Jude turned eleven, discouraged that the church problem was never resolved, she determined that she needed to understand the differences in these two churches and make a decision as to which was right and which was wrong. Red pen in hand, for underlining what she might need to reference for this decision, she set out to study her American Standard Version Bible in depth. She knew a detailed level of understanding would be called for if she was going to explain to both her parents the basis of her conclusion.

Eventually, feeling confused and overwhelmed, she decided to put most of her focus on the words of Jesus in red in her Bible. After much study and deliberation, she decided on her mother's church. She listed seven reasons for her decision, six of them based on her pre-teen logical assessment of who these early Christians were and how they practiced their religion. Number seven stated that this was her mom's church and her Grandad's, who was also the County Superintendent of Schools and the most educated man she knew. He had a library upstairs with all kinds of reference Bibles. There was yet another unlisted and rather emotional reason. In fact, it was what finally made her decide she had to resolve this religious conflict once and for all. Just that summer she had attended the Vacation Bible School at her dad's family church, as she did every summer, with her two brothers and numerous cousins. The preacher was yelling his warnings of "hellfire and brimstone" as the small congregation of students and teachers sang "Just as I Am" over and over. Finally, her two youngest cousins, twin girls age five, thinking they needed to be saved for their sins or they would go to hell, went forward sobbing. She could feel her brothers, ages thirteen and fourteen, getting very tense and uncomfortable. Three younger cousins and Adam, who was her age, stood beside her. She also felt their discomfort, and it was her nature to feel responsible for all of them. She made a decision. Suddenly, she raised her hand. The preacher expectantly came back to her seat. He bent down putting his hand on Jude's shoulder asking "My child, do you want to be saved?"

Jude angrily blurted out, "Why are you scaring all these little kids?" then added with strong emphasis, "Don't you know that Jesus says 'of such is the kingdom of heaven?' All little children are already children of God!"

A look of shock came over the preacher's face. Speechless, he returned to his podium. Her brothers relaxed, and Jude felt a great deal of relief herself. Her Grandma Hayward and the pianist, Mrs. Bailey, didn't press her about joining their church after that, and her dad never spoke of it.

At age sixteen she was baptized in her mother's church. She shared her list of reasons for joining the church with her mom, but she never spoke of them with her dad. She didn't want to hurt his feelings. She left her Grandma Hayward a note listing the reasons for her decision with the exception of number seven.

Though Jude had made an important decision for herself, her questioning didn't end there. She struggled with why her chosen church didn't allow instrumental music in the service or paintings of Jesus and his followers on the walls. A very creative child, Jude played her guitar and sang almost daily and loved to paint and draw. Why wouldn't God want you to praise Him with every gift you had? It didn't quite make sense to her.

II

Jude was aware that this reminiscing about her childhood questions concerning religion and God was triggered by her relationship with Andrew. Andrew was a fundamentalist. Though there were more liberal branches of his Baptist denomination, he struggled with making a change. He was visiting other churches hoping he would find one that fit his views more closely and one that Jude would agree to attend with him. That he could accept Jude as being totally detached from a church was beginning to look unlikely. He constantly urged her to go to church with him, and he often talked about his church and how wonderful the people were that attended. Somehow, Andrew's need to push his beliefs only served to assure Jude that the direction she had taken was the right one for her. She felt no need to change Andrew. But neither did she like dealing with his urgency to change her. Andrew couldn't seem to leave her alone about this. He ended each Saturday evening, usually after they shared a lovely dinner, with an invitation to visit a local Baptist Church on Sunday. "Can't we just go to church together then discuss the experience over lunch? I really want to know your reaction."

Jude felt she had long ago dealt with these issues and resolved them, at least to her personal satisfaction, and she was beginning to feel some irritation at Andrew's constant badgering. Andrew had a lot of questions himself, but he seemed to deal with those questions by holding all the more firmly to what his parents had taught him. It was as if convincing Jude to believe as he did would be his confirmation that what he believed was right.

Jude was a believer, though certainly not very traditional. She had stopped going to church when she and Edward divorced. Before this, she had participated in a not so short list of Protestant denominations as well as a Catholic charismatic group. Through her varied experiences, some institutional and some personally spiritual, she had come to the place where she felt she fit. Her connection with the Divine came through meditation, long periods of solitude in nature, and the act of creating. She had explored all the major religions as well as the philosophy of her Native American heritage. There were common truths, she concluded, that ran like threads through all of these great religions, as if humans were created knowing certain things, the necessary things. Arguing over the unnecessary was, well, the scripture that came to Jude's mind, "like straining at a gnat and swallowing a camel." Most recently Jude had been surprised to hear Pope Francis' statement that all great religions are paths to the same God. The leader of the world-wide Catholic Church had come to a very similar conclusion to her own. She wondered if Andrew could accept her having such concepts. Could he accept her as she was? That was the question she began to ask herself as their relationship grew more intimate, and Andrew's need to involve her in his church grew more desperate.

"I'd have a real problem if you told me you were an atheist," Andrew was saying. They were sitting on the outdoor patio of one of Chicago's finest restaurants, sharing a before dinner drink. Here is the real glory of God; Jude found herself thinking as she watched the colors build and wane as the sun dropped toward the horizon. Not arguing over some dogma.

"Andrew, I have come to believe that God is so much more than we can comprehend, and it seems arrogant to think we can know Him so thoroughly, so specifically that we think we have the edge on every other seeker of truth."

Andrew cleared his throat. "We can only serve God to the best of our understanding with the Bible as our reference. We're not to add to it or take away from it. We can only search the scriptures and live according to what it teaches."

"But Andrew, so many people sincerely search and study and still can't agree on exactly what the Bible is saying. Don't you think it might be more important to learn acceptance and tolerance, and especially love for one another?"

"Well, you can't love the sinner into heaven," Andrew responded in exasperation.

Jude had tried to explain to Andrew how she had come to view God, but she wasn't sure that he actually heard her. She saw religion as an attempt to define a Higher Power that man has always seemed to sense existed. But to Jude, attempting to define that power was like trying to put something inexplicable into a neat little box. That she said she believed there was a God had been enough for Andrew. Or perhaps it was all he chose to hear.

"You know the Baptists were the only original Christians who didn't get caught up in Catholicism?" he continued. "That's why they're considered the true Christians today." Jude wanted to add, "But it's only Baptists who consider Baptists the 'true' Christians, and not even all of them, at that." Instead she kept quiet. Certainly what Pope Francis had declared would hold no credibility for Andrew. He continued, "I've been asked to be the President of our Gideon Group here in Chicago. I said yes. I'm passionate about the importance of every person having access to a Bible. It is our only hope for ever coming together as Christians."

Jude's mind wandered. Andrew asserted his faith over and over, but if she responded with her own ideas it often resulted in tension at best. Yet, Andrew was unhappy with his church. The new pastor would not allow a divorced man to be a part of the leadership. Because Andrew was divorced, he was excluded, yet he would not consider finding a church that was more liberal. When Jude tried to talk to Andrew about choices, he quickly changed the subject. From his perspective, there was no alternative; he was doing what he had to do. She was becoming his sounding board for venting his frustrations, and it didn't feel good to her.

Jude listened halfheartedly to Andrew's complaints as they drove the thirty miles to the newly renovated Applewood Ranch house. The open great room was finished and the kitchen was complete with stainless steel appliances. Andrew had volunteered to help Jude shop for the dishes, pots and pans, and other utensils needed to make it a working kitchen; they would make the first Applewood dinner together. Jude forgot her irritation with Andrew as the conversation changed to how to arrange the kitchen to make it most convenient. They did work well together on most things.

Andrew loved to cook, which was not the least of what Jude found attractive in him. He mixed and whipped, salted and seasoned while Jude kept on top of the dishes as he finished with bowls and measuring cups. She wrapped her arms around him as he wrapped sweet potatoes in foil readying them for grilling. He turned smearing her nose with butter with his finger then proceeded to kiss it clean. This was the kind of distraction she loved from a man.

The meal, in spite of much playfulness, came together rather quickly. Chicken grilled slowly with Andrew's special Chipotle sauce, buttered baked sweet potatoes, and asparagus sprinkled with olive oil and Parmesan, roasted in a foil pouch on the grill. Jude removed fresh baked bread from the newly purchased bread maker as a final touch.

The table was set with new dinnerware, and candles burned in thick clear glass candle holders. Lights reflected off the lake from Andrew's home across the way. They looked at each other and smiled. It was perfect.

III

Jude knew by this time in life that the only person one can ever hope to change is oneself. She either had to accept Andrew as he was, or she had to choose not to be with him. She found solace in knowing she always had a choice. This fact had been reinforced on several occasions. In spite of all they had together, Edward would not let go of his mistress, so Jude had to make the choice not to live in a triangle. And though the thought of Xander examining her paintings at the opening still sent a chill up her arms, Jude could not again be with a man who found it easier to lie than to tell the truth. She had made the choice not to remain in relationship with him as well.

She had known Xander for more than thirteen years! It had been a shock when he showed up at the gala, Jude smiled at the thought of him. He still had an effect on her. They had met at the Chicago Theater when

Jude and Greg Galliano, a San Diego musician she was dating, were holding auditions for a musical Greg had written and Jude had arranged to be performed at the theater.

"Can you tell me what's happening here?" Xander greeted her as she entered through the side door on that day nearly fourteen years ago.

"There's a lot going on here. What specifically are you referring to?" Jude responded with a smile that didn't go unnoticed by the rather handsome stranger with the flirtatious smile and foreign accent.

"Well, I have an appointment with the manager of this theater, but he's nowhere to be found." Jude could feel the irritation in Xander's voice.

"Hold on, let me find him for you."

She produced Sam Wilder, the manager, introduced them, and went on her way. But that had not been the end of it. The next week she received a dozen red roses with a thank you and an invitation.

"I can't seem to forget the woman whose hair was on fire with sunlight as she walked through those theater doors," Xander had written in the note that accompanied the roses.

"I have to know more about her. Will she have dinner with me?"

Xander had left an impression on her as well. He was tall, just under six feet, dark eyes and dark hair, and spoke with a charming accent that she couldn't quite place. German, maybe? She accepted his invitation.

Over dinner, she learned that his accent was actually Dutch, and that he was also fluent in German, French, Spanish and English. Jude was impressed with his intelligence and wit. He was a neuroscientist on staff at University Hospital doing brain chemistry research, a tenured professor, and a married man. She wondered why she had assumed he was single.

Xander's research took up most of his time; however, he had a serious interest in the arts, ceramics specifically, and found throwing pots and experimenting with glazes a great stress reducer. His second hobby was Bonsai, if you could call either a hobby. Xander brought great intensity to anything he did, including getting to know Jude. He was not only brilliant, he was fun and adventurous. It didn't hurt that the chemistry between them was palpable. Jude still could not see him without experiencing it.

They became friends, but Jude would not consider more than friendship. It was a few years later, after Xander moved back to the Netherlands, and his marriage dissolved, that they became lovers. He had called to tell Jude he was getting a divorce and was on his way to her. He timed his arrival so that he could again sit in on the ending of Jude's evening class. He brought a bottle of expensive wine.

"Can we sit and enjoy this together?" he asked. "My divorce is final today, and I have come a very long way to celebrate with someone special, and that's you. It's a $100 bottle of wine."

"I have a better idea; bring it along to my home studio," Jude had suggested. "I have the perfect view for celebrating."

It was Xander's first time to see Jude's modest suburban home and studio space. The evening was warm and clear; Jude opened the sliding doors to the sound of the creek. Xander poured the wine.

"I'm curious about the art scene in Europe, Xander. Did you get a chance to visit many galleries?

"I did. I even took some oil painting classes." He laughed shaking his head.

"Did you bring your paintings with you? I'd love to see them. I've never even seen one of your drawings!"

"And most likely you never will," Xander teased. "I am much better with clay between my fingers than a paint brush."

"I'd love to have a showing in Paris one day." Jude was curious if her work would be well received. The conversation led to a rather intense discussion on what was and what was not art.

"I'm not sure you can fully know the validity of a piece of art without knowing what the artist was thinking and feeling." Jude found herself defending the wide range of creations that could be found in contemporary art galleries.

"I just think some of these artists are trying to do whatever shocks or what is so mysterious that the meaning is questionable," Xander responded.

"Well, I can't defend all the art I see exhibited. I'm thinking about the string tacked to the wall in a zig zag pattern at the Art Institute right now. Is it art? Obviously it is some artist's expression that critics have labeled art. So who am I to say it is not, just because I may not understand it. Some art has value for the thought it provokes."

Xander shook his head. "We won't solve this, will we? And it has always been cutting edge art that brings about change."

"And reflects the changes happening in society at the time," Jude added.

Xander walked to the window and stood looking out on the garden.

"Are you going to tell me what happened to end your marriage?" Jude asked.

"It hasn't been pretty," Xander replied. "I guess I knew it was inevitable when we moved back to The Netherlands. I wasn't happy."

Jude poured them each another glass of wine as Xander began to share how his marriage had fallen apart. Jude had just ended what she hoped might have been a long term relationship with Brandon Wilson. "Come and sit," Jude suggested. Xander joined Jude on the sofa that faced the windows. They sipped wine and looked out into Jude's small Japanese garden.

"I've made the decision to move back to the States," Xander announced. "I'll work part time at the university until they allow me a full professorship again. But the real reason I'm moving here is you, Jude. I think we need to find out what this is between us."

She had to admit that she too was curious if the chemistry between them might grow into something more.

"When will you be moving?" she asked.

"I've already packed a container. It will be on its way in a few weeks. I'm here to stay. I have all I need with me. I'll stay in one of those extended-stay hotels until my stuff arrives, then I'll find an apartment."

Jude was receptive. No, it was more than that. She realized that they would have become involved when they first met had Xander not been married. She was excited to explore a relationship with him. They had a lot in common, and his experiences as one born in another culture and traveling the world felt expansive to her.

"Our first trip together will be to Paris. Would you like that?" Xander asked.

"I would love that! But let's take some time to see how this feels....us being together romantically." If she were honest she had imagined being with Xander for a long time, had fantasized about how well they might fit. Her thoughts went back to those seeds she had planted as a child, how they always leaned and grew toward the sunshine. She had learned something about herself. If she allowed her thoughts to hold someone close in fantasy, she too, would grow toward them, and they toward her. She worried that she might be responsible in some way for the failure of Xander's marriage.

"Your feelings for me didn't play into your divorce, did it?" she asked nervously.

"No, I wouldn't say that," Xander responded. "Things have not been good between Imma and me for some time. I almost stayed behind when she was offered the position back home. This is an incredible view!" Xander said, changing the subject and turning his intense gaze away from Jude. He stood again to look out the window. "I had no idea you had such an amazing space. Your garden only needs a few bonsai here and there as a finishing touch. I could take care of that for you." He smiled that smile with the lifted right brow.

They were standing side by side, wine glasses in hand, watching fireflies doing their dance around the garden. Xander put his arm around Jude and pulled her close. She felt the fit of her body under his arm, against his warm thigh. She turned to look into his eyes. He was watching her, "Feels good, eh?" His eyes were teasing. "We are a fit, eh?" Jude nodded a yes, and he leaned down to kiss her.

The kiss had led them to the chaise by the windows. Xander touched her gently, teasing her with his fingers, his lips….slowly he led her to the most incredible, yet playful, sex she had ever experienced. They giggled, wrestled and made love most of the night, so freely, so crazily that at one point they literally fell off the chaise in laughter. Jude had the thought that she was literally "falling" in love. Indeed, she fell in love with Xander Voss.

But Xander had proven to have a very different concept of relationship than Jude. It seemed that just when they were getting the closest, he was off for Europe to take care of his sister or other family business, or to New Zealand to check on property he owned there…most often without Jude. The relationship just didn't move forward.

Jude halted her thoughts. Xander had not been right for her. He was her past. Andrew was here now. And in spite of their different spiritual philosophies, Andrew's values were more in line with hers. She was learning to trust him. There was a consistency about him, and he, too, was full of life and fun and was right across the lake. That was the perfect scenario for Jude; there would be no hurry to move in together or to marry. They could take all the time needed to truly get to know one another, to see how they fit. She had learned the hard way with both Edward and Xander that a whirlwind romance was not to be trusted.

CHAPTER 8

It just takes getting out of the way so the magic can happen. –Jan Groenemann

MAY 27 WAS **the second anniversary of Jude's mother's death.** She had only occasionally sensed her mom's presence after that night over a year ago, when it had seemed so clear that it was her mother who had sent Andrew into her life. Perhaps that's why Jude continued to hang on to a relationship with a man with whom she had some major philosophical and theological differences. Ironically, Andrew's strong faith in God made her feel safe, made her feel that maybe he was like the trustworthy people she had grown up with. People like her mother. And meeting Andrew had helped Jude adjust to losing her mother. He was someone with whom she communicated daily, someone who had her best interest at heart, who loved her, and needed her. And she and Andrew were creating things in common. They loved to meet in the middle of the lake and kayak its perimeter, or to hike the trails through the adjoining park. Cooking together was proving to be a lot of fun. They also shared a love of horses and often rode the lake trails on their matching roan mounts racing back to the stables at full speed. Andrew was generous. He had given her a kayak; and Gandolf, her fox trotter, was a gift from him as well. He loved to tease and play. Most of the time he was positive and upbeat, and certainly, he was attentive. And finally, Jude realized that it was but a dream that she would find a man with whom she could discuss mysticism and spirituality. There would always be that part of her only she could connect with, only she could comprehend. She found some consolation in thinking that was the case for most, if not everyone. No one could know what went on within the deepest recesses of another's soul. Why did she feel such a need to share the fullness of herself with another? She had to admit that part of her would, no doubt, scare many men away.

It was a beautiful spring Saturday. She and Andrew spent the day riding with Jennifer and her husband, Doug. They had moved into Applewood bringing with them their horses, two dogs and two cats. Jennifer was the picture of health with her diabetes under good control. Living on the ranch allowed her much time outdoors. She and Doug grew fresh fruits and vegetables, and their horses were right outside the door. This was Jennifer's dream come true, and Jude had watched the stress melt away from her daughter's face in the months at Applewood. Jennifer never allowed her health issues to inhibit her enjoyment of life, but Jude knew the difficulties her daughter dealt with daily. Jude turned over the management of the ranch to the two of them. Now Jennifer could work from home organizing retreats and workshops and keeping Jude's schedule running smoothly. With Jennifer and Doug living at Applewood, Jude also knew the property was monitored and ready for guests. Doug took care of needed maintenance, and he cooked amazing meals. The arrangement seemed to benefit everyone involved.

"I do love spending time with your kids," Andrew said. Jude detected a bit of regret in his voice. He and his wife had not had children, though they had wanted them.

"I'm happy to share my family with you, Andrew." She reached to hug his waist as they walked from the stables. "I'm anxious for you to meet Grant. I just know you two will hit it off."

Jude's son, Grant, was now finished with his internship and had accepted a residency at top ranked Northwestern Memorial Hospital in Chicago. He was in the process of moving to the area and would soon be spending more time at Applewood. He was single and loved to travel, but found the ranch a great get away. And he was dating a lovely young woman from the Chicago area.

Religious and political discussions would probably have to be off limits, but otherwise Andrew seemed to fit in well.

Jude stared into her mirror as she combed her hair. She had let it grow longer because Andrew liked it that way. She had read somewhere that older women should keep their hair short. Nor should older women wear large hoop earrings. Tonight she wore both. Her hair dresser had put in a few strands of pale blonde along the right side. Jude smiled to herself. She liked shaking things up, making changes. She would not be where she stood today had she been afraid to make her own choices. She straightened her skirt and did a couple of twirls to imagine how it might flow as she danced. Andrew was taking her to dinner then dancing on a classy party barge on Lake Michigan. He had promised, when they first met, that he would take ballroom dancing lessons with her, and he had made good on that promise. That was another thing they now had in common. She had bought special dance shoes with heels. Stilettos just didn't cut it for serious dancing. And of course, older women did not wear stilettos. Jude laughed aloud. She refused to think of herself as an older woman. She was looking forward to the evening.

The doorbell rang as she put on a fresh layer of lipstick. It rang three more times before she could get to the door. Only Andrew was so impatient.

"When will you learn to give me time to get to the door?" she breathlessly scolded. Andrew wore his most charming smile. Darn, he did remind her of the Sundance Kid and ageing well. His smile was teasing and bright; only the Stetson was missing.

Andrew ran his fingers through his hair. Jude laughed aloud.

"I do make you laugh, still," he teased.

Jude led him to the sofa, "Come on in and have a glass of wine before we leave. I need to let down a bit. I've had a rather stressful day." She stepped to the bar to pour the wine. "The gallery was hectic."

"A shower gave me a second wind," Andrew said. "Do you need a shoulder rub?"

"No, just a glass of wine and some relaxing conversation. I know what a shoulder rub leads to." She gave Andrew a big smile. "And I don't want to mess up my makeup." They laughed together as Jude handed Andrew a glass of Chardonnay.

"How has your week been?"

Andrew settled back into the sofa, "Good. I helped Greg fix the damage to his race car yesterday. All went well until that disgusting woman he lives with came home. She started in on him, and everything went to hell."

Jude rarely heard Andrew talk like this except when speaking of the live-in girlfriend of his employee who helped with the care of the horses. It wasn't exactly relaxing conversation or the way she wanted to start the evening. And she had heard all this over and over, how much he disliked this woman. She, according to Andrew, did nothing to help Greg. She had even, at times, been physically abusive. Yes, women could be physically abusive, too. Jude didn't doubt this. But Andrew's employee chose to stay with her, and they had two children together.

"Andrew, I'm sorry. I do feel bad for Greg, and I know how much his girlfriend upsets you. But you have to accept his choices. Can we not get into that tonight? I'm so excited to have a fun evening. Our first night out dancing!"

"It's just that I can't tolerate that woman. She just wraps him around her fat little finger. I can't believe a good looking guy like Greg stays with her."

"I know how much she upsets you. Maybe he stays because of the kids?"

"Yeah, if they even are his kids. Nothing would surprise me with her." Andrew grumbled.

"Come on. Get your mind on something positive. I get how upsetting it is to you. It's much like some of the situations among our Woman Space artists. But there's nothing you can do to change it."

Andrew reached over and took her hand. "You're right. You're good for me, Jude. You help me get a different perspective on things. When I'm with you everything feels right."

She too, felt comfortable in this relationship. And it had certainly taken her long enough to recognize and accept her own strengths and to choose to remove herself from bad situations in the past. Edward. Brandon. Xander. Sometimes people just had to get hit with the facts over and over before they admitted the facts hurt as much as a fist, enough to refuse to be hit again. And she had spent more than her share of energy worrying over a child. She had kept her diabetic daughter alive for most of her life. She remembered how hard it was to give up trying to control what Jennifer ate and when and how closely she monitored her blood sugar. There came a time, however, that Jude had to accept that Jennifer needed to live her own life, even if she made choices that were not the best. Jude leaned over and kissed Andrew. He's a good man, she thought.

It was a perfect evening for dinner and dancing on Lake Michigan. As they sat in elegant surroundings on the deck of the party barge, a warm breeze gave a messy, sexy look to Andrew's hair. The stars were visible, a rare sight with all the bright lights from the city. Andrew had pre-ordered a lobster dinner, and though the wine was not familiar to Jude, she could tell by the mellow taste that it was expensive.

"Here's to the new Applewood!" Andrew lifted his glass toward Jude. "I'm so pleased with all the changes you've made there, that I've been thinking of some changes I want to make to my ranch house. Your remodeling of Applewood has inspired me. I want to expand the house, give myself a better view of the lake, and build an entertainment area on the water. It would be a good investment if I ever decide to sell. You're good with visualizing and designing. I'd like your input."

"Of course, I'll help you make a plan," Jude responded. "You know how I love that kind of project."

"You're one gifted lady," Andrew whispered as he took Jude's hands in his. Jude smiled, appreciating his compliments, but there was something different in the way he was looking at her.

Suddenly, he was down on one knee. "Jude, I'm so in love with you. You're the most passionate woman I've ever known, about everything! I can't imagine not having you in my life. I want you as part of every project I'll ever do. Will you marry me? Will you be my wife and let me be there for you, protect you, take care of you?"

Jude was deeply touched, and very surprised at his proposal. He actually got on his knee! She wasn't sure men really did that outside movies or romance novels. Had she ever had a man who was there for her, who protected her, took care of her? Not for the long haul at least. Andrew's proposal did sound enticing. She loved Andrew, but after all this time could she be married again?

Andrew was waiting for a response. "Jude, I know you love me. You know we're good together, and we aren't getting any younger."

Jude laughed. "Okay, Andrew, that reminder about age sort of spoiled the mood. But yes, I think so, if we can just go slowly, if we can have a long engagement." Her last statement, "can we have a long engagement?" triggered a memory of the last time she had been proposed to. No, she could not think about that. She trusted Andrew.

With her response, Andrew jumped to his feet, scooped her into his arms and spun her around. "You won't be sorry, baby. I'm so happy!"

"Me, too," Jude whispered, but a pang of something she couldn't quite identify went through her. Once again, she found herself wondering why she couldn't just trust what was happening and be happy.

Andrew reached into his pocket and pulled out a ring box. He opened it to reveal an elaborate setting supporting three large diamonds. "For today, tomorrow and forever, my love," he whispered, as he put it on her ring finger. It was a perfect fit. "It took me a long time to find you, but then God moved you right across the lake where I couldn't miss you. This is destiny, Jude, yours and mine."

Jude felt the tears welling up in her eyes. She had begun to think she was destined to live the rest of her life alone; perhaps a man was a distraction from the work she was here to do. Their arms encircled each other. She did feel she had come home. Her memories of all those she grew up trusting most deeply were manifest in this embrace, this moment.

Andrew's excitement was contagious. The night was a celebration, a joyous occasion. The dance lessons paid off, and the two of them danced as if they had danced together for years. Andrew brought Jude home, happy and a bit high.

"Here, let me take your coat while you get out of those shoes." Andrew pulled her light jacket from her shoulders as Jude walked to the bedroom. She was removing her second shoe as he appeared wearing only that incredible smile. Jude laughed as he reached for her pulling her up and against him. He was kissing her neck, her shoulders and working his way all over her body, with no signs of stopping, as she struggled to get out of her own clothing. Her skirt slid down over her hips as he found her lips and pushed her gently back on the bed. Tonight Andrew's love making was intense and demanding. Jude found herself opening to him, body and soul, as she had not opened to a man in so very long.

II

Jude's work schedule had grown very full. She was scheduled for a solo show, an invitational, at the Ameringer Gallery, a prestigious New York gallery located in Chelsea. In less than two months she needed to produce two more pieces in order to fill the space. She was painting every minute she could manage and depending on Maggie to keep Woman Space running smoothly. In the last few months, sales in the gallery had been the highest ever. It was September, and clients had already begun their holiday shopping. She had been engaged to Andrew for more than three months, a fourth of a year. He seemed much less moody. And she was happy, too.

Jude now spent several days of each week in her studio on the water at Applewood. Her creativity was enhanced by the bright, airy studio space, abundance of window walls, and compelling view of the lake. The large open room was furnished with two comfortable overstuffed chairs. One wall was lined with shelves filled with her favorite books. Near the window wall stood her large easel and a substantial wooden work table. She pulled one of the chairs to the middle of the room for a clear view of the painting in progress. Holding her cup of fresh coffee with both hands, she settled into the chair to study her progress. She wasn't satisfied with the way this piece was developing. She'd been painting on it for over a month and something wasn't working. Maybe she was too distracted with all that was happening in her life. She stood, moved across the studio, and out onto the deck. She had pushed the sliding glass wall fully open, allowing the studio to become part of the outdoors. A perfect calm lay across the lake. The buzz of a bee momentarily caught her attention, then she noticed a breeze so slight it made no impression on the grasses at the edge of the water. She imagined being in her kayak paddling the circumference of the lake. Maybe she needed a break. She felt restless. She picked up her phone to check messages. It rang in her hands, startling her. "Jude Bennett," she answered. There was a pause.

"Hello? Jude?"

"Yes," she replied. The voice was familiar.

"Jude, it's Xander. Do you have a few minutes?" She felt her heart skip a beat. Why was he calling? She hadn't heard from him since he showed up unannounced at the gala.

"Xander? What is it?" Her voice tightened.

"Did you like my gift?" he asked.

"Yes," Jude said, thinking of the rhodonite stone he had given her the night of the gala. "It's lovely, and appropriate."

"Jude, I've not been able to get you nor your new series of paintings out of my mind since I saw you. Your work must be seen in Europe! I've been in touch with a gallery owner that I know in Belgium; I gave him your website link and he's interested in seeing your work in person. He's suggesting a solo show in his gallery just based upon your web site. It could mean more international recognition for you. You already have enough pieces in *Exploring the Goddess* series to fill his feature gallery. I'm just taking the chance that you won't allow our history to prevent you from taking advantage of this opportunity. I think you might sell out across the pond. Europeans love abstract paintings. He says he could get you featured in *Art Review.* They would highlight your work and your Woman Space gallery. It would be some great publicity for the artists you support."

How could she turn down something like this? But could she work with Xander? It had been years since they were involved, and she was happily engaged to Andrew. So, maybe? "Yes, yes. How could I refuse something like this? What an exciting opportunity! I appreciate you making the referral."

"Well, I figure I owe you, Jude." He seemed sincere. But then, Xander was very good at sincere. Still, he kept the conversation business-like. Maybe he had changed. Whatever the case, Jude knew what an important thing this could be for her career as well as the gallery and all the artists she was representing there. An international venue for her work would be an important step toward taking Woman Space opportunities international.

"I will call you with details as soon as I know when he can fly over to see your work and your gallery. His name is Petra von Hessen; you can google him: Von Hessen Galleries in Antwerp. I will be in touch soon, Jude. You won't regret this, I promise."

Jude held the phone to her chest. Could this really be happening? An international solo show in a prestigious gallery? And Xander was making it happen? Well, yes, he does owe me, she thought. He had led her to believe they were building toward a life together when he had still been a married man. But she had never expected this.

Xander had betrayed her, hurt her deeply, but she no longer held it against him. She knew him; she had not entered into a relationship with him with eyes closed. She once wrote in her journal that she loved Xander, and she was willing to take the risk with him, knowing full well that he might not be able to live in a committed, monogamous relationship. If not, well, she would have at least given it a chance. She had no regrets.

Again, the phone rang in Jude's hands, startling her back to the present. "Hi baby. Are you busy?" It was Andrew.

"Not too busy for you. What do you need?"

"Just to see you. Want to take a spin around the lake? There's no wind."

"Were you reading my mind? That's exactly what I need," Jude exclaimed. "I'll meet you in the middle of the lake in twenty minutes!"

III

The sky was a deep Cobalt blue, so clear it seemed to Jude that she was sucked into its depths as she kayaked out into the lake. The still air was a perfect 75 degrees. She and Andrew glided around the perimeter of the lake teasing and laughing, splashing one another until both were literally soaked. It took them two hours at a brisk pace, a good workout. Jude felt invigorated as they pulled their kayaks onto the shore next to her dock. Andrew was in a good mood. She loved his playfulness.

"Andrew, this was the perfect break. Thanks for getting me away from my work for a while. But I do have to get back to it." She dried her arms and legs with a large towel. Andrew moved close, pulling her to him, nuzzling her neck. He smelled of soap and shaving cream with a hint of sweat from the workout.

"Baby, I'd like to keep you away longer. I'm thinking of a nice early dinner at Georgie's with wine followed with a little romance." He was smiling that brilliant smile of his.

She had to resist. "Got to finish this painting tonight, sweetie. I really must go." She pulled away from him as he leaned in for a kiss. It was a peck on the lips instead of what he had in mind. Fortunately, he laughed aloud and let her go.

"I love you. Hope the painting comes together easily."

Jude smiled and whispered, "Thank you; I love you, Andrew." She blew him a kiss and turned to walk to the studio feeling his eyes on her. He really was good about the demands this solo show was making on her time. He seemed to understand.

A text from Xander was waiting when she got inside. Von Hessen would fly in a week from Monday. It was Thursday. Xander would call with specifics when he had them. The gallery was closed on Mondays, so that would mean she would have the time to walk Von Hessen through the gallery uninterrupted and to discuss ideas for a show in his gallery.

Back at her easel, her painting finally began to come together. One brush stroke led to the next. This was the creative zone she loved to fall into as she worked. As she painted, the glow of sunset spread across the still sparkling water. The days were getting longer. The ringing of her phone broke the silence.

"Jude, my girl, where are you?" It was Kim, one of her best friends and part of her Dream Weavers group. Jude had forgotten they had a meeting at Kim's home tonight.

"Kim! Oh, I am so sorry! What time is it? I got so caught up in this painting that I totally lost track of time."

"It's 8:15 dear, you can still make it. Just come as you are."

"But I'm so not prepared!" Jude hesitated.

"Not to worry. I have a special project I want us to address tonight, anyway. Just get your paint-spattered self over here!"

"Okay, I'll be there ASAP." Jude laughed. "Pour me a big glass of wine."

Jude stood back from the painting. "It is finished," she declared aloud. She could sign it tomorrow. She felt a pang of guilt as she dropped her brushes into a container of turpentine. It wasn't good on brushes to leave them that way, but there was no time. She grabbed a long sweater from her closet, slipped on a pair of Crocs, and ran out the door, locking it behind her.

The drive to Kim's gave her some time for thought. She must talk with Andrew about this new development. She wanted to be totally up front with him, fill him in on her history with Xander, to assure him there was no threat in her working with Xander on an international possibility.

The girls were in a state of excitement when she arrived and happy to see her. Including Jude, there were five of them: Kim Prather, an investment lawyer; Allison Wallace, a southern belle type with a Ph.D. in psychology; Amy Carson, the musician, a graduate of Julliard; Gracie Wetherby, a successful businesswoman who, with her husband, owned the building in which Jude was leasing the gallery and her studio apartment. They had been meeting together monthly from the time Jude inherited the Emily Rosen Galleries. The Dream Weavers, as they called themselves, were her support group, as well as great friends. The five of them had met at a women's conference and immediately clicked. Each had been instrumental in Jude's blossoming success, and each had been there for her through every disappointment and every high as she struggled to transform Rosen Galleries into the not-for-profit Woman Space. They now formed her board of directors. Jude owed them, though she knew they'd never think of it in that way. These women were her family now, her sisters, and her close friends.

"Come here, girl," Allison said as she opened her arms for a hug. In seconds everyone joined in for their traditional group hug ritual. As always it ended in laughter. What was it about these women that they could truly love and support each other, could create such supportive community? She never sensed the slightest pang of jealousy from any one of them.

"Okay, now for business," Kim announced, handing Jude a glass of some exotic Merlo. Kim always served the best wine. Jude took a sip and sighed as the semi dry smoothness of Kim's latest favorite slid down her throat.

"What is this, Kim?"

"Tenuta dell 'Ornellaia Masseto, Tuscany, 2007," Kim said smiling. "I bought it when we stayed in that villa near Florence and have been keeping it for a very special occasion." Kim beamed.

"Okay, then." Jude had to admit that Kim's very expensive taste was always easy to enjoy even though she'd never remember the name of the wine. "What is this project, and what is the occasion?"

"Well, you know I've been staying in touch with Luca."

The rest of the group oohed teasingly. Luca was a handsome Italian who had followed Kim around the entire time she had last been in Italy. He was also very married.

"Now, nothing like that is going on," Kim continued. "Luca and I are only friends!" She emphasized the only. "But," she continued, "he has something in the works that I think we should get in on; I know it would benefit Woman Space, Jude."

"Okay, I'm all ears," Jude set down her wine glass to give Kim her full attention.

"Well, Luca is friends with a well-known but struggling Italian artist who would love an international venue. She recently divorced her husband of fifteen years. He was the one with the money, and there was a nasty pre-nup. So, she needs some help boosting her income in order to make it on her own. Luca insists her work is awesome. She could be our first international artist to sponsor, and I thought we could make it a Dream Weaver project to get her over here, let her stay in our homes, you know, sort of host her."

"That's a great idea, Kim," Allison exclaimed.

"I agree," chimed in Gracie.

"Me, too," Amy added. They had obviously been discussing this before Jude arrived.

Gracie walked around the table and hugged Jude. "This is just what you need to put Woman Space fully into the international spotlight!"

"So," Kim interjected, "you like my special occasion? We can make this our special project?"

"You do have to allow me to see her work and her bio before we make a decision." Jude interjected.

"Yes, of course," Kim lifted her wine glass. "As soon as Jude approves the quality of her work, we will move on this!" The others cheered, lifting their glasses in unison.

Jude could hardly believe her good fortune. If she could connect with this artist and get a specific go ahead, she could share this with Von Hessen when she met with him. Perhaps this news would inspire him to suggest a Belgian artist in a similar situation. Things were happening fast. The possibility of her own international solo show and taking Woman Space to an international level, all in the same day! It was time to share with the girls her news of the solo invitation. This was more reason to celebrate.

"One more thing," Jude clanked her glass with her pen. "I got a call from Xander today telling me he wants to connect me with a gallery owner in Antwerp, Belgium. Just by viewing my work on my website, this man is considering featuring my art in a solo show. So, we have two international possibilities in one day!"

The girls cheered again. "A toast to manifesting what we felt should come next," Kim interjected.

"It does seem that setting the intention to go international has immediately started the ball rolling," Jude added. "I hope we can keep up with it."

"Well, I say we contact Luca and get things moving. I told him I had to run this by you first." Kim pulled out her cell phone and dialed. "Luca, it's Kim. I'm here with my group, and we need to see your artist's work. Can you send me an email sampling or the link to her website?"

Luca immediately sent a link to Leona Fratelle's website. There were beautiful photos of elaborate sculptures in wood and metal. The artist had rave reviews from previous galleries as well, and her artist's statement was impressive. Jude agreed her work and her philosophy would fit with the Woman Space vision. The women spent the next two hours brainstorming ideas and pinning down a timeline while Luca verified that his artist friend could make the chosen dates. The artist, forty-one-year-old Leona, a mother of two, was as excited as the Weavers. Before the evening was over, all was arranged. Jude would share the news with Von Hessen when she met him a week from Monday.

IV

Being with the Dream Weavers, caught up in the excitement of featuring an Italian artist at Woman Space, left Jude energized and feeling good. She wasn't sure what she would do without this group of women in her life. They were so supportive. It was nearing 2:00 AM when she arrived back at the loft. She was so excited that she couldn't immediately get to sleep. The next morning she slept in, then did yoga and meditation. As she was about to make a journal entry, an email from

Andrew came in. "Good morning. Where in the world were you last night? I called several times."

Jude reached for her cell phone. There were six messages from Andrew. She had gotten so caught up in the excitement that she had forgotten to check messages. She pushed #3 for Andrew.

"Hello?" Andrew answered. Jude sensed the tension in his voice.

"Hi, I'm so sorry you were worried last night. I finished—"

Andrew interrupted, anger apparent in his voice. "How can you do that to me? You know I worry."

"Andrew, let me explain." It hit her that she seemed to always be explaining. "I had just finished the painting, and Kim called, reminding me that I was late to my Dream Weavers get together. You know we do this monthly. I simply grabbed my things and rushed out the door. Oh, and I have some exciting—"

Again he interrupted. "Jude, if I am going to be an important part of your life, then you have to learn to give some priority to keeping me informed."

She knew he was right. It was only fair that she let him know where she was going so he wouldn't worry. But she had totally forgotten about the get-together herself.

"I am sorry, Andrew, I didn't mean to worry you. You do know that, right? And let me tell you my exciting news." There was silence. "Kim heard from a friend in Italy," Jude continued, "and he has a wonderful artist friend wanting to come to Woman Space as our first international artist. It's all set… Andrew?"

"Yes, I heard you. That's great. But that still doesn't excuse you for ignoring my calls last night."

"Honey, I didn't ignore you. I simply got so caught up in the moment that I didn't hear the phone. It was in my purse and on vibrate. I had to see samples of the artist's work to be sure she was a fit with Woman Space. Then we had to determine dates and get those agreed on, and with the time difference we were dealing with, I lost track of time. By the time I got home, it was too late to call you."

Andrew was obviously upset. Jude shook her head in frustration. He would just have to get used to this. Sometimes things came up that she had to deal with.

"Am I forgiven?" She thought she sensed Andrew softening.

"This time. Just be more considerate next time." The phone went dead.

Had he really hung up on her? This was ridiculous! She would not honor such a move by calling him back. She would just give him time to cool down.

V

Xander was early. Jude caught his eye and waved as she locked her car. He was in the outdoor seating sipping coffee and watching for her. She entered the remodeled foyer of the Western Springs Pracino's taking note of the live edge wood slab table tops. It was a habit she had, noticing the slightest change in décor. The tables were a new addition, and they must have been all of four inches thick. Something like this would work great in the entry to the gallery. Xander stood to greet her with that mischievous twinkle in his eyes. He took her hand and kissed her cheek.

"I'll never forget that perfume." he teased.

Jude shook her head. "If we're going to work together, you must keep this professional, Xander." He pulled a chair out for her, performing an elaborate bow. She could not help but laugh. There was no way to avoid the play of energy between them. She may as well enjoy it. But she did know what she wanted, and it didn't include getting involved with Xander.

"I have some news for you that will fit perfectly with Von Hessen's international exhibition idea."

"Yeah, and what is that?"

"We've lined up our first artist for the international program, an Italian woman who does wonderful sculptures in wood and metal. Do you think Von Hessen will be impressed?"

"Well, that works very well into our plans, Jude. You see, this is meant to be." Xander reached for her hands, leaning across the table to capture her full eye contact. "You are a creative genius, my dear. And I am here to help you make an international splash! I have a lot to make up to you, and finally things have come together so I can."

"I would rather you think of this as setting a friend up with a great opportunity, Xander. I don't need pay back. I just need an honest friendship."

"However it works for you." Xander leaned back as Jude pulled her hands away. "Now, here is the itinerary from Petra."

"Petra is Von Hessen's first name?"

"Yes, Petra von Hessen III, in fact. So, here." He pulled a folded paper from his jacket. "I will pick you up at 5:00 AM on Saturday, and we will fly to meet Von Hessen in Manhattan. Plan to be gone for the weekend. I promise to return you home to your apartment and gallery on Monday morning where Petra will join us in order to see the work in person."

"Wait, what is this change in plans? Why do we have to meet him in New York for the weekend?" Jude was immediately suspicious. And she had not yet had an opportunity to discuss all this with Andrew. "You said he would fly here on Monday."

"Because this is the way he works, my dear. He will wine and dine you, take you on a tour of his New York gallery, then come to see your Woman Space."

"He has a New York gallery as well?" It seemed Xander had failed to fill her in on some of the details.

"Yes, apparently he has just purchased it. I didn't know about it myself until I got his itinerary late yesterday. He wants to feature your work there also. I told him that you have a showing in New York in a few weeks, so he wants to move your work from the Ameringer to his gallery at the end of that run. It will go from there to Belgium. Of course, you will have to have enough work to replace anything sold. His gallery is at least as large as the Ameringer."

"Okay, this is feeling a bit overwhelming." Jude felt her face flush.

"Well, you had better get ready! This is it." Xander touched her cheek with his forefinger. "You are tearing up? Your dreams are coming true, eh?"

Jude began to laugh and cry at once, tears staining her blushing cheeks.

"You are still so beautiful." Xander whispered.

She was shaken. And she was obviously still not totally immune to Xander. This was even more than she'd imagined. She'd been dreaming of having her work in demand in New York and European galleries for as long as she had been exhibiting. It was her hope that if she just kept doing what she loved and supporting others like herself in doing what they loved she would be ready for whatever it blossomed into. She had used that word often. Blossoming—letting things develop at their natural pace, their natural course.

"This is your blossoming, eh?" Xander said, as if reading her thoughts. She saw that Xander's eyes were glassy as well. He remembered.

VI

The flight to New York was uneventful. Jude read for most of it. Xander slept. The two of them could have been an old married couple. There was a comfort level that put Jude's mind at ease.

It had not been easy convincing Andrew that this was strictly business. "It isn't you I don't trust," Andrew assured Jude. "It's this Xander guy. You can't convince me that he doesn't have more than business in mind. You two were in a serious relationship." But in the end he drove Jude to the airport and whispered, "I do trust you," as he kissed her goodbye.

Von Hessen had arranged for a car to meet Jude and Xander at the airport and drop them at a lovely hotel near the gallery. They were to enjoy dinner and a show, Von Hessen's treat, and then get some rest. The car would be there in the morning to take them to meet Von Hessen for breakfast.

"Freshen up and take some time to rest; I will call for you in about an hour and a half," Xander said, leaving Jude and her luggage at her room. His room was across the hall.

Jude unpacked her bag, hung some clothing in the closet, and opened the curtains to let in the afternoon light. The room faced the west. The sun was beginning to set, spreading an aura of color across the city. She looked out over a view of lower Manhattan. She wondered if they were near the Highline. It would be fun to walk there if she and Xander had some time to themselves while here. She left the curtains open and lay across the bed.

She had not intended to fall asleep, but she was suddenly awakened by a knock at her door. She jumped up, rather disoriented, and walked to peer through the peep hole. There was Xander's distorted face. Laughing aloud she opened the door to him.

"What's so funny?" he asked with a look of irritation on his face.

"You're just so handsome with the oval convex face," Jude said giggling.

Xander grabbed her in a bear hug and began to tickle her. For a moment she flashed back to the years of wrestling and lovemaking with this man.

"Whoa," Jude exclaimed, regaining her perspective. She pulled herself free of Xander and closed the door.

"Sorry," Xander smiled sheepishly. "It was just my natural instinct."

"I know," Jude said, and began laughing again.

"There will always be that magic between us, Jude."

"Well, we just have to learn to deal with it, then," Jude replied. "Make yourself comfortable while I freshen up. I fell asleep."

Xander walked to the corner chair and flipped the remote to CNN. "I'll just catch up on the events of the day."

"Probably just more news of terrorism," she said, taking her makeup bag with her into the bathroom. Would she never stop being affected by this man? More memories played in her head as she began touching up her powder and blush. She brushed her thick hair, gave it a couple of tosses with her fingers, and sprayed a fresh spritz of perfume. That would have to do.

"Ok, I'm ready," she announced as she entered the room.

The restaurant was on the top floor of the hotel with breathtaking views of the city. The haze that hovered was tinted pink and the sky above it a deep Cerulean blue. The pattern of buildings dotted with white and yellow lights stood silhouetted in black against this horizon. Von Hessen had spared no cost. An expensive champagne, the real thing, was brought to their table in a crystal bucket. Together they toasted the sunset.

"To you, famous artist, and your blossoming," Xander lifted his glass a second time.

Jude touched her glass to his. "And to you, my friend, who has made this whole thing possible." They each took a long sip. Their eyes met over the rim of their glasses. Xander smiled that mischievous smile again with the lifted right brow. Lowering his glass he spoke. "I'm so privileged to be here sharing this with you, Jude. I feared you would not allow it."

"We do have a history, don't we?" Jude replied. "But I'm happy that you're here, and I do appreciate that you've made this possible. Thank you."

Setting his glass aside Xander reached for Jude's free hand. "Don't panic," he began, "I just need to say something to you, and I think this is the time." He took her hand in both hands. "I am so very sorry for the way I hurt you, Jude. I loved you, and still, I blew it with you. I am well aware of that. I loved you then, and I love you now. But I know you have moved on. You are engaged to marry another man, and I promise to respect that. You don't have to be on guard with me. Okay?"

"Okay," Jude replied. There was a slight trembling in her voice which she sensed Xander didn't miss. She would always have to be on guard with Xander. "I just ask that we not discuss this further. Okay?"

"Okay." Xander replied.

Dinner was delicious and delightfully served by a waiter in coattails and a bow tie. Xander's apology seemed to have cleared the air; their conversation was comfortable and easy.

"It's happening!" "Jude said excitedly. "I can feel it Xander. Woman Space is going to help women worldwide, and my artwork will get greater exposure as well. It just feels so unreal. And I can't tell you how much I appreciate your role in this."

"It's an honor to be of help." Xander smiled. "I'll do what I can to make it happen. By the way, I have some rather exciting news of my own. Are you aware that President Obama has instituted a BRAIN initiative through the National Institute of Health?"

"No." Jude shook her head. "I've been so caught up in what was happening with Woman Space. I missed that."

"Well, I've been asked to be a part of this new study. The aim is to generate a comprehensive picture of the human brain and its function. I am really excited about it, Jude."

"That's great, Xander! Congratulations! Talk about an honor! Looks like we're both going to be very busy doing what we love! What exactly will this project involve?"

"We have an unprecedented opportunity to develop new technologies that will allow us to map the circuits of the brain, measure brain activity, and understand how the brain maintains health and modulates human behavior."

"So," Jude began with a deeply thoughtful look, "do you think this might one day help determine how to deal with terrorism in the modern world?"

Xander shook his head affirmatively. "And so many other problems," he added.

"It's strange how we sort of fall into this place of acceptance concerning the fact that a growing group of people would like to destroy the entire Western culture. It just seems beyond what I can wrap my mind around." Sadness overwhelmed Jude as she spoke.

"I know," Xander responded. "When I'm in Belgium, I am very aware of this threat. We have so many rumored terrorist cells hiding out there…." Then he broke a silent pause, "But on a lighter note, I have been doing some research concerning the Belgian art markets."

"And?"

"And I feel sure your work is going to be a hit and sales will be significant."

"You're thinking this is going to work then?" Jude asked.

"Yes. It is definitely going to work."

VII

Sitting in comfort while a driver smoothly navigated the traffic in Von Hessen's limo added still another dimension to the fascinating energy of New York City. Jude felt like an official jet-setter as she and Xander were dropped at Norma's on 56th Street for breakfast.

Von Hessen was already seated and had ordered juice and coffee. He stood to greet them, taking Jude's hand and lifting it to his lips as he bowed. "You are simply elegant," he said to Jude as he pulled back the chair for her to be seated.

And Jude did look elegant in her black mid-calf pencil skirt and three quarter sleeve top. She wore understated jewelry and a black and charcoal gray wrap. It was cool enough that she chose knee high boots with a dressy heel, also in black. She was happy to see that Xander had a black suit with a gray shirt and understated tie. She knew they were a handsome couple who would look at home in any major city in the world, whether on business or a romantic getaway.

"Thank you, Mr. Von Hessen," Jude replied. The gallery owner was what Jude would call worldly handsome. His features were rugged, and he had an air of having been around and in charge for a long time. His suit was expensive and perfectly tailored. For a man who was at least in his early seventies he was still attractive and appeared in good shape.

"I will suggest the blueberry pancakes. They are superb," Von Hessen said.

"Blueberry pancakes are a favorite of mine," Jude responded.

"I find their cinnamon crepes incredible," Xander said.

How did he always have the scoop on everything? Jude wondered. Xander never ceased to amaze her.

It was a lovely breakfast complete with orange juice laced with champagne, and Von Hessen quickly put Jude at ease with his gentle manner and wit. His eyes danced as he obviously flirted, though in a very gentlemanly manner. Jude felt sure it was innocent enough, but she was quick to mention Andrew and their engagement when Von Hessen asked about her future plans. His question gave her the opportunity to share her dream of taking Woman Space to an international audience and her excitement over the Italian artist who was already on the calendar to be featured at Woman Space.

"I am most impressed with your project, Ms. Bennett!" Von Hessen said enthusiastically. "Xander speaks so highly of you as well. I do want to be a part of your work, first by featuring your original paintings in my New York and Antwerp galleries, but also, I would like to offer a sizeable donation toward your not-for-profit. I look for worthwhile charities annually, and I will pledge to yours for next year." He slid a note to the center of the table with the proposed amount of $1.5 million.

Jude could not hide her shock. "Mr. Von Hessen, I don't know what to say. I…I'm speechless!"

Von Hessen patted Jude's hand. "I am happy to help. I find your work a very worthy cause, Ms. Bennett. And it has a personal meaning for me as well. When I was only nine years of age my mother was beaten to death by my father when she tried to leave him. She got us children to safety before she announced to him that she was divorcing him; otherwise, I might not be here today."

"I am so sorry! I promise you that I will make the best use possible of your generosity, and in your name. I am so sorry about your mother. I've had to add security to my staff in order to adequately protect the women involved in Woman Space. In addition, I hope to expand my staff to include free therapy as well as medical and legal services for all of my artists who could benefit from it. This generous contribution assures that I will be able to make these services available much sooner than expected."

"My mother's name was Norma," he whispered. "Could you include her name in some way?"

Jude saw his eyes turn glassy. "Yes, yes, of course," she said, reaching to touch Von Hessen's hand.

"I had no idea," Xander responded. "I am so sorry. Is there a connection with your mother and this restaurant?"

"Only that I first came here because of the name," Von Hessen replied. "Now I also come because the food is superb."

Jude felt a wave of compassion for this wealthy, worldly man with such a soft and compassionate interior.

"Okay," Von Hessen said, trying to move beyond the mood that was settling over them. "If you are ready, let's get going. I have a wonderful gallery to show you, and some plans for promoting your show that I feel sure you will approve of."

The gallery was beautiful with light gray walls professionally designed so as to best highlight each piece of art on display. A large comfortable sectional was arranged in the center of the open space where clients could sit and observe their favorite selections from a rolling wall with special lighting. A massive coffee table, a center cut from a large walnut tree set on a welded metal frame, made an impressive center piece where drinks and hors d'oeuvres were served. Jude could see that Von Hessen would spare no expense to properly present her work to the New York art world.

Jude sat sipping a flavored coffee as she looked through Von Hessen's plan for an opening celebration. The plan included a feature article in *Art Review*. She was living a dream.

After an excellent dinner that went late into the evening, Von Hessen instructed his driver to drop Xander and Jude back at their hotel. "We will talk in the morning." Xander smiled and kissed Jude's cheek at her door. "I don't know about you, but I am exhausted and more than a little tipsy."

Jude giggled. "Yes, I definitely need a shower and bed. What time for breakfast?"

"I'll call you when I wake, okay? I'm too tired to think about that right now."

Xander's call didn't come until almost 10:00 AM. Jude was still enjoying dozing between thoughts of the previous day. It felt wonderful to sleep in.

"Are you awake?" Xander asked, when Jude answered the phone. "Are you ready to decide on breakfast and how you want to spend our day in New York City?"

Jude's response was sleepy and slow. "I would love some quaint and quirky breakfast spot where we can discuss the day. Do you know such a place?"

Xander laughed. "I know just the place. Can you be ready in an hour?"

"Yes, an hour will be perfect."

Over breakfast they decided to spend the first part of their day visiting galleries where Jude would get ideas and inspiration for both art and décor. Then, after a leisurely vendor packed picnic lunch in Central Park, they would tour the Guggenheim. It was Jude's favorite art museum. Just entering the main lobby and looking upward through the spiraling architecture had been a spiritual experience the first time she had visited.

"I already know where I want to take you for dinner," Xander said. "It will be my surprise."

By lunch time it seemed they had walked for miles. The hotel had packed a picnic basket that included a light weight quilt they could spread on the ground.

"You've got to be kidding," Jude exclaimed, as she unpacked a Petrossian caviar picnic from two slender rectangular containers, each about the size of a child's box of watercolors. There was a big green salad with a few marinated peppers and a tart vinaigrette, but who cared about that? The caviar was the thing, a 30-gram container of sevruga and the same amount of salmon roe, complete with a small tool for prying open the jars, and a mother-of-pearl caviar spoon packed in a blue velvet pouch. A few light crackers were included for the sevruga. For dessert, yes, dessert, there was a delicate, delicious fig genoise and a pillbox of tiny, exquisite chocolates and two small airplane-sized bottles of vodka.

Jude looked up at Xander who was watching her with a mischievous grin. "I don't have any idea what half of this is!"

115

"I wanted today to be special," he said, reaching for the tool to open the salmon roe.

They ate their fill then lay back on the quilt to digest. The sun was warm, and a soft breeze caught the remnants of a colorful yellow ribbon of paper that had been a part of an environmental art installation in the park. Miniature sailboats floated on the small lake nearby. Jude stared up at the windows of the condos that framed the park. What would it be like to live here? She found herself wondering. She had heard that Barbara Streisand lived across from Central Park, and Paul McCartney. Certainly they would have amazing views. Her thoughts were distracted by Xander's soft snoring. She would have to wake him soon if they were to see the remaining galleries on their list.

That evening Xander escorted Jude to Robert Restaurant, located on the 9th floor of the Museum of Arts and Design in Columbus Circle. Here they had their own spectacular view of Central Park. Live jazz accompanied the meal.

"Von Hessen has connections all over Europe, Jude. If he is as impressed with you and your work as he appears to be, he will be an important factor in making your work known throughout the European art world."

"Do you think he really likes my work that much?"

"He wouldn't be making plans to show it both here and in Belgium if he wasn't already sold on it. Yes, he wants to see it in person, but he has already gone to a lot of expense bringing us here. I'd say it's a done deal."

"I'm going to be your interpreter in Belgium, you know." Xander smiled taking a slow sip of his Champagne.

"Well, I'll need one." The thought hit Jude that she was just an Illinois farm girl. How could all this be happening to her?

"I promise to behave myself." Xander added. Jude could see he was a bit tipsy.

"I'm holding you to that promise." She laughed.

Xander grew serious. "Jude, I realize that I really blew it. I hate the idea of you with this other guy. We belong together, always have, always will."

Jude reached across the table and took the glass from his hand. "Enough of this for you, my friend. I believe things happen as they should, and so, we are both exactly where we need to be. You are okay, right?"

Xander smiled slowly. "I am just great. I am behaving."

Jude shook her head and smiled.

They sat silently listening to the wonderful jazz trio that was the after dinner entertainment.

"What an amazing day," Jude exclaimed as the waiter set their bill on the table.

"I know," Xander replied. "I find that I don't want it to end. I have missed spending time with you, Jude. You do me much good."

"And you do me good, too." Jude smiled warmly. "You truly do. You're a good friend. Friends always, right?"

"I would very much like that, Jude." Xander reached for the bill.

Intercepting his reach Jude added, "And I insist that you allow me to buy dinner. Without you I would not have this promissory note for $1.5 million! It is the least I can do."

"Unreal, isn't it? Okay, you can treat me this time."

They took a cab back to the hotel. It wasn't quite the same style as the limo, but it was relaxed.

"Very early morning tomorrow," Xander said as they reached the door.

"Yes," Jude replied as she gave him a hug.

They stood, simply holding one another, neither wanting the evening to end. Finally, Jude pulled away. "Sweet dreams, Xander," she said smiling.

"Sweet dreams," Xander replied. He stood, watching as she entered her room and closed the door.

Jude felt so tired that she fell into bed, opting for a morning shower. But for some reason sleep wouldn't come. Instead, she found herself caught up in nostalgia concerning Xander. She had fallen in love with him as she had Edward. Xander was highly intelligent, witty, charming, and determined. She could claim vulnerability, for certainly she had been hurting from the failed relationship with Brandon. That failure had disturbed those old wounds from her marriage to Edward. And at that time in her life, she was still looking to be rescued. And she had to face it; she was an expert in denial.

Jude took a long shower, and still wrapped in a towel, picked up her phone and dialed Andrew.

CHAPTER 9

You can live a life of either trusting your inner voice or distrusting your inner voice. You can cling to familiar expectations, conventions, and "reasonable" responses or you can listen to the sweet madness in your bones.

—Tama Keeves -author, Harvard lawyer

BACK FROM NEW York for only three days, Jude's head was still in the clouds. Things were moving so fast; she was finding it a bit difficult to wrap her mind around all that was happening. She'd have to enlist Maggie's help in order to stay on top of Woman Space and be ready for both New York and Antwerp solo exhibits. She was sitting at her desk at Applewood trying to focus on a "to do" list.

"Jude, have you seen the hat I wore the last time we went riding?" Andrew asked as he stormed into the house without even a hello. "I get so frustrated that you move my things around."

"Wait a minute, Andrew. I haven't seen nor touched your hat. Why would you think it was over here?"

"Because," Andrew said in a raised voice, "I can't find it anywhere in my house, and you were with me when I rode last."

"Have you checked in the stables? Yours, that is?" Irritation was rising in her own voice. Then Jude laughed aloud and added, "We are sounding like two old married people!"

"Well, that isn't likely to happen with you," Andrew zinged back.

"Okay, Andrew. What's bothering you?" She knew this was a comment aimed at the fact that she wasn't ready to set a wedding date. She walked to stand directly in front of him and reached out to touch his arm.

Andrew sighed and shook his head. "I'm sorry, baby. I've just been feeling disconnected from you. So much is happening with your gallery and your art. I'm feeling there is hardly any time for us."

"Then, doesn't that make it even more important that we make our time together count, keep it positive?"

"Yes, you're right." Andrew took her in his arms and nuzzled her neck. He smelled so good, felt so good to her as she snuggled against him.

"Can we take today for ourselves?" She asked as she pulled back from the embrace. "I think we need to get away from everything and spend the day together."

"I can't today, sweetie." Andrew sighed. "I didn't know if you would be free, so I agreed to meet with a new client who has a horse for me to train. It will take most of the day. That's why I'm desperate to find my hat. He'll be here in thirty minutes."

"Okay, how about a long, leisurely dinner tonight, on the deck, just the two of us? I'll take care of everything."

"That should work; yes, that would be perfect. I really need some alone time with you, Jude. I'll see you then." He added sheepishly, "And I'll check my stables for my hat." With that he was out the door.

Andrew had been so great about her traveling to New York with Xander. And she had another trip with Xander coming up in a couple of weeks to see the Belgium gallery. She really needed to save some time for the two of them. She determined tonight would be special. She picked up her phone and called John, whose number she knew by heart.

"John, would you have time to put together a dinner for two for tonight?"

"Sure, I can squeeze that in, Jude. What would you like?"

"Let's do pecan crusted salmon, sweet potato balls on the side, and a green salad."

"I can do that. Delivery at six?"

"Perfect! Thanks, John." Okay, the food was taken care of. She dialed Andrew's cell, which went immediately to voice mail. "Hi honey, dinner at six. I promise you we'll have quality time together. Enjoy the new horse. I love you."

Now all she needed to do was make a peaches and cream pie for desert and make sure both she and the house looked great. She had once considered herself a wonderful cook. At least others had said she was. But now she teased her family that she was all cooked out. She had lived alone for so long, and with so many more pressing matters to take care of, she had lost her timing for cooking. If anything stressed her when her family came together it was trying to be sure there was enough food. Cooking for one did not keep her in practice. Besides, what fun was it to cook for one? And now that Doug, a real gourmet cook, was at the farm, she seldom cooked at all. Andrew would be surprised, and happy, that she made a homemade pie.

Jude got out her baking supplies. She still knew the recipe by heart. She pulled her mom's handmade apron from a drawer and tied it around her waist. She was reminded of her years as wife and mother. How her life had changed. But these were good times, maybe even the best. She soon found her hands doing what they needed, measuring and stirring. Cooking was a creative art as much as painting, as was gardening or sewing. She found herself enjoying being in the kitchen even as her mind periodically wandered to those "more pressing matters."

Plans for the New York show were going so well. Von Hessen had visited the gallery on the Monday following the trip to New York City, and he loved Jude's work, as well as some of the work of participating Woman Space artists. She could feel that this show in New York followed by one in Belgium would lead to so many other opportunities. To top it all off, Von Hessen had chosen to purchase her most expensive new piece, saying he needed it for his collection and didn't want to take the chance someone might buy it out from under him. It would still be in the exhibit, but would be marked as sold. Because of this sale she had $25,000 more in her bank account. Her plan was to share this news with Andrew tonight.

II

Jude stood in front of her full length mirror. The peaches and cream pie was cooling on the counter, and she was dressed for the evening. She felt confident that Andrew would like her new white eyelet sundress with a sexy low fitted bodice. There was a slight flare to the skirt that came mid-calf, placing emphasis on her new strappy teal sandals. The dress showed off her tan and made her hair a focal point that framed her eyes. She wanted to please him. She loved him. She held out her left hand and studied the beautiful three diamond ring that he had given her the night he proposed. She should be feeling happy, but suddenly she felt totally overwhelmed. She was getting ready for her big New York show while having to visit new galleries in both New York and Belgium. All this while dealing with being around Xander again after so many years. And she was struggling to adjust to the idea of getting married.

Jude wrapped her arms around her head and dropped heavily onto the sofa. The expansive glass wall revealed the serene lake, a flower garden that welcomed a stroll, a studio that any artist would die for. All of this was hers. She needed more time to soak it all up, to enjoy, to process. She needed more time!

Her anxiety was peaking when the doorbell rang. John was early with dinner. She stood, took a deep breath, and straightened her skirt. The doorbell rang a second time. As she walked toward the door, the doorbell rang a third time. That would be Andrew. Why did he always do that? It was so damn irritating.

Jude threw open the door, a look of exasperation on her face. "What?" Andrew asked, looking perplexed.

"First of all, you are forty-five minutes early, and secondly, why can't you give me a minute to get to the door? I absolutely hate the doorbell blasting me as I am trying to get here!"

Andrew made a face and took two steps back. "Sorry. I'm just anxious to see you." He gave Jude a sheepish grin. She shook her head and forced a smile.

"Come on in. John is bringing dinner. I thought that would be him."

Andrew slid inside. His face was pink with fresh sun. He had obviously been outside working the new horse all afternoon, though he was now scrubbed and smelled of soap and cologne. A subtle whiff of his cologne softened Jude's mood, and she smiled. With that he grabbed her in his arms and kissed her. A pang of desire surged through her veins.

"You are so darn...frustrating!" Jude said as she began to laugh. "Get in here and pour us a drink. I see John driving up, so dinner won't be long."

Andrew walked to the bar and poured two glasses of sparkling wine. They sat on the glider enjoying the lake view, sipping the wine while John served up the food.

"Dinner is served," John called. But he had slipped out and on to his next appointment before they walked inside.

"I love you, Jude. I'm sorry I've been difficult." Andrew closed his eyes with a "Mmmm," as he took a bite of the pie.

"I made it. From scratch," Jude whispered.

"Delicious, and the way to a man's heart....Jude, I'm more than a little jealous of all the time you're spending with this old boyfriend. I'm not sure just how to handle it."

"Andrew, you're the man I love. It's you I've agreed to marry. You've nothing to worry about. I ended things with Xander years ago because of who Xander is. That hasn't changed."

"Then marry me now." His eyes locked on hers. She leaned forward and kissed him softly.

"You have to give me time, Andrew. I'm gun shy about marriage, not about you. Can you understand that?"

"Probably not," he smiled. "But I'll take your word for it." He patted her thigh, and they stared across the lake to the sunset.

The quiet that followed dinner was heavy. Maybe Andrew was tired, or maybe he was disappointed in her. But she could only deal with so much at a time, and right now there was too much happening in her life to think about marriage. After all, she had made it clear from the beginning that she needed a long engagement.

"I think I'll turn in early, sweetie," Andrew said as he helped her clear the table. "It's been a long day."

"Tired?" Jude asked.

"Yes, a difficult horse. And a difficult woman." He laughed.

Jude walked him to the door. She realized he was finding her difficult. She just hoped his patience would persevere.

"All is well. Honestly," he whispered as he kissed her forehead. "Get some good rest, and I'll talk to you tomorrow."

Jude closed the door behind him. A wave of tiredness permeated her entire being. She ran water for a hot bath and leaned back in the huge free standing tub. She had so much to do before flying to meet Xander in Belgium. She sighed, realizing she had forgotten to tell Andrew about the sale of the painting. An overwhelming and anxious feeling washed over her again. "One thing at a time," she whispered under her breath and dozed off in the tub.

III

It had been a while since Jude had taken a morning to herself to walk, do some yoga, journal and meditate. That was most likely why she was feeling so much stress. She spread her yoga mat on the deck of the lake studio and spent an hour doing long and intense poses. She felt an emotional release with each asana. Tears were now flowing down her cheeks. She sat looking out over the stillness of the lake. She had to slow her life down. She loved everything that was happening, but she knew she had to take care of herself as well. She had felt so on edge last night after Andrew left. She must have been very tired to have fallen asleep in the tub, not the safest thing to do.

What was stressing her to such a degree? She wondered. Most likely it was the idea of marriage. Andrew was determined, and she was, frankly, unsure marriage was what she wanted.

"It's not about you, Andrew. You are wonderful," she whispered aloud, her thoughts adding, It's about me. I'm not sure what I will gain by marriage to anyone. And if for some reason it doesn't work out, then it becomes a really big mess.

CHAPTER 10

....lay down beside me; make angels, make devils, make who you are.
— Giam Slater "I Am A Small Poem"

ANDREW SEEMED TO **have dealt well with Jude flying to New York with Xander.** But Jude had felt the tension in him as she kissed him goodbye at the airport. She was now on a flight to Belgium where she would be meeting Xander again. But if Jude was going to make this international exhibit happen, she had to act now. Von Hessen had been excited about her work when he visited Woman Space following their meeting in New York City. And Xander was more than cooperative. He respected that Jude was engaged and not available. Not that she would have been available to him anyway, considering all that had happened in the past. This trip to view the Antwerp gallery was simply the next step.

Jude was becoming painfully aware that flying was not as much fun as it once had been, thanks to a nineteen hour flight including layovers. They were perhaps two thirds into the flight, and her back ached, her legs needed to stretch even though she was in first class. She lifted a bite of the chicken breast smothered in some sort of sauce to her dry lips. It was as tasteless as cardboard. She placed the fork back on the plate, prongs down.

At least the wine was good, she thought, as she took another sip of a nameless chardonnay and leaned back and closed her eyes. If only she could get some sleep. She pushed the recline button. She should be thankful for the comfortable seats. If Von Hessen weren't paying for the flight, she would be flying coach, which could really be uncomfortable on a long flight. Shifting and turning in the seat, she finally settled in enough to doze. Once asleep:

> Jude found herself in a large building. She thought Xander was with her, but they had somehow become separated. She had no idea which direction he might have taken. She wandered through several long, sterile hallways. There was no one in sight. The building appeared to be some sort of maze. Suddenly, she felt a strong sense of danger. Was Xander in danger?

> "Xander, please answer if you can hear me!" Nothing. Her sense of danger was growing. She frantically began to open each door only to find one empty room after another.

> Finally, she threw open a door to a dimly lit room filled with partially finished sculptures. Plaster casts used for molding bronze were scattered all around the room. Plaster dust covered every surface. She felt as if she was choking and began to cough.

Jude jerked awake, pulled out of her dream by her own coughing. "Please fasten your seat belts," the captain was saying. "We have a bit of a rough ride ahead."

Jude tightened her belt and brought her seat up. She took a sip of melted ice from a plastic cup. Why was her mouth so dry? The dream had left her with a sense of foreboding. Probably she was just worried about how to find Xander once she landed at the Antwerp airport. She spoke inadequate French and no Dutch. She didn't relish the idea of being in a foreign country without Xander to interpret. What was going on with her? Wasn't she the one who loved an adventure?

Jude closed her eyes again trying to recall more details of the dream. It could have been triggered by the history she shared with Xander. They'd kept running into one another at the Chicago Theater where they first met. The theater was a large building with long white hallways leading to rooms for music practice and acting classes. Xander was there often for meetings for the fund raising project he was a part of. On Thursday evenings Jude taught two classes on creative expression at the center. Xander's meetings finished early; he would often bring Jude a coffee and sit in on the final thirty minutes of her class. Sitting together, sipping coffee, and talking, once the students left for the day, became a regular weekly occurrence. Slowly their friendship deepened until Jude found herself at times fantasizing a romance between them.

Xander was an interesting man, well-traveled, well-educated, a neuroscientist with a passion for the arts. They met at the Art Institute a few times for a special show that he wanted to share with her, and a few times they shared lunch. She found their conversations intellectually stimulating, and they often brainstormed concerning the marketing of Jude's art. Their coming together had been innocent enough in the beginning.

A dis-ease settled over Jude; chills swept across the top of her shoulders. She felt strange. Never had she been so uneasy on a flight. She picked up the book she was reading and tried to concentrate. It would help if she could get lost in the story; it would make the time pass more quickly. But she couldn't focus. Someone had left remnants of a *USA Today* in the seat back. She slowly read through the headlines and settled on a story on Canada's young Prime Minister. From there she played with what was left to solve of a word puzzle. She tried again to nap, but each time she closed her eyes, she saw the long white hallways of the dream and felt a knot grow in her stomach. Finally, she took out her notepad and pen and began a list of the artwork she wanted to have ready for the New York Show, along with some ideas for new work she might need by the time the exhibit was moved to Belgium.

It seemed she had just dozed off when she was disturbed by the drink cart rolling noisily down the aisle. She took a glass of Diet 7 Up, and then asked for water. Jude sighed with relief when the flight attendant finally began collecting trash and reminding people to prepare for landing.

The plane took its landing attitude. Jude watched the buildings surrounding the airport grow larger until the tires screeched a smooth meeting with the tarmac, and the pilot threw the engines into reverse thrust. She sighed. At last she was on Belgian soil. She spotted Xander the instant she walked out of the jetway. He flashed a big smile and waved as Jude made her way toward him on rubbery legs. How did he manage to look so fresh? As she reached him he greeted her with a bear hug; all was well.

"I am so relieved to be on the ground," Jude exclaimed. "It was a strange flight."

Xander took her bags and led the way to the hotel shuttles. "It's important to stay up to a reasonable hour. It will help you make the time adjustment. We'll stop and have a cup of coffee before going up to the room." Jude was yawning. "I promise you will feel better tomorrow," he said with a laugh.

II

"Feels a bit like old times, eh?" Xander said as the server brought two coffees to their table in the small café near the main lobby in their hotel. He gave Jude that engaging smile with the raising of his right eyebrow. She knew the meaning of that look all too well.

"Xander, we are managing to work well together. Don't blow it." She knew that recalling the past would do neither of them any good, and he had promised.

Xander laughed, again lifting his right brow. "You sure know how to shoot a man down, don't you? I was hoping to make better headway on my own turf."

Jude smiled and changed the subject, "Good coffee." She was already fighting jet lag. "Tell me the plan for tomorrow."

"We will have a leisurely breakfast here in the hotel." Xander responded. "Von Hessen has something to take care of in the morning, but he has arranged for a car to take us to the gallery around noon. We'll have time to go over the exhibit plans for both galleries, including the press release and advertising agenda, then we'll have midafternoon drinks followed by a dinner that will most likely last late into the evening. Petra says the restaurant will be a delightful surprise. I have no idea where he plans to take us, but I am sure we will dine in grand style."

"So it will be a very full day."

"Yes." Xander continued, "Tomorrow is all business, but we will have the following day for a tour of the city. I am a very knowledgeable guide, you know. Then we will fly you back home the next day."

Jude was in Xander's hands now. He was her interpreter and tour guide. Though he was born and raised in the Netherlands, he had lived the last several years in Belgium before moving to the states. She found herself wishing there was time to see Amsterdam as well. They traveled a lot together in the past, but he had never taken her to his childhood home. He didn't have good memories there. Xander's mother suffered from bipolar disorder before enough was known about the mental disorder to treat it properly. His childhood was filled with his mother's alternating highs and lows. Her mood swings were not something a young boy could make sense of. Xander's father, rather than protecting his children from their mother's outbursts, played the perfect co-dependent, teaching his children to handle their mother with care, to overlook her behavior while doing their best not to upset her.

There was no doubt that Xander's painful childhood played a big role in his inability to commit in relationship. Jude understood, and she felt badly for him. But it was Xander's choice not to work through it. At one time he convinced Jude he was in therapy. "I am determined to get my head on straight so as not to lose you," he had declared. But Xander never actually entered therapy. When Jude learned the truth, he claimed he was happy with himself as he was.

Jude stood and gathered her things. Xander joined her, and silently they walked to the elevator. They each made an unsuccessful attempt at small talk on the ride to the 15th floor then followed the room numbers in silence. "This is it," Xander finally said, using his key card to unlock the door. He smiled, lifting a single brow.

"Okay, then." Jude was suddenly nervous. "Let's get some rest so we'll be at our best tomorrow." As she reached for her bag Xander kissed her on the cheek then turned to open the adjoining room. Why was it so awkward? She wondered. Was it the idea of the two of them together so far from home?

Jude checked the time as she unpacked her bag. She would not be able to reach Andrew in Chicago at this hour. Instead, she sent a brief text: "Hi, sweetie. I have arrived safely and am about to get to bed. The flight was very long. I miss you already, and will call you tomorrow. I love you!"

III

Von Hessen's limo picked Jude and Xander up at 12:00 PM sharp and delivered them to the gallery. Strangely enough, though the gallery was open when they arrived, there was no one in sight. Together they walked through the gleaming galleries. The walls were a soft gray, brushed aluminum lights and white wood trim gave clean contemporary lines. Everything flowed so that the surroundings were elegant without distracting from the art. Jude sighed.

"Are you okay?" Xander asked.

"Yes, I'm great, just a little overwhelmed, I think."

Xander chuckled and put his hand on her shoulder. "This is where your art belongs. It is all good."

There was a water jug iced and dressed with fruits and cucumber in a small alcove. The glasses stacked in the corner were crystal. Small white fabric napkins stamped with Von Hessen Galleries were neatly stacked nearby. Jude filled a glass for Xander then one for herself and they took a seat in the entry gallery.

"Most likely Von Hessen's meeting went long. I will check his office in the back," Xander said. "Enjoy looking around; see how the gallery feels to you. I'll go find him."

The gallery was an impressive, expansive space, and the lighting had been beautifully designed. The present show was a mix of Impressionism and Abstract Expressionism from modern favorites among collectors. In the entry were paintings from famous modern painters who were no longer living. Jude refilled her water glass and walked across the room to stand in front of an energetic abstract expressionistic piece. It had been painted by Lee Krasner, one titled *Earth* painted in gouache. Lee Krasner. She had loved Jackson Pollack, and he had betrayed her. It was Pollack who got all the attention when they were both living, though many agreed she was perhaps the better artist. But she was a woman. And a woman who often set her art, her needs aside in order to take care of Jackson. Could it actually be that Jude Bennett's work would hang in a gallery with Lee Krasner's? Caught up in the idea and the elegant ambiance Jude was experiencing a growing glow of satisfaction. Her work was actually going to be hanging here, in Belgium, in a first class gallery.

Suddenly there was a loud pop. Then another. It sounded like the backfiring of a car. Or gunshots? Jude felt panic as she ran through the galleries looking for the office door. She found it ajar. As she swung it open, she saw a man splayed on the floor. Plaster dust was still settling as she ran toward him. It was Xander, spread out in the white dust as if making a snow angel.

"Xander! Xander, what happened?!" She heard herself screaming. A pool of blood grew slowly larger, seeping from the back of his head. The pool was dark, almost black in contrast to the plaster. His eyes were closed. It occurred to her that was a good sign. If someone died quickly didn't their eyes stay open? Jude knelt beside him feeling for a pulse. When she could find none, she straightened and took a deep breath, trying to calm herself enough to see if he was breathing. He seemed perfectly still. She knelt low enough to put her eyes level with his chest. "Oh, thank God," she said aloud. There was a slight, slow rise and fall of his chest. He was alive. She scrambled across the floor to where she had dropped her purse and searched frantically for her cell phone. She shook so hard she found it difficult to put her finger to a button. What was Emergency in Belgium? Did they have 911? Did she have to get an operator? She pressed 0 several times beginning to cough from the dust that still hung in the air around her. Finally someone answered the phone.

"This is an emergency. Please send help, 1666 Molenstraat. Someone has been shot. Hurry!" Jude shouted into the phone.

The response was not in English. "Does anyone speak English? Give me someone that speaks English!"

There were sounds of confusion on the other end. Finally someone spoke in English. "What is the trouble?"

"Someone has been shot. Von Hessen Gallery, 1666 Molenstraat. Please Hurry!"

"I will get someone on the way."

She removed her jacket, rolled Xander on his side and compressed it against his head. "Oh, Xander. Don't die!"

The ambulance seemed to take hours to arrive. She fought to hold back the blood that seeped through the white silk of her jacket. Her hand became red and sticky, and she could feel her consciousness blurring.

Finally, the medics pushed her aside. They spoke with urgency in a foreign language. Was it French? Jude couldn't be sure; she couldn't understand a word they were saying. Her panic grew and stuck in her throat. "Is he dying?" Her voice was barely audible. "Someone tell me, is he going to be okay?" No one responded. She was an observer in a surreal world. Medics swarmed around her as if she didn't exist.

The police arrived, and a young policeman touched her on the shoulder and began bombarding her with questions. She had questions of her own.

"Is he shot?" she was asking. "Is he going to be okay? I don't know what happened. I was in the gallery. He went to the office to find the gallery owner. I heard this noise. It was two loud pops, maybe gunshots."

"The bullet just grazed his head," a young officer said in very broken English. "But it looks like he hit his head on one of the statues as he fell. We don't know how serious it is. What were you doing here?"

Jude explained that they had flown in to see the gallery as she was to have an exhibit here in a few months. "Where was Von Hessen? What happened to him? Did he shoot Xander?"

"Von Hessen? Is that the gallery owner?" The officer was writing in his notebook. "There's no sign of him. There has obviously been a scuffle."

"There are two bullets lodged in the wall. Get a ballistics guy over here," another officer shouted.

Jude wasn't sure how she got to the hospital. She didn't remember the ride, but a young woman in what appeared as a nursing uniform handed her a glass filled with water and placed a pill in Jude's left hand. "Take this, it will calm you," she said in fluent English.

Jude took the pill and sipped the water behind it. "Can I see him? I need to know he's going to be okay."

"I'll let you know as soon as I know. They are doing everything possible." The girl touched her shoulder. "I will stay with you as long as you want."

It took several hours to learn that Xander was alive. He had taken a bullet to the left side of his head, but it only grazed the skull. The force of the impact had thrown him backward into a sculpture then onto the concrete floor. He had a concussion, and he was unconscious. How long he stayed unconscious would indicate the seriousness of his injuries. Although his vitals seemed stable and relatively strong, he was put in intensive care and allowed only one visitor for 15 minutes of each hour.

Jude felt as if she had stepped into a nightmare. The flight to Belgium had been long and strange. She had thought all was well once she connected with Xander at the airport. They had checked into the hotel and freshened up. During dinner she had finally relaxed. Xander was on his best behavior and seemed as excited as she about seeing the gallery and finalizing plans for her exhibit. Certainly, neither of them had any indication that they might be in any sort of danger. But then, there had been her dream on the plane.

The rest of the day and evening was a blur. An aide had come to tell her that Xander was in surgery. She would not be able to see him until morning. It had to be serious. Traumatic brain injury, the young nursing assistant said. He would be kept in a medically induced coma for a few days to aid the healing. She had taken a cab back to the hotel, but she didn't sleep. She was back at the hospital before 7 AM.

"Come with me, you can see him now," the aide said. She walked Jude to the intensive care lounge. "You can wait here when you can't be in the room with him."

Jude pushed back the heavy door to Xander's private room. Machines and hoses made breathing noises, beeps and hums. She walked over to stand beside him.

"I will come for you when your time is up," the aide said softly.

"What is your name?" Jude asked.

"Lotte," the girl answered.

"Thanks, Lotte. I so appreciate you."

The door closed, and Jude was alone with Xander. His eyes were closed, his face drained of color. The tears began to flow, and Jude gave way to the sobs when she reached out to stroke Xander's forehead. She was relieved to find at least he was warm. She studied his face, the so familiar face that she had tried so hard to forget. His dark hair, still almost free of gray, was barely visible around the wide bandage. His skin was pale, but almost wrinkle free. Why didn't he seem to age? She leaned forward, her hair brushing his face, and kissed his cheek.

"Xander, please wake up. Please don't die. I love you."

"And I always will," she whispered to herself.

Lotte opened the door and peeked in. Her time was up. She kissed Xander again on the forehead and walked across the hall to the waiting room. She had to call Andrew. She looked at her phone. It was almost 4 PM. That would be what time in Chicago? Nine AM, she thought. She pressed Andrew's number. There were three rings. "Hello, Jude?" At the sound of Andrew's voice she burst into sobs.

"Jude, are you okay? What is it? What's wrong?

"Oh, Andrew, Xander has been shot. He's unconscious."

"Jude, are you okay? Are you hurt?"

"No, no Andrew. I…I'm fine. I was in the gallery, and he went to look for Von Hessen. I don't know who. I don't know what happened. We will have to wait for Xander to wake up to know. I found him on the floor…." Again the sobs over took her.

"Sweetie, it's okay. I'll get on a plane and get there as quickly as I can. I'm here for you. I'll come."

Jude wasn't sure just what Andrew was saying, but no…. "No, Andrew. You don't need to come. He's in the hospital, and the doctors say he will be okay; it may take some time for him to wake. I'll stay here, but you don't need to come. Just take care of things for me there."

"Sweetie, are you sure? You're sure you're okay?"

"Yes, I'm good. I love you Andrew. I'll keep you updated, okay. I have to go."

"I love you, Jude. Call me often, Okay? I love you."

Jude hung up. She didn't need Andrew here. Right now she had to be here for Xander.

IV

The days warped into a week as Jude kept vigil by Xander's side. Each day she saw a bit more color in his face, but he was medicated so that he would remain unconscious. Lotte assured her this would help him to heal more quickly, but Jude worried it wasn't good that so much time had passed.

"Xander," Jude whispered, leaning over him, studying his face. "Xander, can you hear me? I need you to know that I don't want to lose you. You are important to me. I want you in my life."

She studied his features, watched his nostrils expand as he drew in air, and noticed how pale his lips were. She had loved kissing those soft and sensitive lips.

Jude could remember so well, in spite of the years that had passed, how it had felt to walk into Xander's arms, to be held tightly against his muscular body, and how he had pulled her head forward to meet his lips. She could feel, even now, how "at home" his arms had felt to her. Sadness swept over her. They hadn't been able to make it work. Jude finally accepted that they never could, but she still missed all the things she loved about him. She knew he was damaged. And perhaps she was damaged, too. Her ability to trust was all but destroyed by Edward's betrayals. She thought about Andrew and wondered if she could truly trust him. So far, he had given her no reason not to. He made her the focus of his life. Unlike Xander, he seemed able to commit. She loved Andrew. She couldn't let seeing Xander like this make her lose perspective.

Jude's phone buzzed in her hand. It was Andrew. She hesitated, and then answered.

"Hi Andrew."

"Jude, I'm so worried about you. When are you coming home? I don't understand."

Xander's still unconscious. I can't leave him here alone, Andrew. I feel responsible. I talked to Maggie and everything is okay at Woman Space. Just be patient."

"Patient. I am patient. I just want an idea of how long you will be."

"I promise I'll come home as soon as I know Xander is out of the woods. We should know once he is awake. Please try to understand; he was here because of me. This happened because of me."

"Jude, that makes no sense. This had to be an accident. The gallery owner is missing, right? Do they think he did this? Or maybe he was kidnapped? He had a lot of money, you said. You and Xander just happened to be there."

"I know, but we were there because of setting up my show. I have to stay 'til I know he's okay."

"I know," Andrew said with a sigh. "Call me when you can. All is well here."

She knew Andrew was not all right. Would she be all right if the tables were turned? She didn't know. It didn't matter. All that mattered was that Xander survived this, and that she was there when he awoke.

Gradually the doctors increased the time she could spend in Xander's room. The nurses told her that her presence seemed to calm him. It would speed his recovery, they said. She talked daily with Andrew and Jennifer. She didn't know when she would return. Andrew wanted to come to be with her, but she insisted they would not allow a second person in the room. He should stay home and look after things for her there. All she knew was that she had to be with Xander until she knew he was going to be okay.

Jude learned through a news report that Von Hessen's lawyer had received a call. Von Hessen was being held for ransom. He had been kidnapped because he was wealthy and vulnerable and a terrorist group wanted money for their cause. Andrew was right. Xander had simply been in the wrong place at the wrong time. He was lucky to be alive. The bullet was intended to kill. The kidnappers wanted no witnesses. A terrorist cell in Belgium claimed responsibility.

What would happen to Von Hessen? Jude was distraught thinking of the kind man who not only planned to promote Woman Space and her work in two major locations, but who had also given his note for $1.5 million to benefit Woman Space programs. What kind of trauma was he going through? Would he come out of it alive? Seeing what they had done to Xander didn't make it look good for him. She thought of the trauma he had suffered as a child, as well, losing his mother and knowing it was his father who murdered her.

What was happening to the world? Jude wondered. Was there nowhere safe? And now, she, Xander, and Von Hessen were victims of an attack by the present terrorist threat. Innocent people in the wrong place at the wrong time. What if Xander never awoke? What if he died? What if he lived but was brain damaged? She must be here for him.

Jude placed a cool cloth across Xander's pale forehead wondering if she'd see that mischievous smile ever again. "Please, God, let him be okay," she repeated like a mantra.

CHAPTER 11

"you are here,
the moontides are here,
and that's all that matters."

— *Sanober Khan*

THEY HAD GROWN **to be close as friends shortly after they met.** Jude looked forward to their weekly discussions after classes at the Arts Centre. Xander, being European, was more open minded, more liberal than most American men of her generation. They talked art, science, religion, even politics. He teased her that liberals in the US were the conservatives in Europe.

"I have something to tell you that makes me very unhappy," Xander announced late one summer evening as the last student left the room.

Jude straightened her desk and packed away pencils and erasers into her rolling bag. "What is it?"

Xander took her hand and pulled her to a chair next to the table where he had set their coffees. "Imma has been offered a position at a new university in the Netherlands, and we are going to be moving. At least she is going to be moving. I'm hoping you will give me a reason to stay."

"Xander, what do you mean? You're married. Are you thinking of a divorce?"

"Maybe." He stared intensely into Jude's eyes as if looking for the answer there.

"What are you implying, Xander?" Jude's voice was shaky. "We're friends." Then she added with emphasis, "That is all."

Xander scooted his chair close laying his hand over hers. "We both know there is much more than friendship between us. What I need to know is if you want me to stay."

"No," Jude exclaimed. "I can't do this, Xander."

But Xander didn't want to take no for an answer. He reached out and pulled her close in a long hug. Jude's mind filled with thoughts of how alone she felt, betrayed by Edward, abandoned, deserving to be wanted, to be loved. She felt as if she might explode with all the desire she had pushed down each time it welled up from within. Xander took her face in both his hands, looked into her eyes, leaned forward, and kissed her. It was their first kiss. She was still trying to deal with the shock of what he was asking when Xander whispered, "I love you, Jude. I need you." She wanted to pull away, but he kissed her again. She responded. "You need me, too, ma cherie," he whispered. She did need him. She wanted him. She deserved happiness.

"I am staying," Xander said in a determined voice. "Whatever happens, I have to stay. I will never forgive myself if I let you get away."

Jude melted into his arms. A delicious desire swept over her. Almost without realizing it, she had come to love him. He took the handle of her rolling supply bag and followed her to her car. There he reached again for her, stood holding her, kissing her, as if he were afraid if he let her go she would change her mind. She drove home to her lonely, empty house in a daze. Could she do this? She so wanted him. But how could she get involved with Xander? He was a married man.

She honestly hoped he would let it go, that he wouldn't contact her again. Instead, a couple of days later, he called and asked to stop by her home studio to talk. Now, instead of the comfortable, playful friendship she had enjoyed, she felt like a wreck. It was as if all the adrenalin within her was released when she heard the doorbell ring.

Xander stood at the door, that playful, mischievous smile across his face and the lifted right eyebrow. "I'm sorry, Jude. I shouldn't have thrown all my feelings at you out of the blue. But let me have my say. Okay?"

Jude stepped aside to let him in the door. He sat on the chaise near the windows to the garden. The morning sun filtered through the trees creating a pattern of light across his hair. The seriousness of the situation was apparent on his face. Jude poured a cup of coffee, handed it to Xander and sat down in the chair near the chaise.

"I don't want to go." Xander began. "I've been a mess since Imma first told me about her job offer; I like it here in this country, I like my work—most of all, Jude, I find I can't leave you. I feel that all of my life I've done what others felt I should do: go into science, get married, have a child, travel to the US for a research position. But ceramics and you are the two choices I make for myself; they are what I want. I have come to love you Jude. Finding you was like finding a part of me that had been hidden away."

"Xander, I won't be the other woman. I've been the betrayed wife. No one wins. Please, go and figure out what it is you really want; be honest with yourself and your wife. Then, if and when you are available, contact me."

"Fair enough," Xander said, sitting the coffee cup on the small table near the chaise. The patterns of sunlight danced across his arm and hand. A surreal quality engulfed the room as he walked to the door. Jude followed him. They stood, solemnly looking into one another's eyes. She felt herself drawn to him as he leaned forward, his eyes fastened on her lips. He must have seen the fear in her eyes. He pulled back from her. "I know, I must go," he said. And he was gone.

Xander moved with his wife back to Belgium. Jude didn't hear from him again until three years later, the day she was about to walk out the door to see her therapist about the situation that had developed with Brandon. They were engaged and had moved in together, but it was not working out. The phone rang as she was about to lock the door behind her. Why she stopped and went back inside for the phone she didn't know. But she was surprised to hear Xander's voice.

"Jude, it is a voice from your past. You told me to call if I ended up available. I am available, and I am calling."

She could not help but laugh aloud. "What timing!" She explained

139

how she was on her way to talk with her therapist to try to determine what to do about her own relationship.

"I am getting on a plane!" Xander exclaimed. "I am coming to you!" With that he hung up.

They were together almost five years, five fun, wildly chaotic years. The relationship they shared was best described as a roller coaster. She believed he loved her as deeply as she loved him; but just when she felt the closest and the safest with him, he would take a trip to Europe or to New Zealand or Australia, and he would be gone, sometimes for a month. Upon his return he was, still, madly in love with her. He promised he would take her with him the next trip, and sometimes he did. But again he would be off, leaving her alone, as if, in order to survive, he had to periodically escape the intimacy that grew powerfully between them. Jude came to realize that she could not depend on Xander. She watched others meet new love interests, grow and develop together, move in together and marry. But her relationship with Xander was in a perpetual spiral upward then down, upward then down, never moving forward. There were ways that it worked for her. She needed solitude for her own work, so having periods of space was good.

Jude picked Xander up at the airport, watching as he loaded his bag into the back of her car. He had been in Switzerland with his sister who had experienced a psychotic episode. He wore a full length black rain coat that she had not seen before. His shoes were new.

"Next time, I'm going with you," she said.

"I'd love that!" he responded cheerfully, pulling a bag out of a zippered compartment of his suitcase. He turned and handed it to her. "Open it," Xander said smiling.

Jude reached into the plain brown bag and pulled out a small black box. She felt her heart skip a beat. "What is this?"

"Go on, open it." Xander was smiling his mischievous smile. Jude could not help but smile back at him.

She pulled the lid from the box. It wasn't a ring. She had hoped it might be. Instead, she lifted a silver necklace with a diamond pendant. It was beautiful, and it was, no doubt, expensive. "It's wonderful, Xander. But you didn't have to do this."

Xander took the necklace from her hand. "Turn around," he directed.

He fastened the chain around her neck. Three diamonds were set in a vertical row. They reflected the morning sun enhancing the impression they made.

"I love you, Jude," Xander said in barely a whisper. "I've had business to wrap up in Europe, but I promise I'll take you on every trip I take in the future." He reached for Jude, pulled her close, and kissed her cheek.

It would take several more months, but eventually Jude learned that Xander had made this trip to Europe to sign divorce papers. He had not been divorced when he moved back to be with her. His numerous trips abroad were all back to visit his wife. He built an apartment onto his wife's house. He helped his father-in-law renovate his kitchen. He was doing the same dance Jude had been a part of with Edward, except this time she was the other woman.

Xander's lack of ability to commit, to move forward with Jude, had made her question what was going on. She decided to contact Imma Voss. It was easy enough to reach her through the university where she was a professor. Imma didn't seem surprised to learn that Jude had believed Xander to be divorced when he returned to the States. Jude learned their divorce had taken place almost a year and a half later. She had been with a married man for that year and a half.

"I did make a decision. I did choose you. I got a divorce. You are what I want." He begged Jude to understand.

"Xander, what you've done is not okay," she told him. "It's another betrayal. I can never trust you."

"I know I'm a bit messed up, Jude," he admitted, and he reminded her of his mother's mental illness. He promised to get therapy. But within a few months she learned he never entered therapy in spite of the fact that he would pretend to share in detail his "therapy sessions," something she did not want nor ask for. Jude had had it with the lies. She ended the relationship with Xander. Without trust there is no relationship.

Now, sitting beside Xander's hospital bed, all Jude wanted was for him to wake up and be okay.

II

The days passed. Jude, who had been at Xander's bedside almost two weeks now, fell into a routine, with Maggie's help, of running the gallery long distance. Andrew was growing impatient and couldn't understand why Jude had to stay until Xander awoke. Jude was not sure even she understood. She only knew that she couldn't leave, not before she knew he was okay.

"Jude, you're not a family member," Andrew reminded her. "You're mine, I need you here." She could hear the irritation in his voice.

"I know it's difficult for you," Jude tried to explain. "But I somehow feel responsible. Xander was here to help me and Woman Space, Andrew. Please try to understand. He has no one here, and I just need to stay until he is awake and clearly okay."

The deep sigh on the other end of the phone alluded to Andrew's building frustration. She realized that from Andrew's perspective, Xander was her former lover. She did not expect him to like that she had to stay. But she needed him to accept it—to trust her.

Jude had worked on her laptop for most of the night. That evening Xander's doctor had announced that they felt it safe to begin bringing Xander out of the medically induced coma. His brain was healing. He would probably wake within the next twenty-four hours. Jude had not been able to sleep. Whether it was anxiety or anticipation she couldn't determine. It was nearing sunrise. The staff allowed her to sleep on a cot near Xander as he could awaken at any time. All indications were that he was going to have a full recovery, but no one could know for sure until he could communicate for himself.

The door squeaked open. It was Lotte with a coffee in her hand. "I thought you might need a wake up," she whispered.

"I could sure use one." It was a hoarse whisper coming from the bed.

"Xander!" Jude ran to him, taking his hand. His eyes fluttered open and a weak smile spread across his face.

"I'll get the doctor," Lotte said as she ran out the door.

"What happened?" Xander asked.

"Just stay calm." Jude rubbed his hands and kissed his forehead. "I am so happy to see you! Oh, Xander, you're going to be fine!"

He reached his free hand to her cheek. "You are here, Jude. You are here with me."

"Yes, I'm here, Xander, and you're going to be just fine."

"How long? What happened?" Jude put her forefinger to his lips.

"Be patient, I'll tell you everything, but you need to let the doctors check you out first."

Xander sighed deeply and closed his eyes. "I'm so tired," he whispered.

A doctor walked briskly through the door with Lotte close behind.

"Can you wait outside please?" he said.

Jude reluctantly followed Lotte out of the room as a second doctor rushed in.

"Jude, the doctors will need some time," Lotte said. "We can sip our coffee in the cafeteria and maybe have a little breakfast."

How could she possibly eat? But she realized Lotte was being kind, and she needed to be out of the way. Maybe breakfast would help the time go more quickly. She followed Lotte to the elevators in a daze. Soon she would know if Xander was really going to be all right.

It was more than an hour before the doctor came to talk with Jude. Tests showed that Xander should make a full recovery though it could be slow.

"It might be best for you to explain the events that led to his confinement," the doctor said to Jude. "You were there, and it might be less traumatic coming from you."

When Jude pushed open the door to Xander's room, she had combed her hair and put on fresh makeup. Hopefully he wouldn't see she had been crying. At least now she could call them tears of joy.

Xander smiled and reached for her hand as she walked to the side of his bed. "I can't remember a thing," he said. "Are we….you and me, are we together?"

"Well, we were in Belgium together to visit a gallery," Jude said with a smile. "But we are not romantically together. I am engaged to Andrew. Do you remember?" She could see the confusion in his eyes, and something more…..disappointment? "You were kind enough to connect me with a gallery owner here. We had gone to the gallery to meet Von Hessen and take a look at the space when something terrible happened."

Xander shook his head. "How did I end up in a hospital bed?" He felt the bandage still on his head.

"Well, Von Hessen was apparently a kidnapping target, maybe a local terrorist cell who thought he'd be a good source of money. You and I were just in the wrong place at the wrong time."

"Are you okay, Jude? I'd die if I put you in danger."

"No, I'm fine, Xander. But Von Hessen was kidnapped, and you were caught in the middle of it. You were shot. You scared me to death!! I heard the shots then found you on the floor in a pool of blood and covered with plaster dust. You hit your head on a sculpture. I was so scared, Xander! But thank God you're going to be fine!"

"How long have I been here, like this?"

"Almost two weeks," Jude answered. "And I've been right here with you," she said, pointing to the cot where she had been sleeping.

Xander squeezed her hand, closed his eyes, and fell asleep.

A flood of relief rose up within Jude. The worst was over. Xander would recover. She could go back to Chicago in a few days, once she was sure he had adjusted to all that had happened. She picked up the morning newspaper to find Von Hessen's picture on the front page. He had been located and rescued. He was a bit roughed up but not seriously harmed. His kidnappers were in custody. As yet it was unknown exactly what cause they were supporting. What a strange coincidence that Xander had awakened at almost the same time Von Hessen was released. Jude doubted that Von Hessen would be resuming his gallery duties anytime soon. She would probably have to forget about the Belgium solo show, at least for now. And she needed some time to process all that had happened. It would not be easy to just fly home and walk back into her life as it had been before all this. Even the thought of being in the gallery alone stirred fears.

The next day Xander was moved to an open and airy private room with a large window that looked out onto a small garden and pond. It seemed the Belgian doctors knew the role of environment in recovery. Jude knew she needed to get back to the gallery and to Andrew. Each day she was determined to tell Xander she would be leaving, but each day she found herself unable to do so. And then another week passed.

"Here, drink this." Jude handed Xander a cup of hot tea as they sat on a curved bench in the hospital garden. "You are getting some color back in your face; this sunshine will be good for you."

"You're taking good care of me, Jude. But I wonder why it is that you are still here? You have a gallery to run and a fiancée to make up to for all this time I've kept you here."

She felt a flush move across her face and lowered her eyes.

Xander chuckled. "You are blushing, girl. Oh, my god, you are blushing like a young thing."

Jude looked up at him laughing. "I'm no young thing; and I'm certainly too old for this James Bond stuff."

"Thank you, Jude." He took her hands in his, his eyes penetrating. "I do not take this for granted. I needed you, and you were here for me." He wrapped his arms around her. "I won't forget this."

"Hey, that's what friends do for one another," Jude said lightly, pulling away from him.

"And we are that, aren't we?" he whispered, "That and much more."

She looked into his eyes and felt her own fill with tears. "You almost died, Xander."

III

Jude was home. Xander was on medical leave from his university and would stay in Belgium until he was fully recovered. As Jennifer carried her suitcases into the bedroom, Jude walked slowly around the apartment touching familiar objects. She noticed that there was not a speck of dust. Jennifer must have had someone clean. She opened the refrigerator to find it freshly stocked with her basics: fresh orange juice, almond milk, eggs, a new tub of butter. Her daughter was taking good care of her.

"Do you want a glass of juice?" Jude called out to Jennifer as she poured one for herself.

"No, Mom, Doug is picking me up at the front door in just a few minutes. I don't have time."

Jude carried her glass of juice onto the balcony.

"Mom, you don't seem yourself. Are you all right?" Jennifer asked, joining her.

"You are hovering," Jude groaned. "I promise you, I'm just jet lagged, and glad to be home."

"Well, I owe you a bit of hovering," Jennifer laughed. "Just get over it. I've missed you, Mom."

Jude turned to Jennifer and reached for a hug. "I've missed you, too, sweetie. Sorry I seem distracted. It has been a very draining few weeks!"

Yes, Jude had done her share of hovering over Jennifer as she grew up, worrying over her blood sugars, watching out for insulin reactions. "I appreciate your hovering," she said, still holding Jennifer close.

"I'll check on you tomorrow," Jennifer said, kissing her cheek. "I love you, Mom."

"Oh, Jenny, I love you too. And thanks so much for having everything in such good order for me. I just need to crash. I'll talk to you tomorrow."

Jude closed the door behind her daughter. All she needed was some solitude, some processing time. Could she just hide out here a few days? It was unlikely. Andrew knew she was flying in tonight. She would call him tomorrow.

The sun set as she sipped her juice. She was back in her space, back to her life. Why did she feel so out of place? So lost? She had been gone less than a month. She had taken that many weeks as vacation before. But this had been no vacation. Xander had made her dreams blossom, and Xander had almost died. She could still see him lying there as if dead in a pool of blood and plaster dust. She just couldn't get that image out of her head. She would never be the same. And something was very different about Xander as well, something she couldn't put her finger on.

Jude walked inside, leaving the doors open to the fresh air, and turned the faucet on the tub to hot. A hot bath was just what she needed, a long soaking hot bath, then a long night's sleep in her own bed. She had hardly leaned back to get comfortable in the tub when she dozed off.

> She was dressed in a long flowing gown that moved as if the wind was blowing rather strongly, and she was walking down a long corridor of white-washed walls and white lights. They ran together, the walls, the lights. Maybe it was more like a tunnel? She followed the hallways, the light, through twists and turns, like a map or a maze. A

geography of light. It all felt familiar, but where was she going? There were smells, too, flower fragrances, essential oils. And music. Classical. She didn't recognize it, but it, too, seemed familiar. The light grew brighter, so bright that she could see nothing else. And then she saw him. Xander. He was in the light, like a silhouette at first, then, he too, began to glow. He reached both hands out to her, and she reached for him.

Jude jerked awake. The water surrounding her was lukewarm. She must have been so exhausted that she fell immediately into a deep sleep. She reached for the bath towel hanging near her and stepped out of the tub. What a wild dream. And why was Xander reaching for her in the midst of a tunnel of light, like Jesus did for those who had near death experiences? Xander was certainly no Christ. Nor was he an angel. She laughed to herself. "I am obviously too tired," she said aloud as she pulled back the covers on her bed and crawled in.

IV

Jude awoke to the sound of the phone; she recognized it as her ring tone for Andrew. She stretched slowly as she reached to answer. Her eyes felt heavy and sticky, not yet ready to be awake. Emerging from the warmth of her bed she immediately recoiled. It was cold; she had left the balcony doors wide open. Jude pulled the covers back over her shoulders and snuggled into her pillow. Just a few more minutes, she thought. But again, the phone rang. Again, it was Andrew. Groaning she reached across to the cell phone laying on the night stand, fumbling to unplug it and get it to her ear.

"Hello, Andrew." She yawned.

"Am I calling too early?" He sounded apologetic.

"What time is it?" Jude moaned.

"Nine fifty. Did you get in really late?"

"Not too late, but I'm just very tired. Can I call you back after I have a chance to wake and drink a cup of coffee? I'm dealing with jet lag."

"Sure sweetie. I'll be here."

She laid the phone on the floor. Was it disappointment she heard in his voice?

What was she feeling? Why was she not ready to see Andrew, to face him? What had changed for her in these last few weeks sitting in the hospital with Xander. She and Xander were friends, maybe even close friends. But nothing had happened to change her feelings for Andrew. Why did it seem that everything had changed? Seeing someone she knew and cared for lying in a pool of blood, knowing they might die, or worse, that was bound to change her. Things like this happened all the time all over the world. Jude was well aware of that. But this was the first time something so traumatic had happened to her. She had lived all her life in her safe little world, a world where she worried about paying the bills, selling paintings, and teaching others to express themselves creatively. A world where she worried over having a man in her life. What did any of it mean? The words of Solomon came to her mind: *I have seen all the works that are done under the sun; and, behold, all is vanity and a striving after wind.* That hit upon some of what she was feeling, yes, that it was all meaningless, especially international fame, or wealth, or a relationship that made you feel safe and protected. No one was ever protected, really. Security was an illusion.

She had to see Andrew. Maybe just seeing him again, in the flesh, would bring her back to herself.

Her second cup of coffee in hand, Jude picked up the phone and called Andrew's number. "Hi, again. Just give me an hour and then come on over. I'm anxious to see you. I've missed you."

"I'm anxious to see you, too. It's been far too long."

Okay, that was better, she thought to herself as she rolled up again in the covers. She was anxious to see Andrew. She loved him. She was just exhausted.

CHAPTER 12

Those who truly love us will never knowingly ask us to be other than we are.
—*Mark Nepo*

J UDE WAS FEELING **more herself after a few weeks back home**. At first, she felt awkward with Andrew. She wasn't exactly sure why, but she suspected it was knowing he had his own struggle with her staying at Xander's bedside. And all the introspection about the relationship she and Xander once had as she sat beside him worrying over his recovery had affected her deeply. She could admit to herself that she still loved Xander. Or more likely she still loved the fantasy Xander, the Xander she once believed him to be. Who he really was, perhaps not even he knew or was willing to admit. And that was the problem. Jude understood that you could only love another to the degree you could love yourself. And loving yourself depended on how well you knew and accepted yourself. She guessed that Xander didn't really know himself. Otherwise, he would not have been all over the place in relationships. In Xander she had fallen in love with another man not unlike Edward.

Andrew, on the other hand, seemed very self-aware. He was consistent. Perhaps who he was didn't always feel fully compatible with Jude, but at least she could know Andrew. He didn't shape shift into someone else just when she thought she was beginning to understand who he was. There was a comfort in that, a safety. And it had been a very long time since Jude had felt safe with a man. Instead, she learned to create her own safe place in her solitary life. She realized, too, that the more you knew yourself the more comfortable you could be alone with yourself.

Maybe she didn't feel the same passion for Andrew that she once felt for Edward nor for Xander, but she felt trust. She would marry Andrew. She believed they could have something long lasting.

It had taken several weeks for Jude to get caught up at the gallery. Maggie stayed on top of things, but there was just so much an assistant could do. Ultimately, Jude was needed for finalizing decisions and carrying through with plans. It was Friday evening after a long day at Woman Space. Jude pulled down the drive to Applewood where she planned to escape for the weekend. Andrew's truck was parked in the drive. He hadn't bothered to let her know he would meet her there. There goes my plan to just crash for an hour or so before he arrived, she thought.

Jude unpacked two bags of groceries and an overnight bag from her car. Determined to carry everything in in one trip, she put her overnight bag on one arm, her purse on the other, and grabbed a bag of groceries in each.

As she neared the house, she saw that the door was ajar; soft music, Mozart, wafted out into the early evening air mingled with the aroma of something wonderful cooking. She could never feel irritated at Andrew for long, she reminded herself, smiling.

"Do you need help, honey?" Andrew rushed to take the groceries from her arms. "Go take a bath and relax for an hour or so. I know you must be tired." He gave Jude a quick kiss on the forehead and turned toward the kitchen.

She climbed the stairway to the master bedroom. The doors were open to the fresh air, and sheer curtains were softly billowing out into the room. What sane woman would complain about being greeted like this? Andrew was a wonderful man. There were times that she became frustrated with his need to be in control, but his earthy Virgo was a fixed sign to her mutable and fiery Sagittarius. In relationship you had to be willing to compromise. She couldn't always do whatever she felt the urge to do. And she was getting her hour to bathe and let down, wasn't she? And while her man fixed a wonderful dinner.

As Jude stooped to turn on the hot water for her bath, she noticed a large vase of fresh flowers reflected in the bathroom mirror. She turned to look behind her. On the dresser, directly across from the entrance to the bathroom, was a beautiful and very large bouquet of wild flowers. She smiled, and tears pooled in her eyes. Andrew, you are a hopeless romantic, she thought to herself. He had brought her wildflowers the day she bought Applewood….wildflowers and a picnic lunch. Oh, dear, today was the second anniversary of that day. He had remembered. "I do love you, Andrew." Jude whispered.

Jude went downstairs after a leisurely bath dressed in fresh comfortable clothes and only a touch of makeup. The wonderful live edge table in the center of the dining room had become the centerpiece for the entire room with more flowers, several candles in glass containers, and a table setting fit for a TV cooking show. Andrew was seated by a lamp reading.

"What can I say? You have outdone yourself tonight!" Jude exclaimed as she entered the room. "It's our Applewood anniversary."

Andrew came to greet her. Taking her in his arms he danced her around the room to Nora Jones singing *Don't Know Why*. He then led her to her seat at the table. "I'm just so happy to have you home," he whispered as he leaned forward to push her chair beneath her. "You have no idea how much I've missed you."

"I missed you, too," Jude responded. "I do hope you understand. It's so great to be home. And I think I'm about to get caught up with all the back-up at the gallery."

Andrew filled their plates with grilled salmon drizzled with molasses, a baked sweet potato and freshly roasted Brussels sprouts and mushrooms sprinkled with parmesan. This has to be as good as it gets. She leaned over to kiss Andrew lightly on the cheek. "I love the way you take care of me," she whispered. I truly do, she thought. "And I remembered, too. I have a little something for you." She handed him a gift wrapped in brown paper stamped with horses and tied with raffia. That wonderful smile spread across his face as he carefully unwrapped a book. "*The Horse Whisper's Guide to the Universe?*" He laughed as he opened to the center of the book and read: "It is said that the horse whisperer helps people with horse problems, but the truth is he helps horses with people problems." Andrew laughed aloud. "How true this is. Thank you Jude. I'll enjoy reading through this."

Andrew took Jude's hand and pulled her up into a hug. "I love you, sweet lady."

"I love you, Andrew, and thank you for remembering, and for the flowers, and this amazing meal. There's a gift card just inside the book…..your favorite restaurant."

Conversation was light and cheery, and the food delighted the pallet. As Andrew filled their wine glasses for a second time, he smiled sheepishly then began, "Jude, I have something I want to discuss with you tonight."

A bit of panic rose from somewhere deep within Jude. "What is it? You sound so very serious."

"Well," Andrew began, "As of tonight we have been together for two years, and we've been engaged almost a year. I thought this would be a good time to set a wedding date. What do you think?"

There was that panic, this time growing even more distinct. It was now a specific knot right in the center of Jude's breast bone. She could feel it beginning to pulse with every heartbeat. Okay, she thought, just calm down. She took a deep breath that came out in a sigh.

"Oh, that sounds ominous." Andrew laughed.

Thankfully this allowed Jude to relax a bit. "Andrew, I don't think I'm ready for this. I've just been through a trauma in Belgium. I saw a man almost die. And since I've returned home, I've had my nose to the grindstone trying to catch up. Why now?"

"Why now?" Andrew repeated her question. "Because, Jude, I've been through a trauma as well knowing that you were sitting at the bedside of a man you once loved, and for all I know may still love. Week after week I was stuck here, trying to carry on without you, hoping every week that you would return to me, and yes, at times, fearing you never would. That is why now. I think you owe it to me to set a wedding date."

Jude could feel the rebel that lies beneath the cheery optimist in every Sagittarius begin to rise within her. It joined the ball of panic that was by now the size of a fist in the center of her upper belly.

"Am I hearing you right, Andrew?" Jude began. "You're telling me we need to set a wedding date tonight because I owe it to you? Is that really a good reason to be setting a wedding date? Do you think that makes me feel what I should be feeling when we do set a date?"

"Okay, Jude, that didn't come out right. Don't get all riled up." Andrew stood and began clearing away the dishes from the table.

"Please, Andrew. Just sit down." Jude was trying to calm herself realizing that she was probably overreacting.

Andrew seated himself and turned to Jude. "Do you love me, Jude?" He asked in a much softer tone. "Am I the man you want?"

Jude softened. "Yes, I love you, Andrew. Yes, you are the man I want. But I'm just stressed out with all that has happened. The way you put this to me just felt like more pressure. I'm sorry. I overreacted."

Andrew stood taking Jude's hand and pulling her up to him, wrapping her in his arms. "I'm sorry, too, Jude. I think all those weeks of thinking of you there with Xander just made me feel desperate."

"I'm home, now," Jude whispered. "I'm home with you. Isn't that enough for right now?"

"I guess," Andrew replied. But Jude felt his body stiffen slightly. It wasn't enough, she could feel that. But she couldn't be pressured into setting a wedding date right now. Not yet.

II

They made it through the evening, but three weeks passed, and they had not discussed setting a wedding date since. Jude knew it was a sort of stalemate that they had come to. She had made it clear to Andrew, when he proposed, that she needed a long engagement. They had known one another a total of two years. She didn't think of that as long. That meant they'd been engaged one year. One year does not a long engagement make, Jude thought. This from the girl who married Edward after knowing him only six months? Is it something wrong with me? She found herself questioning. What am I afraid of? Why am I so reluctant to set a wedding date? Am I so damaged that I can't commit? She determined to make an appointment with a therapist. Allison would know a good one.

Jude was at Applewood for another two-day weekend. She had asked Andrew for a day of solitude to finish a new painting she'd been working on since her return from Belgium. Between Woman Space and Andrew, whose urgency now seemed to permeate everything they did, she was having difficulty finding time for painting.

Today she had painted for four hours straight; her stomach was signaling that she needed a break. There was hummus in the fridge, and some carrots, if they weren't stale. She didn't want to walk to the house for food. She just needed something to calm the jitters. Water was her drink of choice, but she'd already had three glasses. Maybe a glass of wine would be good for a change. She searched through the cabinet for a bottle of red, but there was none to be found. She checked the fridge again. There was a chunk of Colby cheese and an opened bottle of an inexpensive Chardonnay; that would do. She poured the wine and carried the glass and cheese onto the deck. The view was beautiful, and the stillness calmed her. A soft breeze was coming across the lake from the direction of Andrew's house. It occurred to Jude that Andrew was probably stewing about the fact that she didn't want to see him today. How was she going to work this out once they were married? Would she have to fight for every hour of solitude?

There was that knot building again in the pit of her stomach. It had not totally dissipated since the night Andrew pressed to set a wedding date. It would fade, almost disappear, but each time she questioned how it might be to be married to Andrew she felt it growing again. Normally, Jude would be meditating and journaling around the fear the knot represented, but she hardly had a moment to herself since her return home. Was that what she needed to spend time on today, rather than painting?

Jude nibbled on the cheese and sipped the wine as she sat cross legged on the edge of the deck. The water was directly below her, clear and undisturbed. She recalled, at one time, sitting here feeling a quiet clarity within herself. But something was definitely disturbing her now. She didn't feel at peace. Instead, there was a sense of dread. A great blue heron flew across in front of her. The great blue heron, Jude recalled from her study of animal totems, reflected the innate wisdom of being able to maneuver through life and control life circumstances. To have a great blue heron cross your path was a reminder to follow your own innate wisdom and path of self-determination. Trust that you know what is best for you and follow it, rather than following the prompting of others.

Jude repeated aloud, "You know what is best for you and should follow it, rather than the prompting of others." She closed her eyes in contemplation. Her thoughts began to swirl around the questions she had asked herself earlier. Was she afraid of commitment? Or, what was it called? Fear of intimacy? Had she fallen once too often for an untrustworthy man, and now she couldn't even commit to a good man? Or, was the heron speaking to her? Was she so caught up in the pressure of Andrew's urgency to get married, that she was not focusing on what was best for her. Was this what was so disturbing? Was marrying Andrew not what was best for her? She began to breathe deeply allowing her body and mind to fully relax. She found herself falling into the calm of meditation.

CHAPTER 13

"It is difficult to exaggerate the adverse influence of the precepts and practices of religion upon the status and happiness of woman. — Hypatia Bradlaugh Bonner

I**T WAS A bright spring Sunday morning; Andrew had convinced Jude to go with him to his new church.** He assured her this church was more liberal, more accepting. He had been asked to be a deacon and even to speak occasionally. Since her return from Belgium, she sensed a discontent in him. He had shared with her the turmoil he felt when she was with Xander in the Belgium hospital, and he was not happy that Jude refused to set a wedding date. There was a change in her, she admitted that, though she was not sure exactly what it was. All Jude could conclude was that she needed time to recover from the traumatic events that had occurred at Von Hessen's gallery. And maybe, she also needed time to determine if marriage was the right thing for her. She couldn't allow Andrew to push her into something she wasn't ready for; to push her to make a life changing decision that was counter to her inner self.

Jude shifted uncomfortably in her seat. What was she doing here? She had not been in church for several years. Instead, she had a daily spiritual practice of an early morning walk, journaling (her way of talking to God), a yoga practice, and meditation (her way of listening to God). She began to admit to the truth. She was trying to make up to Andrew for being away so long, for being away with Xander, and for refusing to set a date for their wedding.

She was doing this for Andrew, but she was struggling within to control a growing outrage as the preacher elaborated on the scripture, Ephesians 5:23: "The husband, therefore, is the head of the wife even as Christ is the head of the Church." Had Andrew known this was the subject of this week's sermon? The preacher approached these lines from every social perspective, concluding that the wife's place was in the home, cooking, cleaning, raising children, and helping with grandchildren. The husband was to take care of the big decisions and to provide for her and the children. This was the problem with today's society, the preacher asserted. No one was home with the children. And women were no longer obedient or submissive to their husbands.

"If men will step up and take their rightful place in the household, and if wives will allow their men to be men in the eyes of God, the world will quickly right itself!" the preacher spoke, raising his voice another octave. "It's selfishness, sinfulness, pure and simple, that has everything out of order. Be submissive to your men, if you would be women of God!" He seemed to be yelling. Jude recalled similar sermons as a child, and not just in her father's church; this message was also a part of the teachings in her mother's church where women were not even allowed to participate in leadership positions during worship, nor were they allowed to teach anyone other than small children. Therefore, her dad felt entitled to determine what they watched on TV and when, whether or not they bought a new car or another fifty acres (he made all financial decisions), and even whether or not Jude could spend the night with a friend. That her mom resisted going to his church, and instead, went to her family church when he was on his milk route, branded her as a rebellious woman. Jude's dad walked into her room one Sunday morning, awakened her, his Bible opened to this very passage in Ephesians.

"Read this," he said, thrusting it in her face. "Your mom is walking across the field to go to that church with her aunt and uncle rather than going with me. Do you think she's finding favor with God? A woman is to be submissive to her husband!"

Jude had not responded. Her father laid the Bible, still opened, on her bed, turned and walked angrily out of her room. She burst into tears. She felt scared and hurt that her mom had not taken her with her.

Jude turned to watch Andrew as he listened intently to the sermon. It was clear that the preacher's teachings were what he believed. For the first time it fully hit her. This was who Andrew was. And this was what he hoped to convince her was the truth. Why had she not seen it clearly before? Andrew stood for the very ultra conservative beliefs that incensed Jude and inspired her to create a place in Woman Space that helped women become fully independent from the controlling and abusive men in their lives. She was sure Andrew would not support a woman's right to choose whether or not to have an abortion under any circumstances. He might even agree with those who felt women were somehow at fault when a rape occurred. And certainly, there was no need for birth control. You had to trust God in those matters. And didn't he already support the candidates who voted against equal pay for women? Yes, he was so patient, gently nudging her to try this church or that church so they could have discussions over dinner. But the truth was she felt manipulated. He had no idea how infuriating such beliefs were to her.

As a young woman, Jude had been submissive to her father, yet only her brother's college fees were paid. She had to get through college by working part time and applying for student loans. Her father bought her oldest brother a new Ford Mustang while he was still in high school, and her middle brother was given a nearly new Chevrolet Camaro for his high school graduation. Jude had to wait to buy her own car once she had her first job out of college. She was submissive to the elders and deacons, and worried if her creative talents where sinful since they were not recognized in the church. She had been submissive to her ex-husband, and he played the role of the godly church going man. He was even a deacon in the church, while at the same time involved in several affairs at his work place.

Yes, there were good men, and many good men were in these churches, Jude reminded herself. But that did not make these teachings any more acceptable. These teachings did women a terrible disservice: a woman must be submissive to her man; she must trust that he knows what is best for her. No matter what; women were not to get out of line. They were to build their world around their husbands so that they might be saved.

But what happened if the man was a liar, if he cheated on his wife, and left her? And though adultery was technically grounds for divorce, in fact, the only grounds, divorce was not at all socially acceptable. It was a shame to be divorced. Jude remembered a young divorced woman who was a church member in her mother's church. She was treated as a second class member, just as Andrew had not been allowed to be in a leadership position in his previous church. And it was questionable as to whether there was such a thing as rape in marriage because the wife's body belonged to the husband. Jude could feel her blood pressure rising.

What if you were a woman without a man…..a woman alone? Then you had little value at all. The females in the church looked upon you with suspicion, as you might be a threat to their own marriages, while the male leaders of the church kept a careful eye on you under the guise of shepherding you.

She had gotten lost in her thoughts. The preacher's voice had softened. "This is why we must be sure that a woman doesn't become our next President. It would be the ultimate insult to the men of our nation."

"Enough!" Had she said it aloud? Jude closed the song book she held on her lap. She glanced at Andrew. Thankfully, it had only been a strong thought. Andrew was fully focused on what the preacher was saying. Jude must have blocked his final words, for suddenly the congregation was standing to sing the invitational hymn. She quickly stood beside Andrew. Her mind was racing. How could she marry a man who supported this way of thinking? A man who actually believed she should think like this? She could not!

Once the service was ended they drove silently to a lovely outdoor restaruant that overlooked the lake. Andrew was cheerful. He asked for a table near the water. He pulled Jude's chair out for her, his eyes meeting hers directly, a searching look. She knew he was anxious to know what she thought of the service. For the last half hour, while Andrew introduced her to a few friends, and they shook hands with the preacher, Jude had been contemplating the pending conversation. She knew she must be honest.

"Well," Andrew began, "What did you think?"

"Andrew, if you truly believe all that was said in that sermon, then we must have a serious conversation. If that is what you need from me, that I be your sweet submissive wife, cook and clean for you, wrap my life around you, then we just do not fit. I grew up with those same teachings.

I even lived my marriage within those guidelines, but that is no longer who I am. Being submissive to a man will never be who I am. Can you understand that?"

"Jude, you know I love you. I want to marry you. I appreciate who you are and all you have built in Woman Space and as an artist. I don't want to change you. But yes, I do believe that God intends that a man be the final authority, that he is to take care of and protect his wife, and she is to respect his authority before God. I don't feel that conflicts with who we are as individuals."

"And you agree that a woman has no business being President, that it would be an insult to men in this country?"

"Well," Andrew stuttered, "basically, yes, I agree. It should be a man who holds the most powerful position in the world. I don't believe women are built for such a stressful job. Women are too emotional for such a position of authority."

Jude thought of her mom's assertion that a woman had no business being President. She had to remember that even she had been taught this; that she should wrap her life around a man, should accept his decisions as final. And didn't Paul teach this in his New Testament writings? Yes. Andrew came about his beliefs honestly. She could not fault him for this. But she could not marry him either.

"Andrew, I need a partner, someone who considers me an equal. Can you see that we just don't fit? I can't marry you."

"Jude, you're a Christian, aren't you?"

"I'm not sure if I meet that definition according to your criteria, Andrew."

"Are you telling me you don't believe the Word of God? It's the Bible that tells us women are to be submissive to their husbands, that a man is the head of the woman as Christ is the head of the Church. What do I do with that?"

Jude took a deep breath. "Andrew, I think you simply let me be who I am."

II

They had driven home in silence. Jude guessed they both had a lot of thinking to do before taking this conversation any further. It was Tuesday, and still she had not heard from Andrew. She had stayed at the loft with the excuse that the gallery was so busy she needed to catch up on paper work. The truth was she didn't know what she wanted to say to Andrew. She loved him. But how could she be with a man who saw her, who saw all women, as inferior beings, a man whose belief system she had grown beyond so many years ago? She knew the prejudices that went with Andrew's way of thinking. She couldn't go backward.

She was shutting off the lights, about to go out the door of the apartment, when her cell phone rang. It was Andrew's ringtone. It was time to deal with this.

"Hi Andrew," she said as cheerfully as she could.

"Jude, can we have dinner tonight? My place?"

"I can do that. It's time we confronted this thing, isn't it?

"Yes," he chuckled nervously. "We've put it off long enough."

"I should be able to be there by seven, will that work?"

"Seven is perfect. Bring that wine you love. I'll do the rest."

"Andrew...."

"Yes?"

"I do love you."

"I love you, Jude. See you tonight."

III

"Don't you understand?" his voice was raised an octave. "I love you. What if you are wrong, Jude? What if you are being disobedient to God?"

Jude studied his face. His eyes were filling with tears. She saw how sincerely he believed what he was saying. "Andrew, I do believe in a Divine Being, a God. But I don't believe this God sees men as superior to women. What about the words in the Bible that specifically say, 'there is neither Jew nor Greek, nor male nor female.' Who discusses that scripture, Andrew? And how does that fit with the male superiority sermon I just heard? Can't you see that even my work with Woman Space is a statement against such beliefs?"

She knew it was no use to argue. Neither would change what the other believed. They must simply accept that they had differing beliefs. The question was whether or not either of them could live with that. Could she live with a man who needed her to be inferior and feared she might go to hell if she were not? Submissive and inferior.

"Do you understand, Andrew? I can't accept that the man I marry must see me as inferior. I can accept that you feel that. But I can't marry you."

Andrew nervously stroked his chin. His eyes became glassy. "I was so sure that we were meant to be. So sure. I just knew you would come around, that you would be touched in your heart, that I could love you enough."

"Enough?"

"Enough that you would welcome me as the head of our household."

Jude put her hand on Andrew's arm, fighting back her own tears. "It's okay, Andrew." She slowly removed the ring from her finger, took his left hand and placed the ring in his palm, closing his fingers over it.

"I leave you with no hard feelings," she said as she stood. "I hope you find the right woman."

With this, he looked up at her but said nothing. Jude smiled, though tears were beginning to slip down her cheeks.

"I think I should go," she said.

Once in the car the tears flowed freely. Perhaps she was destined to live out the rest of her life without a partner. Andrew was a good man, but she couldn't be with him. She had her children, her friends, and her work. More than this, she had herself.

Most likely, it was these very teachings that repelled her now and the hypocrisy that surrounded them that had compelled her to create Woman Space. Her mind flashed back to Mr. Crane slapping his worn Bible down on her office desk as if it gave him the authority for his mean behavior.

Jude loved men. She knew many men were kind, honest, loved their families, were good to their wives. She just had not married such a man. Thankfully Edward's abuse was more of the emotional kind, though it might have been easier to leave him had he hit her. She was sure, had that been the case, she would not have stayed on so long trying with everything she knew to keep her marriage together. Jude felt she was open to the possibility of meeting a man who could love her for all that she was and be a "rest of her life" partner. But it just didn't appear that was going to happen.

These teachings that had inspired her independence, even her success, would move her on to her next phase of life, but it wouldn't be with Andrew. She couldn't go backward. She had grown beyond those beliefs, and she would never return. She could feel inclusive and understanding of those who still held to those old belief systems, but she knew they could not accept her.

"God is inclusive," Jude whispered to herself. "Love is inclusive —unconditional."

But it was clear that to those of her old faith she had crossed the line. Andrew was compelled to "save" her. She could not agree, but she understood.

Jude pulled up to the lake house. She sat for a few minutes and just allowed the tears to come. A full moon hung low in the sky. She was reminded of watching that moon as a child, feeling God's presence and the "knowing" that had come to her. She had to trust that "knowing." She could trust it. She wiped her tears on her jacket sleeve, opened the car door and stood bathing in the moonlight. She took a deep breath, sighed, and then walked through the house to the old sycamore beside the lake. She was trembling as she stood staring out over the water. But she knew it would be okay.

CHAPTER 14

"You only need one man to love you. But him to love you free like a wildfire, crazy like the moon, always like tomorrow, sudden like an inhale and overcoming like the tides. Only one man and all of this."

—C. JoyBell C.

MAYBE IT WAS **naiveté.** Jude had always managed to convince herself that everything happened for a purpose, happened as it needed for her ultimate growth and good. But having broken off her engagement to Andrew, she was struggling to identify the good in that decision. She did feel some sort of relief. It had been a gut feeling that something wasn't quite right with the idea of marrying Andrew. But she felt more alone than ever before. She thought of her mom. Oh, how she missed her. She realized that she had sort of replaced her mom with Andrew. He had reminded her of her mom in so many ways. Now she found herself not only grieving Andrew but again grieving her mother.

Get your act together, she thought as she tossed in her vast, empty king-sized bed. You're alone again. You'll always be alone. No man has ever truly loved you. What's wrong with you? Why can't you have a normal relationship? The voice in her head wouldn't go away. She curled into a fetal position and felt the tears coming. What does it say about you that you fall for the wrong men, men who are not right for you?

She gave into the sobs, her body shaking for their intensity. She didn't care if everything worked out for her ultimate good. Right now she was feeling more pain than she wanted to feel. She needed the pain to be over. With that thought, a fresh wave of sobs swept through her.

Was she going to totally lose it? "Mom," she spoke aloud. "Did you send this man into my life? I was so sure it was you. I so wanted him to be right."

The truth was, she now reminded herself, that her mom had often said, "Jude, why do you think you need a man? You have such an abundant life, and you have the freedom to do whatever you choose."

But freedom based on having no one to check in with, no one to share with, seemed to Jude a shaky freedom. Conflicting thoughts battled within her. We are creatures of community and family and significant others. Why couldn't she have someone to share her wonderful life with? Why did she have to be alone?

But what was that uncomfortable feeling that reared its head each time Andrew had pressed for marriage? Something never felt just right.

Jude locked herself away at Applewood. She asked Maggie to handle her calls, to tell people she was away on business. She told Jennifer and Grant she was writing and needed a block of solitude. Her family was used to Mom hiding away in her studio for days at a time when she had a show coming up. It was rather easy to disappear.

No one will even miss you. It was that voice again, that crazy voice. Why was this affecting her so deeply? She had loved Andrew, but it was a different love than she felt for Edward or for Xander. It was less intense, more mature, with fewer expectations. So if she was more mature, what was this she was experiencing right now?

II

Maybe it was something like withdrawal from an addiction, this terrible tearing away from the idea of a "rest-of-my-life" with Andrew. With a lover, a companion. She had to stop thinking her life was incomplete without a man in it. She'd had long periods of time without a man, so why was this different? She was older, with more to share; she felt that the next logical step was to experience spiritual growth in relationship to a partner, the "Other." She had to admit, it was a great disappointment to think she might spend the rest of her life alone. If that was what had to be, then so be it, she thought with resolve. She had to get out of the house.

Jude turned Gandolf, her roan fox trotter, down the trail toward the woods. Andrew had given her Gandolf, but she would not be riding with Andrew again. She would not be in a relationship with a man again. The thought hit her hard. This was what felt different. It was as if she knew the quest to find Mr. Right was over for good.

"It's over because you allow men to be a distraction, and you have work to do." The voice was audible. She turned around to look behind her, but there were only silent oaks and hickory and a smattering of cedar. Now I am losing it, she thought.

"Get over it," the voice spoke again, distinctly male. "And don't try to label me....I have no gender. Are you forgetting why you ended it with Andrew? Do you want to go backward? Do you need to flirt with being controlled?"

Jude began to laugh aloud. Gandolf's ears were perked backward. Had he heard the voice, too?

"Enough is enough," she yelled as she urged Gandolf into a canter. She had been crying and whining and beating herself up for more than two weeks. This had, after all, been her decision. She could not marry Andrew. She didn't want to marry Andrew. So why was she making such a big deal of acting on that decision? What was this insatiable need she had for a man in her life? Perhaps her expectations were the problem.

"Go!" She signaled Gandolf, and he leapt into a full gallop through the woods, up a long length of hillside, and back down again, jumping the creek at the bottom of the grade without hesitation. Jude felt life pulsing through her veins. She was alive. She was free. She didn't have to be something inauthentic to herself in order to please someone else.

"I'm free!" she yelled out. "Free, free, free!"

She allowed Gandolf his head; he ran at top speed the last half mile back to the stables. Jennifer came around the corner of the barn as Jude pulled a sweaty, snorting Gandolf to a halt. "Mom, what are you doing? You could hurt yourself!"

Jude laughed. "I just felt a need to let go."

"Well, let me have Gandolf," she said reaching for the reins. "I'll cool him down for you. Maggie needs to talk to you; you'd better give her a call."

Jude climbed down from the saddle and gave Jennifer an exuberant hug. Jennifer shook her head and smiled. She was used to her mother's wild whims. Jude turned for the house feeling renewed, ready. She'd better get back to Woman Space to give Maggie a hand. Jude wanted to get caught up on business. Maggie had been carrying quite a load at the gallery while Jude hid out grieving her break up with Andrew. She felt a bit disgusted with herself.

CHAPTER 15

No serious work can be accomplished without great solitude. —*Picasso*

S MALL WHITE BILLOWY **clouds peppered the sky as Jude slowly paddled the perimeter of the lake.** A large blue heron lazily flapped its way across in front of her, as unconcerned as if she were part of the landscape. It had been the heron that reminded her to be true to herself. And she did feel a part of this world that she joyfully joined as often as she could keep the morning for herself. She watched as fish circles decorated the water's surface, and skimmer bugs skated away from the prow of her kayak. She had pretty much recovered from her break up with Andrew. She was not unhappy alone, and she was growing more comfortable with long periods of solitude. She loved awakening to the stillness of the lake; she would return to the dock for yoga and journaling. This morning ritual gave her a sense of balance and a trust that her own intuition would not lead her astray. By learning to act on her own inner guidance, she would avoid a lot of pain and indecision. She sensed an inner shift, an assuaging of that longing, that ache of life. She had at first become aware of a subtle shift when she returned from Belgium after Xander's injury. At first she feared she had lost something, some motivation to accomplish her dreams, or maybe she had lost herself. But she began to understand that she had simply been made more aware of what was really important. She felt an even greater sense of that shift once she adjusted to breaking off with Andrew and accepted being single again. Things were moving quickly with Woman Space, yet Jude felt an inner calm that manifested itself in a need for even more tranquility and a slower pace.

II

Maggie walked into the office with a paper in her hand. "Jude, do you have a minute?" she asked.

"Of course," Jude said, motioning to the chair near her desk. "What is it, Maggie?"

"We got this letter from the university, and I think it's something you'll be interested in. They have a young Syrian woman enrolled who needs some help. She comes from the University of Damascus, and as you can imagine, education has been totally interrupted there with the war going on in Aleppo. This woman is in her third year in International Business and has been accepted as a part of the Illinois Syrian Scholarship Program. These scholarships are like an emergency fund for students affected by the breakdown of higher education in Syria. She has a Syria Consortium Scholarship, full ride. But her original sponsor has some financial difficulties and is pulling out; she needs a sponsor. They thought of us because she happens to be quite a talented artist as well as a very bright business student."

Jude reached for the letter. It was from Mariam Brosner, a friend of hers, who was involved with the Alumni Scholarship Program. She read through the letter. "Ayr Hanadi," she said as she finished. "It could be perfect timing. We could use another person here in the gallery, and she might eventually be someone who could head up the international aspect of our outreach program."

"That was my thought exactly," Maggie responded.

"Okay, let me give Miriam a call. I'm sure she has more details on Ayr and this program."

"I'm going to finish uncrating Leona Fratelli's work that just arrived from Italy," Maggie said, rising from her chair. "Jude, hiring Ayr could be an exciting opportunity. I've felt a need to do something concerning the Syrian crisis. Maybe this will also open some doors in that respect."

"I'll see if I can set up a time to meet this young woman. I want you to be there, too, Maggie."

"Yes, I'd like that."

The interview revealed a lovely young woman with a sparkle in her eyes and a passion for art. Jude watched Ayr's excitement as she and Maggie explained the purpose and intent of Woman Space. By the end of the interview, Jude was convinced that Ayr was a fit. She was hired to work part time as an assistant for Maggie while she completed her Bachelor's Degree, and there was the possibility they might have a scholarship for her if she continued toward her MBA in International Business. The gallery would also promote her beautiful mosaics.

Ayr's story was very touching. She had taught herself English watching soap operas, of all things, before she was allowed to go to school. She was intelligent, and once in school she advanced so quickly that a wealthy aunt took notice and brought her to live with her and her family so she could attend the University of Damascus. That same family member taught her the ancient Syrian art of mosaics. Tragically, the aunt and her family had been killed when their home was bombed. Ayr had been in class and was fortunate to manage to escape to Turkey. She had not been able to get in touch with her parents and two sisters who lived in a small village several miles north of Aleppo.

With Ayr available to help Maggie, Jude could now reduce her time at the gallery to three or four days of her week, which allowed for a morning spiritual practice and more time for both painting and writing. She would need the painting time as Von Hessen had contacted her to assure her that the Belgium exhibit would happen. He suggested a date for early the following year. The trauma he suffered had not allowed a quick recovery. But he had followed through with the grant and the New York exhibit which had been quite successful. Jude thought often of Xander, who remained in Belgium, but she heard from him only occasionally. There was something different about him that she could sense from his emails. Maybe he, too, was having trouble recovering from the trauma.

Leona Fratelli's show had also been quite successful and led to contacts that would build a consistent flow of international artists to Woman

Space. In addition, Jude received more international invitations to show her own work. Money was flowing in for grants and scholarships for needy artists as well. A new program providing free psychological counseling, medical care, and legal services for participating artists was put in place with the contribution Von Hessen had made, and the Norma von Hessen Scholarship was established. Woman Space was expanding.

Grant was married. His lovely wife, a financial planner for Ameriprise, convinced Grant of the importance of being near both of their families. They were expecting a boy, Jude's first grandchild.

Jennifer and Doug chose not to have children, but they were growing the retreat aspect of Applewood at a rapid pace. They were now paid Co-Directors for retreat programs, and a larger conference center was in the plans to be built at the far end of the property, complete with dorms and classrooms.

Jude enjoyed more privacy in her Applewood house, as she directed more of her energies inward. She felt a need to avoid the limelight. At times, she wondered if she was becoming a recluse. She scooped her over-medium eggs from the skillet and carried her plate outside onto the deck to enjoy her breakfast. She took a deep breath, looking out over the stillness of water, drinking it all in. I am so grateful, she thought; then slowly ate her eggs and toast as if partaking of bread and wine. A monk. I'm becoming a monk. That thought caused her to laugh to herself. With all that was going on in her life there was not much danger of that. But she knew something was changing within her. She no longer wanted to be involved in the interviews and publicity and was grateful that there were others who could take care of the public relations for the gallery. Her priorities were shifting.

Juniper, the newest family member, a red golden retriever, lay at Jude's feet. Jude leaned to pick up a twig that had fallen from a tree overhead. "Go fetch, girl!" she yelled as she gave the stick a throw. Juniper bounded to life getting to the stick as it bounced on the ground, then ran quickly back, stick in mouth, and placed it in Jude's hand. "Good girl, Juniper." The eager-to-please canine begged for another throw. As she watched Juniper swim to retrieve she looked across the lake at the now empty house. Andrew's absence still triggered some sadness.

"Okay girl, that's all my arm can take. Time to go." Jude carried her plate inside, rinsed it, and left it in the sink. As she grabbed her paint shirt, Juniper ran to heel and together they walked briskly to the studio.

Jude glanced across the lake. Andrew had sold his ranch and moved to South Carolina with a woman he met online. He and Jude parted friendly. He apologized, admitting he wanted Jude to be what he wanted rather than who she was, and that was not fair to her. But Jude had been just as guilty of the same charge, and she told him so.

"It was that Robert Redford look you have going for you. I just couldn't resist it. I would pretend not to see anything that got in the way of how I enjoyed that."

Andrew laughed. "I do love you, Jude. You are a most amazing lady. I realize that you are somehow religious without being religious, and I just can't wrap my mind around that."

"I love you too Andrew. Be happy. That southern lady is very lucky. Baptist too?"

Andrew nodded his head.

They laughed, stood for a moment smiling at one another then hugged goodbye.

Jude had not met the new owners of Andrew's ranch but heard from Jennifer that they were a young family. Jennifer and the wife had connected over coffee and conversation centered on horses. They were doing some renovating before moving in.

"So, what do I really want the next phase of my life to look like?" Jude wrote the question in her journal. She needed to do some serious thinking on that. Too often she'd been guilty of believing someone would change for her. That was one of her most difficult lessons, accepting that one could only change oneself. It seemed so simple now, but she had loved a few men in spite of knowing they were very different from her at the core. They were sometimes men who pretended to be exactly what she wanted, and sometimes even wanted to be what she wanted. Had she believed she could love them enough that they would change? And then there was Andrew who was sure he could love her enough to change her. But it just didn't work that way.

To see the good in another and to love the other is wonderful. But one must be honest with oneself when that other has a very different world view from one's own. To love someone is to accept them for who they truly are; but to love someone does not mean they will fit as a life partner.

Edward once said that Jude had changed, and he had not. Once they went their separate ways, Jude felt that Edward regressed, becoming more black and white in his thinking, but more likely, he just became more his real self.

Jude continued to feel a need for more time for introspection, to process how much her own core had changed, how she, herself, had grown. Change was the one constant in life, and it was an essential for remaining vital and vibrant. She wanted to be growing and changing until she took her last breath. She wanted to move toward a deeper spirituality and all that might entail. That was to be her top priority. If it meant that she must grow old without a significant other or even a lover, then that was the way it would be.

Inner peace would be her top priority; inner peace came from being authentic and aware. Simply put, she had to be true to herself. But what did that mean? Looking back over her life she could see how that seemed to mean different things at different times. What was that old original dream? Meet the man of your dreams, fall in love, have children, and live happily ever after. That dream, for Jude, also included being an artist. But at that point in her life, she really had no idea what being an artist meant. Now, her dream was to discover and be her authentic self. Every life experience had either served to show her who she was or who she was not.

Thinking back to her childhood, it seemed to Jude that she had lived several lives within this one life: innocent country girl who was an "A" student and most popular in school, who went away to college on a scholarship intent upon living her dream of being an artist even if it required rebelling against her father; young wife, stay at home mother of two beautiful children, one with a chronic, life threatening illness; mature wife, planning for an empty nest by restarting her career and growing a business, planning to travel and bike with Edward; divorced mid-life woman starting from scratch and struggling to make ends meet. Now, she found herself a very successful business woman and a well-known artist, established and financially secure. Each experience had prepared her for the next. Where did she go from here? That was the question she was now asking.

Before meeting Andrew, Jude had thought there was only one thing missing from her life. She had met many men in her post-divorce single years. She loved a few. She almost married two of them. And yet, for some reason, she remained a woman alone.

CHAPTER 16

"Empowered Women 101: Forgive yourself for having chosen to expose yourself to people who don't care about your feelings and help others to do the same." —Shannon L. Alder

THE NEW PAINTING **was very different from anything she had painted before.** Jude turned it 180 degrees on the easel. No. She liked it better the other way. Maybe she should sign it in a circle. She had designed a stamp of her name that allowed for that. She lifted the canvas and turned it another 90 degrees. Ah, that was even better. The colors melded in waves of rich earth tones until they seemed to crescendo to a deep red the color of a fine wine. This became the focal point. Staring at the painting did something in the pit of her stomach, as if the painting was attempting to speak to her on some deep level. What was it saying?

She had learned years ago that painting connected her with something beyond her present understanding, a knowing. It was as if her painting knew more than she knew on a conscious level, as if when painting she was channeling something greater than herself. Perhaps she was channeling the goddess or a feminine expression of the Divine. This new piece was certainly trying to speak to her. And she did have questions. She felt again at a crossroads of some sort. This painting felt like a breakthrough, one she didn't yet understand.

Jude stood back from the easel, pulled a comfortable upholstered chair from the corner of the room, and sat, not taking her eyes off the painting. A restless energy seemed to fill her, a dis-ease. Most likely the intensity of the recent political climate was getting to her. She was obsessed with watching the news to see what inappropriate thing presidential candidate Donald Trump did next. She had felt, under Obama, that the country was evolving to a new and higher level of consciousness. And she was hoping to see the first female elected President of the U.S. in the pending election. But Trump was turning the election process into a circus. I can't think about this right now, she thought. I have to stay focused. She switched off the TV.

Jude forced her attention back to the painting. If she looked at it as a landscape, she could see what appeared to be bluffs of rich neutral tones sandwiched between sky and water. It could be a coast line, she thought. It was too rugged and energetic to be a lake. Certainly the message she was getting was not to relax, sit back, and go with the flow. There was something she was supposed to do. Needed to do.

Jude sighed deeply and reached for the cup of barely warm coffee next to her chair. Whatever the painting's message, and it would come to her, she loved the finished composition. Whatever it was saying to her, she felt it signaled a change. Maybe what she needed was to get away by herself so that she could fully hear what this new work was speaking to her. It felt like the beginning of a new series, and perhaps, also a new period of growth.

The phone rang. "This is Jude."

"Hey, girlfriend." It was Kim. "Are you free for lunch? I need to talk."

"Of course," Jude replied. "Come to the lake studio. I'm here working, and I need a break! I'll fix a salad. It's so warm we can sit by the water."

"I'll be there in twenty." Kim hung up.

Jude removed her chambray paint shirt and laid it across the chair. Thinking she might end up spending the afternoon with Kim, she decided to clean her brushes. She had just finished when she saw Kim coming down the path to the studio. Jude dried her hands and walked to the door. Kim was walking rapidly with her head down and one hand on her sunglasses. Something was wrong.

As Kim neared Jude, she pulled off her sunglasses revealing a red swollen eye that was beginning to turn black and blue.

"What in the world?" Jude exclaimed.

Kim burst into tears and reached for Jude who wrapped her arms around her. Kim was trembling. For a moment they simply stood holding one another. Kim began to sob. Jude held her until she seemed to calm, then pushed her back enough that she could get a look at her.

"Kim, what happened? How did you get a black eye? Who did this to you?"

Kim looked embarrassed. "It was that great guy I've been telling you about. We met at the Diversity Conference I attended in New York. Remember me telling you about him?"

"Roger? Roger did this? Oh, my God, Kim! What happened? You thought he was such a nice man."

"He is…or it seemed that he was. We've been seeing a lot of each other. He's such a charismatic guy. I was really falling for him, Jude." The tears started again, and Jude gave her another hug.

"It's okay, come inside and sit. Do you need something to drink?"

"No….no." Kim sat stiffly on the overstuffed chair, and Jude sat in a chair beside her.

"Last night I saw a side to him that was a total shock. We had a date for dinner, but when he arrived he was angry and irritable. He claimed he was upset over a case he was working on. He took issue with everything I said or did. Finally I confronted him, told him his behavior wasn't acceptable and asked him to leave. Instead of leaving, he grabbed me and pulled me to him saying, 'You know you don't want me to leave. I know you want me.' He forced a demanding kiss on me and proceeded to tear at my clothes. I fought him off; hit him over the head with my copy of Janson's *World Art History*."

"Kim, that's a huge book!"

Kim could not contain a chuckle. "At least it shocked him into stopping, but he swung at me, like a reflex, yelled some obscenities and stormed out. Thank God. I thought he was going to rape me, Jude!" The sobs came again. Jude hugged her.

"Hold on, you need some ice on that eye." Jude walked to the kitchen, poured Baileys in two mugs of coffee and got an ice pack from the freezer.

"Tell me the details." Jude handed Kim the cup of coffee and the ice.

Kim leaned back in the chair compressing the ice pack to her eye. "I just can't believe this, Jude. I thought he was one of the greatest guys I'd ever met. We really had some in depth and intimate conversations over lovely dinners. He's so intelligent, seemed such a gentleman...until last night. This mood change was out of the blue."

"He sounds like he has some serious issues," Jude replied. "Kim, do you think he'll stalk you?"

"I haven't heard from him since he left last night. Maybe he'll just disappear. I'm sure there are many women he can easily charm. He's so good looking, and wealthy." She began to tear up again. "I'm so embarrassed."

"Kim, how could you have known? You talked about how great he was, how sweet he was to you. You can't blame yourself for this."

"Maybe," Kim mumbled through her sobs. "I just keep thinking I must have missed something. I just feel so, so shot down. But I know I'm also lucky. It could have been much worse than a black eye."

"I think maybe what you need now is a glass of wine." Jude went to the cabinet. Knowing how much Kim appreciated a really fine wine, she found a bottle she had been saving for a special occasion and poured them each a glass.

"Here lady. This will reinstate your self-worth." Jude laughed as she handed Kim the wine. "Well, at least it might relax you a bit. You won't let some screwed up man mess with your mind. Besides, he's an angry abusive man, and thank God you now know who he really is. When I divorced Edward, I did a lot of study on narcissism, Kim. And I remember reading that if a narcissist sets his sights on a woman he can be the most charming, perfect gentleman you can imagine. It would be a rare woman that could resist him. But once he thinks he has you hooked, it's just a matter of time until you see the real warped person."

"I thought about that," Kim said in a low voice. "I could have found out after I married him. I was falling in love with him."

"You're a very savvy woman, Kim. I'm sure he was thinking he had a good thing. But obviously he couldn't control his sickness long enough to hook you. You're lucky! Let's just celebrate that! To revelations!" Jude tipped her glass to Kim.

"What would I do without you, Jude?" Kim said after a long sip of wine.

"The feeling is so mutual my dear friend. Do you want to report this to the police?"

"No. One incident like this won't make a case," Kim responded. "But if he tries to come around or keeps contacting me, I'll file a restraining order. He's a lawyer, but knowing that I'm a lawyer as well, I think he's smart enough not to bother me. I yelled after him that I'd better not see or hear from him again."

"How about staying with me a few days?" Jude suggested. "When you feel a little better we'll drive over and get your things. Okay?"

"Okay," Kim whispered, and the tears began again.

What was it with men like that? Jude thought to herself. They could certainly control their anger in order to get what they wanted, a job, a woman, a deal. Or maybe even President? The thought creeped her out. She knew her own experiences with men like Roger were what made her so nervous about Trump. Both fit the profile for Narcissistic Personality Disorder perfectly. When men like this started to get in too deep emotionally all hell broke loose. Thank God this guy blew up before Kim was in a more vulnerable position with him. So often the angry man beneath that wonderful guy appeared only after a woman married him, and from her experience with women at Woman Space, it was often not before there was a child.

II

Kim stayed at the ranch with Jude for four days. She had one text from Roger asserting how very sorry he was, begging her forgiveness. Kim responded with a threat to report him if she heard from him again. She had not. Most likely he wouldn't pursue things further, knowing Kim would not hesitate to take legal steps against him if he did.

Jude worked from the lake studio while Kim kept mostly to herself, reading, resting, and making phone calls. She started a new painting, taking advantage of the solitude and quiet that was becoming more difficult to come by at the loft.

"I feel I'm ready to go back to my place," Kim announced over dinner the fourth evening. "I feel stronger, and I know how to deal with Roger if I have to. I'm betting on him knowing this and leaving me alone."

"Are you sure? You know you're welcome for as long as you want, Kim. I know you can deal with him. I just hope you don't have to."

"Jude, thanks so much. This has been just what I needed. It's so quiet and peaceful here. It really helped me to get my head on straight. I do know that I was in no way to blame for any of this. And there's no danger he will suck me in to allowing him back into my life."

"You certainly don't need someone like that around," Jude asserted. "Just know if you feel uncomfortable at home alone in any way, just come back. Okay?"

"I will, I promise."

The next morning Kim packed her bags and left for work and for home. Jude knew how devastating it was to have someone you had grown to love and trust turn on you. She had experienced this once with Edward. His mistress had called him at home asking to speak to Jude. Edward hung over Jude as she talked to Helen, both women realizing they were being lied to. Hearing Jude's end of the conversation incensed him. He grabbed the phone from her hands and yelled "I don't need either of you!" He began poking hard at her chest with his index finger. She was frozen in place, looking at him, thinking, "My God, I'm dealing with a crazy man. He is crazy!" It had scared her and had shaken her self-confidence deeply. Edward's anger had not left her with something as blatant as a black eye, but she had ended up with a sprinkling of finger bruises on her chest.

How grateful she felt at this moment to have no man's craziness or chaos clouding her life. She was free of that; she was free to paint like a mad woman if she wanted, or to simply sit and stare out onto the lake. She was at peace.

As Kim drove away, Jude slipped on her paint shirt and walked out into the silence of the morning; the lake was still, not even a leaf stirred in the overhanging trees. She walked down the flower lined path to her studio thinking that she had best be very grateful for all her blessings. This is as good as it gets, she thought.

III

"Abusive men are often, at least initially, the most brilliant, charming, charismatic men you would ever meet," Allison said to Jude as they walked the trail around the lake. "What such a man can do to a woman's self-esteem, even if he does little damage to her body, is brutal. It is, in fact, labeled 'crazy-making.' Trying to figure out what's going on can drive you crazy because there's no logic to his behavior." Allison was involved again in her therapy practice and saw this often. Even Jude saw this with the women connected with Woman Space. But she had not expected to see one of her closest friends experience abuse. Kim was an intelligent, strong woman and a brilliant lawyer. Her experience was proof that no woman was immune to such a man.

"Do you think Kim is okay now?" Allison asked.

"I think so. She seems pretty angry too, so I think no guy is going to get the best of her."

"Men," Allison sighed. "I married one of the good ones, not that we don't have our conflicts at times."

"You and Gene have always been such a team."

"Well, he can be very supportive of me. We both agreed it was important for me to be a stay-at-home mom while the kids were small. But there are times I still think I'm going to starve to death for intellectual conversation. Gene can get lost in his own little world of golf and fishing. Our conversation seems limited to what's going on with the kids or where he will be golfing next week. If I try to discuss some of the latest studies or more recent philosophies his eyes glaze over. And we absolutely cannot discuss politics. I finally told him if he's going to vote for Trump I don't want to know. It would affect how I feel about him, Jude."

"I'm sorry to hear this, Allison. Don't you feel it's important that you talk about everything?"

"Thirty four years, Jude. We've talked about a lot of things, but you also have to accept your differences."

Jude took Allison by the arm and they continued down the trail. "Well, you can always talk to me about politics, girlfriend."

"You do have to pick your battles," Allison said, and they both laughed aloud.

"For sure!" Jude gave Allison a hug.

Feeling alone is not just a condition of being single, Jude thought to herself. She was sure there were many good marriages; Gracie and John certainly had one, and Allison was an example of making a relationship work even with major differences between partners. So funny how she had once thought the right man would be the final door to complete happiness. What a surprise to learn that happiness resides behind the door to self. Why had she never been taught this? Instead she'd had to discover it by a lifetime of throwing open the wrong doors.

IV

The fall wind carried a chill that nipped at Jude's cheeks. She wrapped herself a little more tightly in her wool shawl. Large yellow leaves floated from the outstretched Sycamore branches and settled on the wind-whipped waters of the lake. The smells, the freshness of the air, the severe clarity of the atmosphere that created a sky of deep blue, everything seemed normal. But it wasn't. She had this gnawing feeling that if the presidential election, now only weeks away, went the wrong way, things would never be normal again.

Her mind wandered back to Kim and how devastated her friend had felt to find the wonderful man she was falling for was not at all as he had led her to believe. Jude knew that feeling. She had felt it when she first discovered that Edward was cheating on her and again when she learned that Xander had lied to her, had not been divorced when he came back to the States to woo her. Why was it that a man would try so hard to impress you, to convince you how right he was for you when he knew he was lying, knew he was something very different?

Jude couldn't escape the thought that this was the kind of man who was running for President. She recognized him. There were times when she watched him as he was speaking, and his face morphed into Edward's face. He was fooling so many people, but she knew his type. A sick feeling moved through Jude's stomach and knotted in the center of her upper belly. She picked up a stone that lay beside her and threw it as hard as she could out into the lake. The smooth flat stone fell into the choppy water without a trace. The futility, the frustration of having no effect. She had felt this often as a woman. Trump was stirring hatred even within her! She had had it with men who assumed superiority and asserted power over women. It angered her that this type of man felt he could do whatever he wanted to a woman. And Trump had even said this publically. Old resentments were being triggered. Jude knew there were good men, honest men who respected others. Many men were just as upset over the idea of a Trump Presidency as she. They represented positive masculine energy. Besides, she claimed to trust that things happened for a purpose. If she believed this she would have to apply this same attitude to a Trump Presidency. Certainly he had opened a fresh discussion concerning sexism and what constitutes sexual assault.

Most likely, to the privileged, white, chauvinist male, Trump represented the fear that somehow, having lost the sanctity of marriage to gays and lesbians, having to compete in the work place with women, having lost the power over a woman's reproductive rights, and having already lost the most powerful position in the world to a man of color, allowing a woman to become President would be the ultimate insult. It might mean the white American male's place at the top of the ladder was lost forever.

She experienced an "aha" moment. Donald Trump was symbolic. He was the perfect opponent to be defeated by the first woman to attain the highest office in this land and the world. He represented the Edwards, the Xanders, the Rogers, all negative male energy, the racism, the bigotry, the misogyny, the lies and the fear that holds hostage not just women, but all of humanity. You only had to know a little history or look to the Middle East to see how effective this repressive energy could be. Oh, God, she prayed Hillary would defeat him.

Jude thought again of the words of Paul that often gave her comfort when confronted with any sort of inequality. "There is neither Jew nor Gentile, neither slave nor free, nor is there male and female...." In direct opposition to the superiority of man, the Apostol Paul asserted that all humans are equal. We are not locked into some hierarchy according to culture, race, gender, or sexual preference.

A wave of relief fell over her. The knot in her stomach dissipated. It could be that Trump's candidacy would point out the inequalities in our culture in such a way that more would be awakened. He had insulted a disabled journalist, swore to ban Muslims from entering the country, and proclaimed that immigrants crossing the Mexican border were criminals and rapists. He seemed to have no self-control. He became a sexual predator, critic or abuser of every woman he met, depending on how effectively they stroked his ego or whether he saw them as a two or a ten. He managed to stoke every fear of the right wing as he preached of a rigged system, fake media and a variety of conspiracy theories.

It was those on the extreme right who considered themselves most Christian. She had once been of like mind: self-righteous, so sure of her truth. Again a knot formed in her stomach. She had been so sincerely wrong. She wondered, sitting under her majestic tree, the sun shining bright in a clear fall sky, what else was she wrong about?

What she needed was to get away from everything and have some time to herself to paint, write….think.

CHAPTER 17

"...there are no wrong turns, only unexpected paths." —*Mark Nepo*

J UDE WAS DRIVING **south from San Francisco on the Pacific Coastal Highway.** She had decided to act on her need to get away, away from the demands of Woman Space and Applewood. She needed some distance between her and all the reminders of Andrew. Highway One undulated and curved through terrain that inspired caution and awe in a chaotic mix. Jude had rented a convertible, a teal Mustang with an ivory interior. Her first car had been a Mustang, and it seemed appropriate to splurge on one as a rental. She knew it would hug the ribbon of winding road she had to traverse. Her red hair was pulled back in a ponytail that was tucked through a white cap with WILD embroidered in silver thread on the brim. She figured it stood for the book and movie about the woman who hiked the Pacific Rim Trail alone. It fit her mood. She had long dreamed of taking a trip out here alone so that she could fully enjoy what she considered one of the most beautiful places in the world. She had been here before, but never on "her trip."

Jude was still a bit raw from breaking off her engagement to Andrew almost four months earlier. It had been the right thing to do, but that didn't mean she didn't miss him. Three weeks on Big Sur might not totally get her beyond that disappointment, but it surely wouldn't hurt. Besides, those books that had been written about people who escaped to the wilderness to forget their grief were about a different breed than she. Jude was escaping to the wild to celebrate her freedom. She felt no domesticity outside a relationship. There was no specific time she had to get up, or fix dinner, or get to bed. If she wanted to get away from work, she simply had to make a few arrangements with Maggie. The further she drove the more she felt the discipline of daily routine drain from her.

She had booked a treehouse for a bargain price at a place called Coastal Ranch Inn. Maggie's uncle, who was the maitre d' at the Inn's restaurant, had managed to get Jude a significant discount. She would be there three weeks. Even with the discount it was no small amount of money, but the New York show had been a great success. The address was Big Sur, so this would be further south from Carmel than she had been before. She would enjoy the views, hike the trails, and spend as much time as she wished painting and writing.

That is if she ever got there. She pulled off the road again to stretch her legs and take in the incredible view. If her GPS was correct she had another fifty miles to go. But the view around each curve seemed more amazing than the last, and, after all, one goal of this trip was to fully experience the Pacific Coastal Highway and Big Sur.

A stiff wind tugged at her cap; she adjusted it to fit tighter on her head. The waves were coming in high, which meant there were storms far out at sea in spite of the bright sunshine and scattered cirrus sky along the coastline. The mountains fell at almost a ninety degree angle into the ocean, and huge rocks scattered out from where the mountains and ocean met. She could hear the crashing of the waves even though she was high above the beach line.

She took out her cell phone and snapped a few more photos. She might use them as inspiration for painting, though she doubted it. After all, she would be painting plein air for the next few weeks. There was no phone service here, nor had there been for most of the drive.

Jude took another deep breath of the fresh salt-tinged air and got back into the Mustang. As she pulled onto the highway, a silver BMW motorcycle pulled into her space. The driver honked and waved. This kind of majestic landscape seemed to make everyone friendly. She waved back and focused on the roller coaster highway. If she didn't stop again, she should be checked into her ocean view room by 5:00 PM, plenty of time to catch the sunset.

In spite of her best intentions, Jude stopped one more time at a high overlook with a view of a private beach far below. The soft sun-warmed sand between two huge outcroppings of dark rock reminded her of the first time she had seen the Pacific Coast. She had traveled with Edward to Monterey where he was teaching a course in Structures for employees of his company who were working toward an advanced engineering degree. They drove along the Pacific Coastal Highway south from San Francisco, stopping for the views, and at times, walking down to the water. They found a beach similar to the one she was now overlooking and climbed down the rocks to get their feet in the sand. They had been playing there for a while when Jude noticed an unusually large wave building out in the distance.

"Edward, does that wave look dangerously high?" she asked, drawing his attention to a towering swell that was growing by the second.

Edward grabbed Jude by the arm, yelling, "Run! Get to higher ground!" They made it half way up the rocks when the wave completely engulfed their little beach. The adrenalin was pumping as they watched from above. Edward wrapped his arms around Jude, and they stood watching the water until it slowly drained away revealing the beach again. At the same time they turned to look at one another, the awe of the moment still in their eyes. Edward leaned down and kissed her. "I love you, Jude," he whispered. Years later she learned Edward was having an affair with one of the female students in the program; she had not been happy that Jude came along.

Jude had experienced this beautiful area another time on a trip with a friend. The first trip had been all about Edward, his wants, his timeline, and even his mistress. On the second trip Jude's friend, who was worried over health issues, was tired and irritable. Jude determined, after that second trip, one day she would come here alone on a trip that would allow her a full experience. That she was standing here, at this moment, made her want to pinch herself. She giggled aloud as she got back into the Mustang.

Coastal Ranch Inn was even more inspiring than Jude had imagined. It sat out on a point overlooking the ocean with a view every bit as amazing as those she had stopped to enjoy on the drive down. Her treehouse sat on one of the best vantage points, near the trail head that led to a small beach below.

Jude unloaded her suitcases and rolled them up the ramp into the living area. She could see straight through to a view of myriad blues in water and sky. She pulled the suitcases into the bedroom, a large master with a king bed, a sitting area, and plenty of storage. The bath was designed to allow a view from a large soaker tub. Jude walked to the window and could see the gnarly limbs that held the small frame building as much as sixty feet off the ground at the steepest point and much further above the rocky beach. A deck wrapped around the entire ocean side of the room.

Once everything was unloaded, including food from her cooler which would serve as dinner, she ran a tub of hot water, undressed and slipped into the luxurious bath. She surely would not fall asleep in this tub, in spite of the fact that she had driven all day. The view from the floor to ceiling windows was invigorating. But she set her timer just in case; she wanted to watch the sunset from the deck, where there would be nothing between her and the sun slipping into the vast ocean.

II

On the first morning after her arrival, a heavy fog whitewashed the view from the treehouse. Cozy and dry inside, Jude sipped her coffee. The expanse of glass allowed panoramic ocean views, but on this morning it felt as if she looked out through waxed-paper windows. By noon the fog had lifted, and Jude walked up the mountain side to the small breakfast cottage she had found on the map of the resort. She smiled seeing the silver BMW parked outside the restaurant. Wondering if she might recognize the owner, though his head was hidden under a helmet when she had seen him on the road, she entered the room and scanned the clientele.

"Can I help you?" the hostess asked, menu in hand.

"Oh...yes, please. A table with your best view," Jude answered with a smile.

"No bad views here," the slim dark-haired woman in her forty's responded.

She led Jude to a corner window. "Ben will be serving you," she said, laying the menu in front of Jude.

"Oh, can you point out the owner of the silver motorcycle? Just curious, as I saw him on the way here."

"That's Ben. Little man, big bike." The woman laughed as she left Jude.

Jude scanned the menu and decided on a breakfast parfait with yogurt, granola and fruit. She was ready for a cup of coffee. Deciding on her order she turned to scan the view.

"Good morning," a cheerful male voice greeted her. She turned to smile at a middle-aged man with sharp Italian features and dark dancing eyes. "I'm Ben. Don't you love that view?"

Jude's smile widened. What great energy this man had. "Incredible," she answered. "And hello, Ben. I think we met on the way here yesterday. You have the silver motorcycle, right?"

"You must be the lady in the Mustang!"

"That I am. I thought I'd never get here as I had to keep stopping to see the views."

Ben laughed. "I have the same problem. Takes me forever to get to work."

They laughed together. "Would you like coffee?"

"Yes, I need coffee. And I think I'll have the breakfast parfait."

"Great choice. I'll have that coffee here right away."

Jude watched as Ben walked away with an energetic stride. She turned again to enjoy the drop of the mountain into the vastness of ocean. She could see to where the boulders dipped into the water and found the constant licking and lapping of the Pacific against the rocks hypnotic.

"Here you go. Best coffee on the coast. My special blend," Ben announced, setting a handmade ceramic mug before her.

"Thank you, Ben. Your blend? Impressive."

Ben laughed. "This is my place, my dream. I took early retirement from a professorship at Berkeley in order to design and build this place. You like it?"

"You designed this cottage?" Jude asked. "You're an architect?"

"Designed the entire Lodge, every building, every treehouse. I own it with a couple of friends."

"I am impressed!" Jude exclaimed. "So, what are you doing serving me coffee?"

"I like to know firsthand what's going on with my business." Ben laughed. "But the truth is, I've too much restless energy to retire, so I move about doing various jobs at the lodge."

Jude was delighted. "Then, I'm so honored to be served my breakfast by the owner of this amazing place."

Ben smiled and headed back to the kitchen to get her parfait.

Jude finished her breakfast and walked back to the treehouse to pack up her sketch book before setting out to explore the area. There were several trails leading down to the water's edge. Signs warning about the unpredictable surf dotted the pathway. She decided it would be best to set up her easel on higher ground. The restaurant and lounge sat higher up the mountain. That, too, had breathtaking views. She discovered several lookout points and explored the main lodge. The fine dining was located there; this was where Maggie's uncle would be. She had read the food was as incredible as the views. Maggie had assured her that her uncle George was an excellent chef. At Maggie's request he would give special attention to Jude.

Two huge stone fireplaces stood at either end of the lodge lounge, and in the cool evenings, fires burned brightly, inviting guests to sit and mingle. Jude arrived early for dinner to enjoy the ambiance.

"You must be Jude," an older man with a contagious smile and wearing a chef's apron said as he approached her.

"I am. And are you the wonderful chef? Mr. George?"

"That I am. Just call me Uncle George. Maggie has told me much about you, Jude. I'm very pleased to meet you."

Jude stood, extending her hand. "I'm so happy to meet you."

Uncle George ignored her hand and gave her a warm hug.

"You're just as Maggie described you, Uncle George."

"I have to get back to the kitchen, but if you need anything, just let me know. Okay?"

"Yes, I will. Thank you Uncle George."

Dinner turned out to be a social time. By the end of the first week, Jude made friends with an interesting couple from Vancouver and a single woman, a writer, from Germany. It was a friendly group, and, when the pianist began to play each evening, the wives seemed happy to share their husbands so that the two single ladies could have a chance to dance as well. Most of the guests had retired for the night, but Jude lingered listening to the pianist playing soft jazz as she sipped a sparkling wine. She sat, looking out over the vastness of the ocean, allowing the music, the wine, the water to lull her.

"May I join you?"

Jude turned to see Ben standing near her. "Of course," she gestured to the seat beside her. A waiter brought a tray with Ben's drink, a plate of cheese tarts, and some exotic seeded crackers.

"Help yourself," he said, as he reached for his drink. "Jude, isn't it?"

"Yes. What job are you handling tonight?"

"Being sure my guests are comfortable and content," he smiled.

"Well, this one certainly is. Don't know when I've felt so relaxed, so mellow."

"And you're the artist, I hear."

"So have you been checking me out?" Jude smiled.

"I check out all of my guests. Tell me about your art and your Chicago gallery."

It was the beginning of a delightful conversation. His name was Ben Casello. He had been a professor of architecture for thirty years, and, like Jude, he was living his dream. Like Jude, he too, was divorced, but he had no children, just three dogs and a cat. Jude was so drawn to him, but perhaps not in a romantic way; it was something more. She walked back to her treehouse anticipating more stimulating conversations with this man.

Jude spent her mornings writing and the afternoons exploring the trails or painting outdoors. It was her desire, not to copy the landscape, but to capture her experience of the awe inspiring views. Her colors reflected the blues, greens, violets and brilliant whites of the wild water.

She had been at the lodge two weeks but had not seen Ben again since the night of their long conversation. Carrying her painting gear, she hiked to a somewhat level surface halfway down the trail to the beach. Here she set up her easel and began to mix paint. From this distance Jude could see the contrast of the fine-grained sand with the rugged, textured outcroppings of lava rock. As she observed the waves consistent and rhythmic caress of the coastline, she suddenly felt lonely. Realizing she wouldn't have such a moment if she was engaged in talk or laughter or even romance, she wondered if this was actually loneliness. Maybe what she felt was the longing that C.S. Lewis had coined as the "inconsolable longing." A longing for the Divine that Lewis believed was a result of the sensed separation that made possible the human experience.

It was solitude that allowed Jude to access that creative zone, where she could experience a sense of purity and flow. Something about the coming together of water and earth touched her deeply. As she began to layer color across the large canvas, a realization rolled over her. She was never alone, she was part of all of this, as much as the lava rock, the foaming sea, and the gulls that played noisily overhead. She felt loved. Unconditionally loved. She belonged. A deep peace settled over her. She mixed three of the colors she could see in the undulating water, took her brush in hand, and began to paint onto the canvas a sense of belonging to the landscape. As she painted, her loneliness began to dissipate.

III

Standing at her easel on the spot she had come to call her perch, Jude put the final touches of white onto a third canvas with broad strokes of a palette knife. Staring down the steep trail, she could see where the sand leveled out to the demanding wash of the waves. There was something sensual about this junction where sand, rock, water, and wave came together. Maybe it was such a place as this where the first life forms crawled out of the sea to adapt to land, driven by the waters rushing in and rolling out, to seek the silence of a warm sandy beach. Here, life could evolve into the abundance she felt surrounding her in this place.

Jude laid her brush across the palette and took her pen and notebook in hand. The trail to the beach was steep. Her sandaled feet picked their way unsteadily among the rocks. At the bottom of the trail, she found a smooth boulder and straddled it like a horse. The sun-heated stone was warm, solid, comforting. She closed her eyes, observing how sounds became more acute, rhythmic. The mix of sea and salt was absorbed in her heightened sense of smell. Her skin tingled with a delicious sensation as the heat of the rock warmed her, building in intensity, filling her until it seemed to split her apart and send her cells spewing out into the atmosphere to dissipate and disappear. She began to write in rhythm with the waves:

The sea, tumbles, rolls, and rises
Compelled by the sensuous stretch of shore.
His constant caress subtly shapes and softens her….

The sensuality of the words surprised Jude. But then, she often found that nature triggered in her a spiritual reaction entwined with sexuality.

He wraps her in his lapis arms,
Prods with silver tongues…

For Jude, the sensual, the creative, the spiritual could not be separated. Her longing encompassed the three in one. Perhaps this was why, regardless of how she might deny it, she still longed for a lover.

Though Jude realized she had grown through each of her relationships, she longed for the stimulation that could come from deep discussion with the "Other" in a setting of unconditional love. How much more might such a relationship spur mutual transformation? The thought again triggered her longing.

She closed her journal. "The Sea" was Jude's fifth poem since her arrival in Big Sur, and she had now finished three paintings. Half way through the third and final week of her vacation, she was grateful for the insights and the opportunity to accomplish something she had felt a need to do for a very long time: to come to this most beautiful place and experience it fully without distraction.

Distraction. Perhaps the men in her life had not been distractions but rather growth experiences as were the endings she had experienced with each. Had she stayed with Andrew, married him, she would never have had this experience. Had she stayed with any of the men who had been in her life, including Edward, and maybe especially Edward, she would never have become known as an international artist, and she certainly wouldn't have created Woman Space.

Things do happen exactly as they need to, she thought, as she made her way back up the path to where her easel stood. Why was it so difficult to remember that?

Just then she distinctly heard her mom's voice: "Jude, my dear girl, you are on the right track."

"Mom?" Tears filled Jude's eyes. It was the first time she had so clearly heard her mother's voice. "Thank you for being here, Mom."

"I'm sorry if I'm interrupting." It was a male voice. Startled, she turned quickly toward the voice, almost knocking over her easel.

"Oh, I'm so sorry. Let me help you with that." A compact man, barely taller than Jude, with long black hair pulled back in a ponytail, reached for her easel. Picking it up, he folded it together.

Jude laughed. "I was in such deep thought that you startled me."

"I know," the man responded. He was somewhat younger with a solemn face. "You were speaking with your mother. She is always near you, you know."

"I do feel that, somehow," Jude said with a questioning look. This man looked so familiar. Where had she seen him before?

"I'm Joseph Wolf," he said, as if she had asked him the question. "So sorry I startled you. We met several years ago when you were on a Spirit Quest in Sedona, Arizona."

"Oh, yes, of course! Joseph Wolf, the shaman." Jude took his hand. "I would never have expected to see you here! Are you on vacation?"

"I'm here to see you." He stared intently into Jude's eyes. "I had a dream that I was to meet with you on a cliff overlooking a vast ocean, a place with treehouses. Since I knew it was somewhere along the Pacific coast, I began to search online and found this location. When I saw this retreat, I knew it was the place in my dream."

"I remember that you found Sedona through a similar dream."

"Yes, I was living in Canada when I had the dream about the red rocks."

"And looked online to find where that might be, as well."

"Yes, I did."

"This is amazing, Joseph. Why were you led to find me? This feels a bit wild!"

"You're at a crossroads, my sister." He reached for Jude's hands and held them gently. "Sometimes, when at such a place of transition, we can use the support of a kindred spirit."

"And we are kindred spirits?" Jude asked.

"Have you forgotten what I told you? You are my sister. You have the same gifts that I have. You know."

Jude did recall the shaman telling her these things when they met in Sedona. But she had hardly felt like a shaman, a seer, as he had called her. Jude smiled at him. "I never did meet that soulmate you told me I was going to meet."

"Oh, you have met him, my sister. Soulmates are not always what we expect. Most of all, they are teachers for us. But first things first. It's time that you learn to trust your gifts."

"I don't know that I understand what you mean by my gifts. I did take some workshops on Shamanism, and they were very helpful. I was amazed to find that I was practicing something similar through meditation and creative visualization."

"This trip, my sister, has prepared you to trust in your inner guide, your higher power. So I've come to journey with you to help you with your new direction."

"New direction?" Jude was feeling a bit overwhelmed. Shaman Joseph Wolf, here in Big Sur, telling her he dreamed where to meet her to share a Shamanic journey.

"Come." Joseph said, as he started down the trail toward the water.

"Wait," called Jude. "I need to take my things back to the treehouse."

"They will be fine where they are. Raven will protect them."

At that moment, a raven flew into the tree beside Jude, letting out a gurgling croak, a softer, more musical call than that of a crow. Jude stood in disbelief. Her mind flashed back to the raven that had followed her as she hiked in Sedona, stopping to meditate at various vortexes of energy. That raven had called to her as if he had some urgent message. And another raven had spoken to her as she worked with horse medicine while on a spirit quest. She knew raven was a reminder that she was exactly at the right place at the exact right time. Suddenly, realizing that Joseph Wolf was almost out of sight, she ran down the rugged trail trying to catch up to him. He veered off the trail onto a barely visible path through thick undergrowth. Jude followed quickly in order not to lose sight of him. She noticed deer tracks in the soft soil, and wondered that she had not noticed this trail in the two and a half weeks she had been walking to the water's edge.

Finally, they came to a tiny clearing where a large, weathered redwood had fallen. The tree was bare of most of its branches, and the trunk was well worn as if many others had sat upon it.

"Sit beside me," Joseph Wolf said.

She took her place beside him on the felled trunk. Her fingers followed a trail of patterns carved carefully into the wood.

"Are you comfortable?" he asked.

"Yes. But what are these carvings? And this place? It feels mystical. I don't understand why I've not noticed it before?"

Joseph smiled and pulled his medicine bag from his pocket without speaking. He began to sprinkle tobacco and sage in a circle around them.

"And I can't believe this is actually you, here, telling me you want to take me on a Shamanic Journey." She laughed nervously.

"I want to go on a journey with you, my sister. There is a specific difference."

He began to breathe in long deep breaths. Jude closed her eyes and fell in rhythm with his breathing. She felt herself relax, and, as her anxiety melted away, she began to feel this strange event was a perfectly normal experience.

"Now we are going to climb this tree, my sister." Joseph Wolf began in his hypnotic voice. "It is standing tall and strong. You can step up the perfectly placed limbs, reaching with your hands and following with your feet, step by step. Higher and higher we are going. Now you can feel yourself in the clouds. It's becoming so dense with clouds that you can only see a bright light where the sun shines above this cloud layer. When you get beyond the cloud layer, you will step out into the Upper World."

Jude was familiar with this term from Shamanic Workshops, but her visits had been mostly to the Lower World. She had attempted reaching the Upper World several times, but had been successful only twice. This time, she felt the bright sun welcome her as she moved through the last bit of the cloud layer. And there, she was able to step onto what seemed like firm ground. The landscape was beautiful and lush with foliage. Jude found herself beside a small lake surrounded by a canopy of trees. This was a familiar place, a place where she waited for a totem animal to come as her guide.

"You will not wait for a guide my sister. For I am with you on this journey. I am your Spirit Guide."

At the sound of his voice, she saw Joseph Wolf standing in front of her. He offered his hand, and she took it. They walked side by side, hand in hand like two children. There was a soft breeze. The air was fresh and made her think of the smell of fresh sheets on a clothesline. The lines to a poem she had written as a child whispered through her mind:

Oh, joy is mine, joy is mine,
Gathering fresh sheets from the line
Feeling the cool of morning dew
Soaking though my tennis shoe....

She was filled with an encompassing sense of joy. Everything around her seemed to glow with life energy. It emanated in visual waves from every surface, and as she walked the energy was disturbed and moved as a wisp of fog.

The clouds had disappeared from the sky as they walked toward an outcropping of rock that was worn smooth and sparkled with some sort of mineral, perhaps mica. It made the soft neutrals in the rocks look silver and bronze. Jude noticed a path of red clay winding up through the rocks and followed Joseph as he began to climb. The path was worn smooth and packed hard. She was so focused on the path she briefly lost sight of Joseph Wolf. When she saw him again he was patiently waiting for her.

"Come, join me," he said.

Jude made the short climb and seated herself beside Joseph at the edge of the path among a carpet of wild flowers.

"Is this as far as we go?" she asked.

"For today." Joseph answered. "This is the place of Seeing."

"What is the meaning of this red path?" Jude asked.

"Black Elk spoke of the 'red road,'" Joseph began. "The 'red road' is the right path. Jude, you are on the right path; it is time for you to see, to know. Just lay back and rest."

With these words, Jude fell into a deep sleep:

She was on the back of a large red tailed hawk as he soared high into the air, allowing her to look down over a large area of earth. Suddenly she was sitting in her treehouse as a child. She watched a fat red squirrel with only half a tail come down the tree and stretch out flat on its belly in a spot of sunshine beside her. As she was marveling at the squirrel, noticing each strand of his shiny coat in variegated colors of red and black-tipped browns, a brilliant red Cardinal flew to a twig hanging just above her head and began to sing. She could literally feel the squirrel enjoying the warmth of the sun. The song of the Cardinal was more beautiful than a symphony. Again, Jude felt an amazing joyfulness rising up from within. I don't want this to end, she thought. But, immediately, she saw, or was she with…? It was impossible to tell which.….. or it was both? She was with Edward, seeing his face as he held Grant for the first time. He looked up at her, and, for a moment, she knew how much he loved her, had always loved her.….would always love her. It was as if there was an "understanding" between them. An overwhelming love for Edward washed over her. Just as quickly the vision was gone, and she was in the depths of woundedness from Edward's betrayals. The pain was so real, so powerful, as if she was experiencing it for the first time. This too, she experienced for only a brief moment, until another joyful, loving moment came as Jennifer was born; then again sadness, and even fear, as she was being told about Jennifer's health issues. This scene morphed into Jennifer's exuberant smile and laughter and more waves of love as each of the loves of her life came into view. One by one, major experiences from her life danced before her, sweeping her with emotion: sadness, then joy, then sadness. She felt the surges of falling in love and the pain of the ending of that love. Yet, in each experience, she knew the love was real. She had loved well, and yes, she had been loved well by family, friends, children. and lovers. The morphing and motion became a dance of colorful prayer flags blowing in the wind. It came to her as a powerful insight that this was Happiness: the rich random patterns of joy, sadness, fear.….and love. All of it. It was clear that every experience in her life had purpose and was part of the tapestry that created a meaningful life.

The hawk began to speak. "We are all one, multifaceted, living Being. We are all Spirit. All labels and dualities intended to separate us are but illusions. We all feel we need love and belonging, but all people need to know that they are Light and Love when they fully let go of their fears. They belong, as one part of a body belongs to all the other parts. The Great Spirit lives and acts….even experiences Itself, through us, but we realize this only when we can get our fearful selves out of the way."

The hawk made a sharp turn; Jude frantically grabbed his wing feathers in order to stay on his back.

"You know Light and Love. You will use your talents and intuition to help others discover this within themselves. You will know how, because you will be guided."

The hawk slowly landed on the outcropping of rock. Jude dismounted and looked into his eyes. It was time for her to let go of the separateness she had lived as a woman alone. She had grown beyond this. She was ready to live as a full human being. She wasn't sure just what this meant. But she did know that everything, whether she labeled it good or bad, had been necessary in order to bring her to this realization.

Jude awoke. Her painting, now finished, stood on the easel. The sun was warm on her back and shoulders, but Joseph Wolf was nowhere in sight. What was she to understand as her new direction? What did it mean to just "Be"? And who was this soulmate that she already knew? She started to sort through the men she had loved: Edward, Brandon, Xander, Andrew, then stopped herself. She had no need to know anything more.

She turned to look at the painting. It was abstract, as was her style, but a wide spread of wings, like those of a hawk, were woven among the colors of the ocean, the rocks, and the red road. It was, she felt sure, one of her most powerful pieces.

Jude gathered her painting, easel and supplies and slowly walked the trail back to her treehouse. Everything around her seemed enhanced. She saw the myriad of greens in the trees and the gradation of blues to greens to violets with heightened senses. The smells of the dirt path, the evergreens, and the freshness of the air were equally intense. It was as if her senses had been asleep and were now fully awakened.

That evening, feeling a need to remain in the soft womb of solitude, she sat alone in a far corner of the lounge. The music for the evening was performed on harp and cello. Jude's heightened senses moved her with the music. Even the fire dancing in the fireplace had taken on an ethereal glow. And the view…oh, the view. It seemed to sweep her literally into another world.

"I found you." It was Ben.

"I hear you had a most unusual and wonderful day."

"How would you know that?" Jude was puzzled. "I've told no one."

"I too, am one who knows," he answered, and his face widened into a broad smile.

She looked into his dancing eyes. Was this for real or had someone slipped something in her drink?

"Oh, it's real." Ben answered her thoughts.

"And now you're reading my mind?"

Ben smiled softly. "You are my sister too, Jude. You are never alone."

"Okay, sit. You are going to explain this to me," Jude insisted.

"We are always surrounded with those here to help us, Jude. You do know this. Sometimes, just a whispered word, sometimes a spiritual teacher, and sometimes just a guy you waved to driving up the Pacific Coastal highway. Just trust this."

"I will," Jude responded. "I definitely will."

"Enjoy the rest of your evening." Ben touched her shoulder, and, drink in hand, walked away.

IV

The hot foaming water of the jet tub swirled around Jude's neck. She allowed her eyes to close as her body relaxed into the contours of the porcelain tub. The sun was settling lower in the sky. Just a few more minutes then she would wrap herself in a towel and take in the sunset. For now, however, she felt both stimulated and completely relaxed. She felt loved.

It was as if finally she knew that love was the energy that sustained her. Love had been expressed to her through every "Other" in her life, through every experience, even through every tree and plant and animal she experienced—every atom and particle. "God is love," she whispered to herself. There was a whole new meaning to this statement. God is everything, love is everything—I am love. I am. I am Goddess.

There was no need to do, do, do. She thought of the scripture in which God said, "I am that I am." Finally it all made sense. She smiled, feeling the warmth of the water like a womb, knowing, without fully understanding, that somehow and in some way, she had been lovingly transformed.

It took effort, but she managed to move from the tub to the lounge chair that sat at the edge of the deck. She looked down into the swirling grays and greens of the water as she sipped her wine slowly. It seemed impossible to sort out the events of this day. She might never know just what had taken place. Had Shaman Joseph Wolf actually joined her and journeyed with her, had he slipped her some sort of hallucinogenic, or had she simply fallen asleep and into a significant dream? It had to be real. And what about Ben? How had he known what had happened to her...was he real? He certainly felt real. Whatever the case, she knew that she was on the "right road." She could feel it deep within. All was exactly as it should be. She was to simply be, and she would be guided. Woman Space would be a place where people came to connect, not just with their creativity and spirituality, but with their very essence. It would be a place for helping others find themselves, which would automatically mean finding meaning in their own lives.

The clouds colored into deep pinks, transparent blues, vibrant violets, and ethereal yellows as the round sphere of fiery light fell below the watery horizon. It was as if Jude saw the sunset for the first time,

The phone rang as the last light of the day disappeared. It had been so silent for these weeks. Jen had been able to get through and ask for some advice on an upcoming retreat. Now, someone else was able to get through. Probably Jen with another question.

"Hello, Jude?" It was Josh Weldon, her dear old friend whom she had not heard from in over a year.

"Josh, how are you? How is Clare?"

"I'm good, Jude, but I felt I should call you to let you know that Clare has passed. She died of a stroke two months ago."

"Oh, no. Josh, I am so sorry. What do I say? I'm just speechless."

"We were hiking on our mountain property, and, suddenly, she collapsed. We thought she was in great health. I guess you just never know." Jude could hardly believe her ears. Clare gone, just like that. They were one couple she had felt had it all, and they were so good to her, helped her so much when she was trying to move on from the divorce.

"Clare was the most wonderful woman in the world. I'm not sure how I will manage without her, Jude." Josh broke into sobs. "We were so far from the road with no phone service. I couldn't get her help in time."

"Josh, I'm so sorry. Are you doing okay? Is there anything I can do for you?"

"No, I just needed to let you know. I'm sorry we sort of lost touch. I didn't know how to reach you, and just recently found Clare's book of contacts."

"I just assumed you were both busy; you've always had so much happening in your lives. I know you were so happy."

"We were, Jude. I loved her so much." Josh sighed deeply. "I certainly didn't expect to get emotional on the phone with you. I just felt you should know. I'm doing okay. I'm staying with Randy and his family for a while, until I feel strong enough to go back to our home alone."

"How are the kids, Josh? I know this has to be very difficult for them."

"They're devastated too, and very supportive of me."

"Josh, let's get together soon. You are such a dear friend, and you and Clare were there for me when I was going through such a terrible time."

"I'd like that, Jude. But give me some time. I have a lot to get settled here. I'll be in touch. I need to go."

"Thanks for calling, Josh. You're in my thoughts and prayers. Do be in touch again soon?"

"I promise I will."

Jude hung up the phone in a state of disbelief. Josh and Clare. Clare dead. A wave of compassion enveloped her. She loved these two people so much. She felt Josh's pain. And she was hit with a realization: there is no romantic happily ever after. That isn't even what we're here for. Happiness is a state of being that comes from within and grows slowly and surely as we come to understand what and who we really are. Situations and circumstances pull us in all directions. Happiness comes from an inner balance that keeps us centered no matter what happens. Josh would find peace and happiness again.

The phone rang in her hand. It was Maggie. There had to be something with the weather that she was getting two phone calls in a row. She was still caught up in the emotions Josh's news had stirred in her. Maggie was saying, "I know it's almost the end of your vacation, so the Dream Weavers and I have a proposal. We were wondering if we could join you for an additional week."

Jude was taken totally by surprise. "How is that possible, Maggie? Don't you have to book Coastal Ranch Inn months in advance?"

"Well, my uncle just called to tell me that the couple who booked your unit for next week had to cancel, and he wondered if you might want it another week. I got in touch with Kim, who called the other girls, and we decided we would come and join you for a week. We'll cover the cost. Uncle George said he would see to it that we had plenty of sleeping space.

"Maggie, that would be wonderful!" This couldn't be a coincidence. She had just had one of the highest experiences of her life and was then confronted with some equally disturbing news. She needed her friends. She needed to share with them, and what better setting than the treehouse. Besides, it had been a rather intense three weeks, and as wonderful as the days of solitude had been, she could use some fun and laughter. She would have three more days to herself then the girls would join her for another week. It would be a perfect way to acclimate back into her normal life. Surely this was another sign that she was being guided.

Early the next morning, Jude dared to explore one of the longer more remote trails. She discovered tiny mushrooms in varied shapes and brilliant colors hidden under pine needles and leaves. They felt magical, as if the act of uncovering them allowed the light itself to paint them. She photographed lichen and moss for their textures and subtle earthy greens and grays. She caught a glimpse of a hawk soaring above her and was captured by the brilliant red of his tail where the sunshine struck it. Her work had included teaching others to see as an artist. Now she realized how blind even she had been. It was as if all her senses had been kicked up a notch. Most of all, she was amazed at how she had missed out on so much of the love in her life because of her fears.

On the last evening before the girls arrived, she had dinner with Ben. They shared what had brought each of them to this place in time. What a joy it was to be able to share so openly with a man, a deeply aware man on his own journey.

"Promise me you'll stay in touch," Ben said, handing Jude his card. "Anytime, anything you need, just call."

Jude put her hand on Ben's wrist. "I'm here for you, too, Ben. You feel like a soulmate. And you must visit me soon. I want you to see Woman Space and my dream property."

"I promise I will." Ben stood, opening his arms for a hug. They held each other for a moment. A wash of loving energy engulfed them.

V

Jude's monastic retreat was over. Maggie and the Dream Weavers ushered in a week of fun, enjoying the views, the food, sharing laughter and sometimes even tears, as only good women friends could do. It was one big sleep over, as they added cots so that everyone could stay in the treehouse.

"Are you sure everything is taken care of?" Jude asked Maggie, who left her young assistant, Ayr, in charge of Woman Space. "It isn't as if anyone can get in touch with us whenever they want."

"Ayr is very capable," Maggie assured her. "She is such an asset and working out so well as my assistant. This will be a good trial run for her. She has both Jen's and Grant's phone numbers if she can't reach us."

"I do worry about her," Jude added. "She is so concerned about her family. They are in constant danger. I wish there was something we could do."

"With the present political climate, who knows what is going to happen."

On their last evening in Big Sur, the group enjoyed a special meal of sea bass with asparagus in a tasty sauce prepared by Maggie's uncle.

Dessert was George's specialty: a croissant bread pudding with a caramel and chocolate sauce. Now, they sat on the treehouse deck and viewed the sun setting over the ocean. There were just enough clouds in the cerulean sky to create an awe inspiring display. And, of course, Kim contributed an expensive French champagne.

"A toast" she said as she lifted her glass. Everyone responded by lifting their own. "This is to Woman Space and beyond, and to being."

"And to my dearest friends and the amazing support they give me." Jude added. They sipped another toast.

Kim lifted her glass a third time, "And here's to Jude without whom none of this would have happened!"

"And….." Jude added before they could toast, "to every person and every experience, both joyful and painful, that brought each of us to this place in time."

Jude shared some wisdom that Joseph Wolf had once shared with her, "Do not regret anything you have chosen to experience, for it has all happened exactly as it should. You have been a teacher, and you have been a student. You have touched lives, and you have been touched by others."

"If only I can apply this to accepting that Donald Trump is now our President," Kim said sadly. They all laughed.

Gracie, in a more serious mood, shook her head. "I just can't believe this has happened. How can he have been chosen as our President?"

"We have worked so hard to help women who have been beaten down to stand up for themselves, to create lives that reflect their worth. It's disheartening to see our nation elect a president who represents old school thinking toward women and minorities," Kim added.

Allison joined in, "He's the alt right candidate….white male supremacy is what they stand for. I feel we've been pushed back 100 years as a culture."

"Let's not spoil this occasion by thinking about that," Jude interjected. "If we truly believe what we claim, we just have to trust there is purpose to this as well. We have to focus on what we can change."

"And be the change…." Allison added.

Jude felt a strange sort of peace. She was as upset as anyone that Hillary had lost the election. But how could she doubt, after this amazing retreat, that everything was happening exactly as it needed to. There had to be some purpose in this.

CHAPTER 18

"No one leaves home unless / home is the mouth of a shark./ You only run for the border / when you see the whole city / running as well." –poet Warsan Shire

I T WAS GOOD **to be home.** Jude had unpacked upon arrival the night before and was enjoying her morning coffee overlooking the peaceful lake from the deck of the main house at Applewood. The wildness of the Big Sur coastline had inspired her. And the encounter with Shaman Joseph Wolf had made her realize it was a way of being, not what she chose to do, that was most important. He had helped her understand we were each doing the best we know to do. That was the key to true forgiveness. Her entire month in Big Sur had been literally magical. It would take some time to process all that had happened. She was ready to again work hard at Woman Space with a renewed passion to help women, who had in ways been beaten down, to stand tall and know their worth. In fact, she was dressed and ready to meet Maggie at the gallery in less than an hour. She had saved her coffee for last in order to enjoy the stillness of the lake, which was inviting after the surge of sea she had witnessed for the last month in Big Sur.

The phone rang.

"Jude, it's Maggie. Can you come in right away? It's Ayr."

"What about Ayr? What's wrong?"

"Something terrible has happened!"

Maggie was speaking so fast that Jude could hardly understand her.

"Maggie, I'm coming, but what's wrong?"

"She couldn't tell me everything. He came into the room, and she couldn't finish what she…what she was trying to say, but she left her phone connected and I could hear."

"Who came into the room? Just tell me what she was saying. What has you so upset?"

"She was whispering, so it was difficult to make out. But it sounded like she was saying 'He has guns and ammunition, call the police.'"

"Who? Maggie, just calm down…..you aren't making sense."

"I think it was her boyfriend. She was saying, 'Please don't do this, Ahmad, please….' She sounded desperate."

"Did you call 911, Maggie?"

"Yes, they're on their way."

"Okay. Ayr was saying her boyfriend has guns and ammunition?"

"Yes, and she was afraid! And she speed dialed me to ask me to get help!"

Jude grabbed her purse and keys and rushed to her car while staying online with Maggie. "So you gave them her address and the boyfriend's name?"

"Goethe St., 171, I think, Lincoln Park. But I've only heard the boyfriend's first name, Ahmad."

"Text it to me; and her phone number…..oh and the correct spelling of Ayr's last name."

Maggie began texting Jude the information.

"Give me any update while I'm on the way to the gallery."

"Okay," Maggie replied. "I'll see you in a few minutes."

Jude dialed 911.

"911. How can I help you?"

"I'm Jude Bennet. I own Woman Space on Michigan Avenue, and my assistant gallery director may be in trouble. My director, Maggie Dennis, made a 911 call a few minutes ago, and you dispatched officers to Ayr Hanadi's apartment at 171 West Goethe Street, near Lincoln Park. It's H A N A D I. Can you give me an update?"

"I haven't had a report back from the officers. But you can contact police headquarters."

Jude jotted down the number the dispatcher gave her then focused on her driving. It had been almost six months since Jude had hired Ayr as Maggie's gallery assistant. She had proven her worth as the one in charge of the gallery while Jude and Maggie were in Big Sur.

Maggie was anxiously waiting at the gallery entrance. It was too early to open up the gallery, so the two of them locked the door and went into the office. Jude dialed the number for police headquarters.

"You'll have to come to the station to get information," a man said in a dry, unfriendly voice.

"Maggie, let's just close for the day and take a cab to the police station. We need to see that Ayr is okay."

"I agree," Maggie said, dialing a cab.

"What do you know about Ayr's boyfriend?" Jude asked.

"Nothing, really. She just started seeing him a couple of months ago. They met at her mosque. I think his first name is Ahmad, but that's all I know. She told me he was very handsome, and that he took her to nice restaurants. She seemed quite taken with him."

At the station, Jude and Maggie found a shaken Ayr. Her face was bruised, and one eye looked as if it would soon turn black. Her wrists were red and swollen.

Maggie removed her jacket and placed it around Ayr's shoulders, giving her a hug. Ayr had no family near; her parents and siblings were still in Syria. They were trying desperately to get out of the country as conditions worsened there. That seemed unlikely now that Trump was President, though their papers had been approved. Maggie had taken on the role of mother, friend, and sister to Ayr since her arrival at Woman Space.

"The police have been questioning me," Ayr cried. "Do they think I had something to do with whatever Ahmad is planning?"

"Tell us what happened." Jude coaxed.

"This morning, I was getting ready to come to work at Woman Space. There was a knock on my door. I went to answer, and when I unlocked the door Ahmad shoved it open almost knocking me over. He started going through my closet and taking out boxes that I had no idea were even there. I knew in my gut that something was terribly wrong. That's when I went into the bathroom, called Maggie on speed dial, and left the phone connected hoping she would hear whatever was said. He was dressed in black and was not at all friendly…. pushing me out of the way and going through everything. I was yelling at him, all the while hoping Maggie could tell something bad was happening and would call the police. I saw guns and ammunition that he must have hidden in my closet when I thought he was moving in his clothes. I tried to talk to him, asking what he was doing, what all of the guns were for….I grabbed his arm and he swung it back and knocked me to the floor. I started for my phone, but he kicked my purse away from me then wrapped a very rough rope around my wrists and tied me to the bed post.

"When he seemed to have gathered everything together that he wanted, he came to me again. With a horrible snarl on his face he tightened the ropes.

"'You've served your purpose,' he said to me. Then he went to my stove and turned on the gas. He left me to die! Had I not been able to reach Maggie I would be dead!" She broke into sobs.

"You're okay, Ayr; we are here now," Maggie said, wrapping her arms around the sobbing girl.

Jude walked to the desk where an officer sat writing. "Can you tell us what is happening? Can we take Ayr Hanadi home with us?"

The pleasant officer looked up. "Let me check to see if they need anything more from her. They're looking for the boyfriend."

Jude walked back to Maggie and Ayr. Soon the female officer came over. "I have some papers for you to fill out," she said to Ayr. "Then I see no reason why you can't leave. Just stay in the Lincoln Park area in case we need to reach you."

Apparently, they had cleared Ayr. Maggie determined to take her home with her rather than back to the apartment. "Give my address as where you will be staying," Maggie directed Ayr. Once the papers were filled out and turned in to the front desk, the three of them took a cab to Maggie's home. Maggie's home was warm, light, and open, and the cheerful environment made the situation they found themselves in seem even more surreal. Jude sat with Ayr while Maggie made tea.

"What do you know about Ahmad?" Jude asked.

"He is the son of one of our leaders at the mosque," Ayr began, still shaken. "He seemed to be such a nice man, a US citizen, though his parents are from Saudi Arabia. I went out with him several weeks ago, and we hit it off so well that I have seen him almost daily since. I was falling in love with him." Ayr struggled to hold back tears. "We were planning for him to move into my apartment, as he was still living with his parents. I gave him a key so he could begin to move his things while I was at work...just last week."

She began to cry again. Maggie handed her a cup of hot tea.

"He was using me," Ayr sobbed. "He was dressed like a terrorist, all in black, and after he turned on the gas, he pulled a black mask over his face. It was so terrible. I knew he was going to kill someone. He intended to kill me!"

Jude walked to Maggie's TV and flipped to CNN. Breaking News was across the bottom of the screen, cameras were in the middle of a scene at a nearby Chicago restaurant. People were scattering, and what appeared to be a SWAT team was storming a burning building. As the women listened, they learned there had been gunfire and an explosion. Fortunately, the police got to the suspect before he was able to fully implement his plan. According to the reporter, four had been wounded, but it appeared no one had been killed. The suspect was in custody. He had been apprehended before he could detonate his explosive device. Or perhaps the device had failed to detonate. They were not yet sure.

Seeing the man in custody, Ayr began to scream. "That is Ahmad! That is him!"

When Maggie's doorbell rang, she opened to a trio of police officers.

"We need Miss Hanadi to come with us, back to the station," a pale officer said without expression.

"We'll come with you," Jude said, taking Ayr by the arm. But the officer pulled Ayr roughly from Jude and slipped hand cuffs on both her wrists.

Maggie grabbed their purses and followed them out, locking the door behind them.

"I'll call a cab," Jude said. "We don't want to worry about parking."

"Jude, I'm calling Dan." Maggie was getting out her phone. Dan Warner was the lawyer for Woman Space.

The officer put Ayr into the squad car, and they pulled away leaving Jude and Maggie waiting for the cab.

II

Jude had conducted a thorough background check on Ayr Hanadi. From her references, she knew she was dependable and a good and conscientious person. Ayr had become a part of the Woman Space family. Jude knew her well and was sure of Ayr's innocence. But she also knew it would be a long time before Ayr got over the betrayal she felt from Ahmad. He had used her to gain access to a place to store his weapons and from which to plan his attack, all while pretending to love her. That the weapons had been stored in Ayr's closet probably implicated her.

Officials soon found evidence that Ahmad Al Zayat was a radicalized citizen of the US. His family was formerly from Saudi Arabia. His father was in a leadership position in the Chicago Muslim community. The entire community was shocked. Ahmad's connection to ISIS had apparently come from a student he had befriended at Northwestern University. That student fled the country, leaving behind his computer showing his communication both with Ahmad and ISIS contacts.

My own alma mater, Jude thought. Who could you trust? These were frightening times. Again, Jude thought of the gallery in Belgium and Xander lying spread eagle, covered in plaster with blood seeping from the wound to his head. She wondered about Xander: where was he? Was he okay? She had not heard from him in quite some time.

Dan managed to get Ayr released after further questioning. There was no evidence to implicate her. But Ayr was going to need help. Jude called her friend and colleague, Allison, a psychologist, one of the Dream Weavers and a member of the Woman Space board of directors. Jude explained in detail what had just taken place. "Allison, could you see Ayr? Or, if you're too busy could you get her in with one of your colleagues?" Jude knew that Ayr was going to find it very difficult getting beyond what had happened.

"Jude, I'll see her myself. It's the least I can do to help her through this. And Jude…."

"Yes, Allison?"

"I want to help get her family here to the States, here to Chicago. I'll call Kim and get her law firm working on this as well."

"I know how much that would mean to her, Allison. Having her family here with her would be the best way to help her through this. It would give her much needed strength."

III

As Jude sat on her loft balcony high above Woman Space, above the city, she thought of the hundreds of thousands of people swarming below. Many of them were, no doubt, angry enough to harm others. And how many might be susceptible to the brain washing of a group such as ISIS? The hatred that created ISIS was not new. Its roots stretched back to the time of the Old Testament, to an ideology that now seethed under the guise of religion, and still no one had any idea what to do about this problem. It was frightening to think about all that might be festering right here in the United States. She wondered how prepared Trump and his new cabinet were to keep the country safe. But to live in fear would only mean that terrorism was winning. There is nothing to fear but fear itself, she reminded herself. Life always brought with it the risk of death. The most profound message that Jude had gleaned from a past life regression experience years ago, was that everything was happening as it needed to happen. There was nothing to fear. It was, after all, more likely she would be killed by a careless driver as she crossed the street than by a terrorist. She thought, too, about the places where people lived their entire lives under the threat of terrorism. How frightening to think that this danger was very present, right now, right here in her city.

She had to help Ayr's family. How sad it would be to allow fear to cause her, to cause the entire country, to turn their backs on the real victims of this terror. Jude recalled the first line of a poem she had seen on the internet written by a Syrian immigrant. She couldn't remember the exact words, but it went something like: *"We would not leave our home was it not the mouth of a shark."*

CHAPTER 19

Language....has created the word "lonely" to express the pain of being alone. And it has created the word "solitude" to express the glory of being alone. —Paul Tillich

J UDE, MAGGIE AND **the Woman Space board, which included all the Dream Weavers, combined their considerable determination and talents in order to bring Ayr's parents and two siblings to Chicago.** This was no small accomplishment considering how difficult the Trump administration had made immigration from several Muslim countries. Fortunately, his ban had been halted by the courts long enough that those whose papers had already been procured were allowed to enter the country. Kim's law firm had been specifically involved, and the fact that the family had obtained visas before the change in administrations had been an important factor. It was with a sigh of relief that Ayr and her group of supporters met her family at the airport with signs and banners. Their reunion was on Jude's mind as she screwed the cap on a large tube of white oil paint. She felt so fortunate to have her own family near.

Her thoughts were interrupted as she heard Grant and Aden noisily coming down the path from the house. There was no mistaking her grandson's laughter. Jude smiled as she flashed back over the last few years and how strongly she had once felt she needed a man in order to be complete, or needed to have retreat property, or for Woman Space and her art to be recognized internationally. Somehow, she had transitioned. Now, hearing Aden's giggle, she was reminded that it is only when we still our noisy desires, when we walk quietly that we can hear the poetry that is in everyday life, and to know no lack. In that calmer life, she had found the real miracle. Of course, her stillness ceased as soon as Grant and Aden crashed through the door. They were racing to see who would get to the studio first. Grant would let Aden, who had just celebrated his second birthday, win the race. Her smile broadened as she opened the door to greet them.

"Wow, you're fast enough to outrun Daddy now!" she shouted, scooping Aden up into her arms.

"I win, Dada!" he exclaimed. He was breathing hard, and as she hugged him she felt his little heart racing.

Aden giggled, and Grant reached to wrap the two of them in a hug.

Jude's heart swelled with love. Grant looked so good, so happy. He and Amy were a great match. They had gifted her with her first grandchild, and another one was on the way. Grant had turned thirty-nine before he met Amy; Jude had wondered if he would ever marry. He was handsome. He had a great personality. But back then he seemed much too busy, getting his medical degree, to fall in love. At the same time, Jude often worried that the break up between she and Edward made Grant hesitant to marry. She was also aware that he and Amy had worried over their decision concerning having children. They felt reluctant to bring an innocent child into a world plagued by so many problems.

"Mom, are you sure you have time to look after Aden for the whole day?" He and Amy were finalizing a deal on a nearby home. Jude was excited, both for the kids and herself. Soon she would have both of her children near.

"Are you kidding?" she laughed. "I have nothing more important to do than play with my grandson." And it was true. Becoming a grandmother had been one of the most wonderful experiences of her life. Aden was so much like Grant. No one had told her that becoming a grandma was like having another child of her own. Aden christened her "Ju Ju," and she could not imagine loving anyone more.

"Okay, we'll pick him up about six."

"Why don't you and Amy stay for dinner? I'll have Doug make extra."

"That would be great," Grant replied. "We can tell you all about the house."

Jude was as excited as Aden; she cleared her schedule so that he would be her full focus for the day. They would cover the table with craft paper and go wild with the finger paints. Kim planned to have her granddaughter, Ella, for the afternoon, and after lunch they would go for a swim in her pool. Doug would be cooking something wonderful for dinner.

This is the life, Jude thought, as she kissed Grant goodbye and set Aden's satchel on the counter; no hassles, no chaos. She so appreciated her days now, doing what she loved to do, working in the gallery, painting, writing, laughing with the Dream Weavers, or playing with Aden. There seemed nothing more she could wish for.

Jennifer and Doug had created a full retreat schedule that still allowed Jude a good deal of freedom. Jennifer's equine therapy program allowed her to work with disabled children, and she and Doug were learning the art of utilizing the horse to read the rider's inner turmoil. Horse Medicine they called it.

Woman Space was now internationally known for helping women, especially struggling, gifted artists, to establish their art careers. Art Therapy and Creativity Coaching were a part of the "Careers in Art Program", and the newest addition was training and support for struggling male artists. "Van Gogh Blues," as the program for men was titled, was getting off the ground. Grant had recently introduced Jude to a young man starting his own practice in psychology who was interested in coordinating the program development.

"Come on big guy." Jude took Aden by the hand and led him to the table. "Let's wrap Ju Ju's table like a big package."

"Yeah, B package!" Aden screamed. Jude rolled the white paper across the table top and handed the roll of tape to Aden. He pulled off a piece of tape and struggled to get it from his fingers to the paper. They both were bent over in laughter before the table was finally covered.

II

The day had been lovely and exhausting. Jude leaned back in her soft studio chair and watched Aden, now sitting in the middle of a large sheet of paper she had spread out on the studio floor, making big swipes of color with washable markers. He still had traces of the finger paint on his tiny hands and various other parts of his body. Not even a couple of hours in Kim's pool had soaked it all off. Jude took a long sip of the pumpkin latte she had picked up on the way home. Aden and Ella had enjoyed splashing and yelling at one another in the pool, while she and Kim hovered over them. Jude took in a deep breath and released it slowly. She was happy.

The studio door swung open; an excited Grant and Amy walked in. "It's done!" Grant called out. "We're the proud owners of our first home!"

Jude rushed to hug the two of them. "Congratulations! I'm so happy for you—all three of you!"

"Mom, are you totally worn out?" Amy teased as she wiped a smudge of blue paint from Jude's forehead.

"Oh, we've had such a fun time," Jude exclaimed. "But yes, I am probably more tired than Aden."

With the sound of his name, Aden began shouting, "Mama, Dada!" Grant scooped him up, fussing over his beautiful art work. Aden scrambled out of his arms and began dancing on the paper, clapping. The three of them joined him, circling the paper in a wild rhythm.

"I think Aden will keep me young," Jude said as she breathlessly threw herself back into the overstuffed chair.

"We really appreciate you keeping him for the day. We'll get the key for the house on Friday. We need to celebrate." Grant exclaimed.

"I have just the thing!" Jude pulled a bottle of French champagne from the cabinet. "Kim sent this!" She opened the bottle, pulled three glasses from the cabinet and poured.

"Make that a fourth glass," Jennifer called as she walked in the door. "Doug says dinner will be ready in fifteen minutes."

"Okay," Jude grabbed the bottle and an extra glass. "We'll take this with us. Doug will want to toast the new house, as well."

After dinner a great peace fell over Jude as she sat with her family watching the sun drop lower over the lake. It did seem as if all of her dreams had come true. She felt enveloped in a gentle web of love that held them close to one another. As they shared an after dinner drink, Aden fell asleep on Jude's mother's handmade quilt.

"I wish your Grandma could be here sharing this with us," Jude said as she reached to pat Grant's arm.

"Me, too, Mom. She would have so enjoyed her great grandson."

Aden never knew when Grant gently took him in his arms, and they left for home. With everyone gone, a different kind of calm came over the Applewood home. Juniper lay at Jude's feet as she finished her glass of wine and watched the sun setting behind the trees on the far side of the lake. She pushed herself slowly in the glider, a soft breeze playing with fine strands of her hair. She noticed the lights on in the house across the lake and thought of Andrew. She hoped he was happy. It still felt strange that someone else was enjoying his home and view. He was out of her life, but she had no regrets. Interesting, she thought, how often she felt that. No regrets.

The birth of Aden had brought Edward back into the family circle. He was a proud Grandpa and adored Aden. She was grateful too, that Edward made it apparent how much he loved his children and now his grandchild. Maybe he was mellowing with age.

"Jude, we did something very right," he had said to her when they met at the hospital to see Aden for the first time.

"Yes, we did," Jude agreed.

Edward hugged her and kissed her cheek. "I think of you so often, especially when I hear of storm warnings and know that your country place is in the path. I always hope you're safe and happy. I still love you, Jude."

"I'm happy, Edward," she replied, "And I love you and want you to be happy, too."

Edward still got emotional seeing her. She wondered what it meant to him that he still loved her. But did it really matter? She smiled, knowing now that he was doing exactly as he needed to do. It had not been her path to stay with Edward. She appreciated that he stayed connected with Jennifer and Grant. She would always feel some pain over all that had happened in the past, if she allowed herself to dwell on it. But the truth was, she had grown, and she was happy.

Jude let out a long sigh as she stretched her arms above her head. No one else can go into our depths completely, she thought. We must travel there alone. Her dream of finding that right partner with whom she could meld sexuality, creativity, and spirituality into some glorious dance had been idealistic. She knew that now. The thought of Ben crossed her mind. She certainly felt a creative and spiritual connection with him, and she felt that same connection with her best friends and her children. She obviously had lessons to learn through her romantic relationships; hopefully she had learned them well. She did trust that, always, like a fountain, what rose up in her replaced what fell away. In retrospect, she could see what had risen as challenges and then turned into opportunities were the very things that revealed her authentic self. By simply being fully in each moment, she was enlivened and transported into the unity of all life. Those brief moments of knowing the Oneness of all things were the very peaks of human existence.

CHAPTER 20

"The further I wake into this life, the more I realize that God is everywhere, and the extraordinary is waiting quietly beneath the skin of all that is ordinary. Light is in both the broken bottle and the diamond, and music is in both the flowing violin and the water dripping from the drainage pipe. Yes, God is under the porch as well as on top of the mountain, and joy is in both the front row and the bleachers, if we are willing to be where we are." —Mark Nepo

IT HAD SEEMED **a long journey, but Jude was more than willing to be where she was, a place of deep contentment, bent over a 6'x6' canvas, spread, un-stretched, on the studio floor overlooking the lake at Applewood.** With a large brush, she slung blobs and splatters of deep purple, green and turquoise paint. She was working on a painting for the solo show scheduled to open in Carmel. Even months later, she still felt inspired from the four weeks she had spent at Coastal Ranch Inn on Big Sur. Unconsciously, she rubbed her lower back trying to assuage the ache that was growing more persistent as she moved around each side of the canvas. Wet colors were running and melding in pleasing patterns, giving the impression of the powerful play of waves against a rocky coast line. Hardly noticing that her hair kept blocking her view, she again pushed it back with her forearm. As dynamic painted forms began to emerge, she was again caught up in the emotions that being on the coast, in the treehouse, looking down into the swirling, crashing waters had triggered in her. Once again, she felt the goddess, connected with that creative consciousness that pulled her forward into each stroke of the brush. The new series was titled "Becoming Sea." The huge stretch of canvas that she hovered over, slinging, brushing and spattering, paint was number twenty-nine of the new series. Her first showing of the work would be in The New Masters Gallery on Ocean Street in Carmel. She had less than two months to be ready, which seemed like ample time, but the gallery had space for as many as thirty paintings. In preparation, she had rearranged her schedule to have even more creative time at Applewood.

Finally, Jude stood and stretched. Walking from the studio to the deck, she took a deep breath of fresh cool air. There were small ripples on the lake surface that shimmered as the sun was beginning to sink on the horizon. Her joy was in the process of creating. She found it interesting that her need for attention or for fame had faded. Maybe this transition from seeking status to internal, personal contentment was simply a part of maturity or ageing. Or, perhaps it was a result of having been there, done that? Jude wasn't sure. But she loved allowing herself to just be, to create for the sake of creating. She painted when her creative energies moved her, from that place of self-appreciation and contentment where she now found herself. Sometimes, she simply sat on the deck staring out over the lake. She once believed an artist's best work came from a place of chaos. But she was producing her best work from a place of peace.

Jude had managed to organize Woman Space so that Maggie and Ayr could keep it going with only occasional decisions on her part, and Jen and Doug now managed the retreat center. She was enjoying semi-retirement. She had not thought of her life in this way before. She signed and whispered aloud, "I like it." She had learned to let go of the attachment to "I am what I do; I am what I have." She no longer felt her identity fully linked to Jude the artist, Jude the creator of Woman Space, not even Jude the mother and grandmother. This was her time to simply "be."

Jude had hovered over her painting, lost to her surroundings, for more than four hours. She needed a break. She filled a glass with water from the fridge and turned on the small TV behind closed doors in a cabinet. Donald Trump was talking to a wild rowdy crowd of his supporters. He still held rallies in spite of now being President. She still could hardly believe he was the President. A woman, for the first time, had vied for the most powerful position in the world! Jude had voted for the first African American President, she had fought hard for Hillary Clinton four years ago, and only a few weeks ago she had voted for the first female President. Hillary Clinton had lost.

She had been a fan of Hillary Clinton since she was first lady and assigned the task of coming up with healthcare reform. Jude recalled how the old Republican guard had hated her even then. It had been hard to accept that the country would choose the likes of Trump over a woman. But Trump had united the right through their dislike and distrust of the government, Obama's policies in particular, and their hatred of the Clintons.

Jude shook her head as Trump spewed his hateful rhetoric. He had not changed. He seemed to still be campaigning rather than being presidential. She switched off the TV and put on Chopin. Feeling a bit restless, she decided to check emails. She was pleasantly surprised to find a message from Xander. She smiled, thinking warmly of him. It had been months since she had heard from him.

"I am going to be in Chicago September nine. Would it be possible to see you?" he wrote.

There was that familiar sense of excitement at the idea. He did have his own issues, but it had been more than five years. Yes, she would love to see Xander. She felt strong, independent. She had dated little since Andrew.

"I would love to see you, Xander," She wrote. "It has been a long time. I'd love you to see my lake house and studio, so do come here. Can I pick you up at the airport?" She kept the message short; there would be time to catch up face to face.

A knot formed in her abdomen. She supposed she still loved him, if only as a special friend. She had panicked at the thought of him dying. But he was not to be trusted, and she hadn't tried to rekindle a relationship with him since breaking off her engagement with Andrew. Perhaps Xander was that sort of soulmate that comes into one's life to teach some difficult lessons. Soulmate didn't necessarily mean a "happily ever after" relationship.

II

Piece number twenty-nine in the "Becoming Sea Series" still lay on the floor. Jude was dressed in black leotard and tights, a paint-spattered chambray shirt with a Ghost Ranch logo pulled over the top. Her hair was pulled back in a ponytail. After yoga on the studio deck, she had an idea for the painting and convinced herself that it would only take a few minutes to apply some deep bronze to the composition. Xander would rent a car at the airport, so she'd have plenty of time to change and start the coffee brewing before he arrived. She was still painting when she heard a knock at her studio door. She opened to a laughing Xander.

"I knew I would find you out here. Your painting always takes priority over your men."

Jude reached out and wrapped her arms around him. "And so you're still one of my men?" She teased.

"Always have been, always will be….." Xander said as he welcomed her hug somewhat timidly.

"I am so glad to see you!" Jude exclaimed. "No more bullets to the head, right?"

"No, no bullets," he smiled, "but you could say something is really messing with my mind."

Jude stood back to observe his face. "What is it? It's not a complication from the concussion, is it?" She asked.

"You might say that," he said feigning a serious look. Then she saw the mischievous grin emerge and knew he was teasing. "I will tell you all about it, but first I want to know how things are with you."

"Where would I even begin? You know I have two grandchildren. And I've had some very successful solo shows. Oh, lots of changes with Woman Space, too."

Should she tell him about her dream, or the visit from Shaman Joseph? She had a pretty good idea of how he would react to that. Even with his appreciation for the arts and for ceramics, he was very much an atheistic scientist.

Xander made himself comfortable in one of the studio chairs as Jude topped off her coffee and poured one for him.

"Oh, this is Aden and Jalee." She reached for a framed photo sitting on the chest near her.

"Cute kids," Xander said as he took the photo from Jude and studied it.

"Woman Space has become quite well known internationally. My artwork too. I have you to thank for that." Jude took the photo and put it back in its place.

"I'm not surprised about Woman Space and your art, but a grandma! No way, Jude Bennett. You do not look like a grandma!"

Jude smiled. "You always know the right thing to say. But I love being a grandma. They are such fun kids. Sometimes I feel I've moved back in time, and they are my little ones."

"I did notice the glow on your face," Xander teased.

Jude laughed then became serious. "After I broke my engagement with Andrew, I took a trip alone to Big Sur. I just needed to get away and process all that had happened. In fact, I'm getting ready for a solo show in Carmel as a result of a connection I made on that trip."

"So that's what this is you are working on? For that show?"

"Yes, I call it 'Becoming Sea.' Xander, the Pacific Coast, especially between Carmel and Big Sur, is one of the most beautiful, powerfully stimulating places in the world."

"I've not been there, but I've heard the Pacific Coast is beautiful."

"You've been to the Amalfi Coast, right? There are similarities."

"Yes, I've been there, and the Isle of Capri. That beautiful, eh?"

"Yes, that beautiful, maybe even more so. And my stay there was, well, magical. Perhaps I'll tell you about it someday."

"I assure you I can handle it, Jude." He smiled warmly as he pushed the hair from her face with his fore finger in an intimate gesture. Jude noticed there was something in his eyes, something different, more gentle.

"Okay then. I had a most unusual thing happen to me while I was in Big Sur. I was visited by a Shaman."

"I've had a few experiences myself since we last were together. Your mystical experiences no longer scare me." He chuckled.

"Well, I sometimes wonder if it was a real visit or a dream," Jude continued.

"I have no doubt your Shaman really visited you, Jude." Compassion swept across his face, and something else she couldn't quite put her finger on. "What does it matter if it was an in-person visit or if he appeared to you in a dream? All of life is a dream, isn't it? And every event can be life changing if we can but see the miracle in it." Jude saw the intensity rise in Xander as he spoke. This wasn't the Xander she knew.

"Everything changed for me when I was shot in Belgium." Xander looked intensely into Jude's eyes.

"I knew something was different about you, Xander." She touched his arm with her hand. "I wasn't sure just what, and it hadn't seemed appropriate to question you at the time. You had been through such a trauma."

"Well, first of all, there was this angel who kept watch over me day after day," Xander said in a whisper. "I can't seem to get her out of my mind."

Jude's expression softened, and she lowered her eyes, feeling discomfort at his intense gaze.

"There is that blush again," he touched her cheek. Jude pulled back slightly.

"Jude, I'm in love with you, still. I need you, want you in my life. Have you forgiven me, even a little?"

A wash of emotion flooded over Jude. What sort of spell did he always seem to have over her that he could so easily stir all the old feelings? She wanted to respond; instead, she pulled back further and changed the subject.

"Tell me what happened. I'm so curious."

"I know you don't trust me, Jude. I have so much to tell you. But first, refill my coffee; get yourself a refill, too. Or maybe you need wine?"

Jude laughed aloud. "Do I seem that uptight?" she said rising from her chair. She took a bottle of champagne from the tiny studio fridge.

Xander joined her, and smiled when he realized she had saved the bottle of Dom Perignon he had brought to the opening of Woman Space. "You've saved it all this time?"

"Who else would appreciate it as much as you?" she said with a sparkle in her eyes.

"You knew I would come back? Make it a nice full glass," Xander teased. "This may take some time."

"Okay, you're really triggering my curiosity now. Come, let's sit on the deck. You'll love the view."

They pulled up two cushioned lounge chairs, side by side.

"Enough stalling! Get to the story." Jude demanded.

Taking a thoughtful moment that ended in a smile and raising of that right brow, Xander began: "I've lived my life with the freedom that comes from believing you do whatever you need to do, whatever you want to do, because there's just this one life you are given to live, and no one but you should decide how you should live it. I've scoffed at the idea of a god. I've marveled that anyone could remotely believe we have life after life in a heaven much less that we might be reincarnated on this earth over and over. As a result, I have basically lived as a hedonist, seeking my own pleasure, and I have not been the best of men. As you know all too well, I've not been the most honest—not even come close. I've loved, yes. And you, Jude, have been my greatest love. But not even for you did I shut down my appetites, my taste for variety or adventure."

Jude interrupted: "You don't have to get into that. I forgave you long ago. Besides, you've more than made that up to me through Von Hessen."

"I know, Jude. I know you no longer hold that against me. But there in Antwerp, with you near me, I found myself fighting for this very life, this only life that I believed in."

Jude reached out and touched Xander's arm. "I was so scared you weren't going to make it." She felt her eyes begin to fill.

"I almost didn't make it, Jude. I found myself floating above my body, seeing it far below me, covered in plaster dust with an expanding pool of the deepest red, my very life's blood slipping away from me. I heard you calling me, searching for me. I watched you come in and find me. I saw your distress, the panic on your face. I heard you say you loved me. I could see and hear you, Jude!"

Jude wiped at a tear that was beginning to trickle down her cheek.

Xander continued. "I was torn, wanting to come back to you but being pulled away, away like a magnet to some powerful magnetic field. When the medics arrived, I floated away toward what drew me, through a hallway of lights that kept blending together into one brilliant light that I couldn't resist. This light spoke to me, Jude. And I'll never be the same."

A wash of emotion enveloped Jude. She had realized that something had changed in Xander. She hadn't considered that he might have had a near death experience. But a near death experience was what he was describing to her. Suddenly she recalled the dream she had upon returning from Belgium. She saw Xander in that tunnel of light. "I knew something had happened, that something had changed in you," she said.

Xander took Jude's hand and lifted it to his lips. Then he continued. "I could hear you, calling for help, begging me not to leave. As I grew nearer to the Light, I also thought of you, and how you knew of this Light and had tried to tell me. I laughed at you. But here I was, seeing it for myself, feeling it for myself, even hearing it. All of my senses were alive like never before. I recognized this as the Light that has so drawn me to your paintings, especially the "Goddess Series". I've thought of those paintings so often and how I made fun of you for calling the light you kept painting the Source. But it is, Jude. It is the Source, and somehow you captured something of it in your work."

"Xander, did you see the spheres?" Jude was thinking of Dr. Eban Alexander who wrote of seeing the spheres in his own near death experience. He described the spheres much as she had experienced them in a past life regression. In fact, she had been a sphere in that regression.

"I did see the spheres, Jude. The ones like you painted. I remember laughing when you told me you were one of these spheres in your past life regression and how you experienced such a joyousness, a bliss when you interacted with the other spheres. What does this woman mean by past life regression? I thought you a bit nuts, you know….the crazy artist type, I thought." He chuckled. "But now I know. One of the spheres came close to me and slowly morphed into a lovely woman. Though she looked younger than I could ever remember her, I recognized her as my mother, Jude. She sort of enveloped me—it was more than a hug. And she said, 'My child, I hope you know how much you are loved. I hope you can forgive all the suffering I put you through.' I can remember everything in minute detail.

"At once I felt that old pain of her abandonment of me and my siblings; then just as suddenly, I felt it melting away. The pain was replaced by a filling, bursting sense of love. I think it's what I now understand as unconditional love.

"I reached for her, but she was again one of those spheres. Like what you have so often painted, Jude. There were so many of them, and they drew me toward them for all the joy they exuded. She joined them as they began to move across above me, emitting a sound that I can only describe as such joy that they would explode if they didn't sing their song. I followed their sound to what seemed the center of this matrix made of gold and silver threads. The threads each led to a center that I don't have words to describe. It seemed it may have been God. It glowed and pulsated, yet had no real form. It radiated a form of light, a brilliance that was at once compelling and overwhelming—like a compelling and overwhelming love. I knew at that moment that all was well."

Xander sighed and looked at Jude as if waiting for a response to what he was sharing. She was speechless. This was so unexpected, and Xander was changed. He was talking about God and Light and Love. This was not the neuroscientist with whom she had often argued theology.

"Jude, I think that Light has to be God or the Divine, whatever you want to call it. It is most of all Love. I have come to know there's nothing to fear. I now know we are here for a purpose. There is meaning, whether or not we ever figure out just what it is. Life is like a puzzle that keeps us occupied in experience after experience, keeps us from getting bored, even pushes us to search for where we came from—where it all began. I'm not sure anyone every figures it out. But we are loved, Jude. So loved."

"Xander, why didn't you tell me when I was in Belgium with you? You know I would have believed you…I would have understood."

"I couldn't tell you what I had experienced right away. I hesitated, at first thinking perhaps my mind had been damaged or even that I had simply lost it. I had to process what had happened to me, research and study it. It was not easy for me; after all, I am a scientist. But I have spent all the years since trying to understand, meeting other people and reading about still more who have had similar experiences. I've been a bit obsessed. I've interviewed hundreds who have had near death experiences. I've studied everything I could find that might remotely speak to what had happened to me, from mysticism to brain imaging. Jude, I know that I died and was given the choice to return. I wanted to return to share this with you, but I needed you to know I wasn't making up some story in order to manipulate you to come back to me. I had to first figure it all out for myself.

"I am a changed man, Jude. I now know, with no doubts at all, that God is real, though nothing like I'd ever been taught. Something beyond our comprehension, and that we, too, are eternal spirits or part of that One Spirit. I came back because I need to tell the people who are important to me and the people that I've misled with my atheism and skepticism. Maybe in a book. I know it may make little or no difference, but I have to try just the same. I came back because I want to love you as you deserve to be loved, to love you as you've loved me. I want to be here with you to grow old and to hold you and comfort you and assure you that you don't ever have to fear nor doubt that spiritual realm you believe in. I now know the reality of it. I, too, have experienced it."

Jude was deeply touched. Tears filled her eyes. She couldn't take her eyes from Xander. She could feel the truth of what he was sharing with her. She took his face in both of her hands and looked into his eyes.

"Xander, what can I say? You've had a most incredible experience. I can't even imagine how it might feel to have seen and felt what you did. I just know that anyone I've ever met who has had a near death experience has told me it was life changing."

"My life is changed, that's for sure. But I love you all the more, Jude. I love you with everything that I am. I'm here for you as your friend, your lover, your fellow traveler in the Spirit. Whatever you want of me. I am here. You're not alone."

Jude studied Xander's face. He seemed to glow with sincerity. Her eyes again filled and she looked out at him through a blur of tears. She saw the love in his eyes as he spoke. It was more than the impassioned love of a man for a woman. She knew that look. This was something that came from a much different place, a deeper level, or maybe a higher level? She could see the authenticity. A wave of chills swept down both her arms. Yes, this was truth, and the chills were always that sure sign. She shook her head slowly, not taking her eyes from his. Smiling, she wrapped her arms around him and smelled his scent as her nose rested against the curve where his neck met his shoulder. She felt his heart beating against her as she pulled tighter against him. This embrace truly was home.

III

The Sun had set hours ago. They had been so deep in conversation that they hardly noticed the subtle changing colors moving from brilliant pinks, reds and oranges then slowly fading into the darkening sky. Now they sat side by side in the lounge chairs, often touching, sometimes staring off to the stars, and other times turning to simply smile at one another. The champagne was long gone, and words had become inadequate. Slowly Xander traced the curve of Jude's forearm with the lightest touch of his forefinger. He let it travel down to her fingers, tracing each separately, the curve between thumb and forefinger, around the forefinger and up the inside line of the middle finger... remembering, too, the creases on the knuckles, the shapes of the nails, then ever so slowly back to the crease at the bend of her arm where the skin is ever so sensitive. Jude lay back, eyes closed, enraptured with the pleasure of it.

"I've come back home, Jude. Can you imagine this when we are 90 years old, pleasuring one another with the lightest touch....."

"You've asked me this before," Jude whispered, remembering when they were lovers.

"Yes, and the idea is still just as wonderful as then, eh?"

Jude smiled. "Yes, it is," she whispered. This must be what Joseph Wolf was telling her was to come.

"My turn." Xander broke the silence again, smiled his mischievous smile and laid his arm on the arm of Jude's chair. Gently he lifted her finger urging her to begin trailing the contour of his arm.

Jude smiled softly. "Whatever happens, Xander, I do love you. I've always loved you."

A shooting star sped across the sky and seemed to disappear into the far end of the lake.

"Did you see that?" Xander sat forward in his chair.

"Make a wish," she whispered.

"My wishes have all just come true." He smiled and turned to kiss Jude softly on the forehead.

CHAPTER 21

No one saves us but ourselves. No one can and no one may. We ourselves must walk the path.

- Buddha

S HE WAS DREAMING; **she was journeying.** Did it really make a difference? She was sitting under the huge Sycamore beside the lake in only her night shirt. Xander was sleeping off his jet lag in the guest room. Jude awoke as the sun was rising and decided to come out by the water to meditate and to process all that had happened the night before. There were some things she felt a need to know, and perhaps meditating would bring some insights. She needed to think hard about Xander and her feelings for him. She had found such peace in being alone; getting involved with him again might distract her from all she had worked for. But then, she had always been involved in some way with Xander, even if only, as in the last five years, a warm breeze of thought across her mind, or an occasional email that subtly lifted her spirits. She was connected to Xander and always would be. But of course, she reminded herself, wasn't she connected to everyone and everything?

Jude began to relax with deep, rhythmic breathing. As she allowed her mind to still, she found herself imagining that she was going down between the roots of her old friend, the Sycamore. Down she went until she imagined she was in the center of the wonderful old tree. It appeared to be hollow, and a silver rope, knotted at its end, hung from somewhere high above. She took the rope in her hands, straddled the huge knot, and began to pull her way upward. At the moment she exerted effort the rope began to lift so that she no longer had to work to rise. As she moved upward she realized she was heading for the Upper World, lifted upward without effort. For an instant she was blinded by a bright light, and then found herself at the top of the tree. When finally her eyes adjusted, she walked out into bright warm sunshine and saw that she was standing at the edge of a lovely small lake. She noticed myriad of colors in the foliage that hung over the water, creating a sense of privacy and protection. Stirred by a soft breeze, the foliage reflected in delightful dancing patterns on the water's surface. Surrounding the lake were wild flowers visited by bees and a ruby throated hummingbird. A pair of brilliant green dragon flies played over the water. Jude seated herself on a large stone at the water's edge, noticing how warm its surface felt to her nearly naked body, and waited for her Spirit Guide to appear. Her meditation had transformed into a Shamanic Journey. As soon as she thought journey, there appeared a dog so soft in color that he seemed almost transparent. He resembled a wolf with a mix of pale grays and browns in his coat. His eyes were the palest blue. Wolf Dog, Jude thought. He greeted Jude with a nudge to her cheek and a whimper. She stood to follow him as he started immediately up a steep red clay path. She was again on the Red Road, Black Elk's red path. It was good to know she was still on that right path. At the top of the grade, she and Wolf Dog came to a large round stone. In her previous Shamanic

Journeys, Jude's chamber doors had always been arched; she wasn't sure why. She found herself wondering if this was a door, as it was round and so small she would have to be on her knees to crawl through. But as Wolf Dog sniffed around the base of the round stone it began to roll open. Immediately inside, rather than a room or chamber, was a well. The stacked stone sides dropped straight downward. She could see what appeared to be water at the bottom. If she went into that well, how was she supposed to get out? Without the slightest hesitation, Wolf Dog slid down the side. Jude realized she could not lose Wolf Dog. She closed her eyes, raised her arms and followed—a leap of faith. At the bottom, rather than a well of water, she found a dry stone and dirt floor and a room shaped as a chamber. The Chamber of Contracts, she suddenly knew. This, she had been taught, was the first chamber on a shamanic journey to the underworld. But this was very different from the Chamber of Contracts she had experienced before. Here there were no contracts to be found, neither new ones to make nor old ones to destroy. She felt confused. Wolf Dog was already leaving the room by way of long, stone stairway that curved upward; Jude had to rush to follow him. As they climbed she noticed that the stones were covered with moss that bloomed in tiny flowers of every hue of pink, red and orange. The flowering moss created a beautiful red path. About half way up the stairs, she noticed an old trunk on a ledge next to the steps. The lid was open, and a fabric in the same wonderful colors as the path was hanging over its sides. Taking the fabric in her hands, she held it closely in order to see the details in the low light. It was loosely woven from a nubby yarn that looked strangely like the flowers on the path, with the same range of pinks, reds and oranges. The fabric was breathtakingly beautiful. Lifting the fabric from the trunk, Jude saw that it was a robe with a hood. Thinking of the saffron robes worn by Tibetan monks, she wrapped it tightly around her and pulled the hood over her head. For some reason, she immediately thought of the Cannas her mom had grown in the side yard of her childhood home. They, too, had grown in all these colors.

"Mom?" she whispered.

"Yes, Judith, I'm here." There was no mistaking her mother's voice.

She wondered what these colors symbolized, and made a mental note to do some research in order to learn what the Saffron dye was made from.

Jude pulled the robe tighter around her; she felt warm and comforted. She both walked and watched, witnessing herself as she made her way up the flowering pink, red and orange steps in her pink, red and orange robe…..*"Red Road,"* she again thought to herself. *"Right Path."*

Jude looked beyond and above her position on the stairs and saw that Wolf Dog was now on a ledge above her, sitting as if waiting. The ledge was covered in the same moss as the path. She climbed up and sat beside Wolf Dog. It appeared that there was nowhere else to go. Her mind began to fill with thoughts and questions. I know I am being told I am on the right path, but how do I know if I am to remain alone. Or am I to be with Xander? I so want to do the right thing. I don't want to lose all I've worked so hard to gain, this peace of mind, this contentment. I have learned so much: that spiritual growth is such an important part of this life; that we grow through every experience and every person—everything is our teacher; that creative expression is the expression of Spirit in the world and it can be expressed through even the most mundane task; that there is absolutely nothing to fear for everything is happening as it needs to happen. I will not be happier with Xander, or more peaceful, for peace and happiness come from within. I don't need Xander to continue my journey. But I do love Xander. And now he understands, he knows. Surely he can finally love me well.

She heard a soft chuckle then a voice, saying, "Simply relax and be. Why do you have such a need to know? Why can't you simply trust? Simply love."

She thought of the Journey with Shaman Joseph in Big Sur. She had been reminded in that journey of all the ways she had loved and been loved. She was reminded that she could not control how others loved. Learning to let go of her fears and love well had been the message. Now she was being shown that loving or being love was all that mattered.

Thoughts flowed through her mind: "It does no good to get caught up in how much another loves me and whether they can be trusted to love me as I wish to be loved. Romantic love is only a faint shadow of what love on a higher level entails. Instead, I am to 'be love.'"

Jude smiled. It didn't matter what she chose or didn't choose to experience. She didn't have to know. She was simply to trust what was rising up and unfolding before her. She was to open herself to Spirit as a conduit for love. Love was all that mattered.

She wrapped her arms around Wolf Dog and whispered in his ear, "Has it always been so simple?" Wolf Dog turned toward her and licked her face.

ABOUT THE AUTHOR

J AN GROENEMANN'S AWARD winning mixed media paintings have been exhibited throughout the United States and in Germany. They are in private and corporate collections in the United States as well as Germany, Belgium and Japan. She is the winner of the *Arty Award for Individual Accomplishment in the Arts* and several *Grumbacher Awards for Excellence*. As an instructor, Jan was also named to *Who's Who Among America's Teachers*. She is the founder of Groenemann Studios and co-founder of Creative Pathways. Jan has also illustrated *The Toad Within* written by Dr. James Worth and *Emotions: Sometimes I have Them, Sometimes They Have Me*, written by Dr. Michael Hall.

Jan was a resident artist for five years at The Foundry Arts Centre in St. Charles, MO and adjunct professor of the Humanities for Lindenwood University for fourteen years. Hundreds of students of all ages have been inspired by her art classes through Groenemann Studios.

Jan's first book, *Through the Inner Eye: Awakening to the Creative Spirit,* was published in 1994 by Islewest Publishing, a division of Carlisle Communications of Dubuque, IA. She has traveled the United States facilitating workshops on creativity and personal growth.

Jan has three sons, two daughters-in-law, and two grandsons. She lives in St. Louis.

Woman Alone is Jan's first novel.

You can contact Jan via email at hokseda@charter.net or her website: www.jangroenemann.com